A PERFECT LIFE

A PERFECT LIFE

JOEL SPRING

ISBN: 0692485783
ISBN 13: 9780692485781
Library of Congress Control Number: 2015946125
Phoenix Books, Mt. Vernon, NY

CONTENTS

Chapter 1 ·1
Chapter 2 ·9
Chapter 3 · 19
Chapter 4 ·27
Chapter 5 ·34
Chapter 6 ·42
Chapter 7 ·49
Chapter 8 ·57
Chapter 9 ·63
Chapter 10 ·73
Chapter 11 ·80
Chapter 12 ·88
Chapter 13 ·96
Chapter 14 · 104
Chapter 15 · 112
Chapter 16 · 121
Chapter 17 · 129
Chapter 18 · 137
Chapter 19 · 146
Chapter 20 · 157

Chapter 21 · 164
Chapter 22 · 172
Chapter 23 · 179
Chapter 24 ·185
Chapter 25 · 194
Chapter 26 ·202
Chapter 27 ·209

Chapter 1

My perfect life began at birth when Dr. Reznick swept me up from my newborn crib and rushed me to the newly inaugurated Perfect Life Room. I was the poster baby for the World Government's promise to provide everyone with a perfect life. As a federation of nations, the Congress of the World Government was controlled by the three hundred highest-earning global corporations. Worried about citizen loyalty, the World Government hoped the Perfect Life Project would win popular support.

My parents, in a panic over their own failed lives, wanted something different for me. In the midst of a shouting match over custody of an unborn child, my mom's divorce lawyer mentioned the Perfect Life Project.

I don't remember the Perfect Life Room. At twenty, while scanning online newspapers for my birthday on March 6, 2020, I found a photo of my smiling pediatrician carrying me through lavish wooden doors with cherubic faces carved into their panels. Above the door a sign invitingly announced, "Welcome to The Perfect Life Room by Biostream and Radiant Technologies." The photo's caption read, "Dr. Flora Reznick carries the first baby into the Perfect Life Room."

"We used Big Data to plan the perfect life," Radiant's CEO, Dan Shriver, explained in the article. "Our social-science team collected past and current data on happiness. Analytics applied to this Big Data set gave us the answers. We've put a computer monitoring chip under Jimmy's skin."

Biostream's CEO, Bo Reddick, added, "We know the body chemistry of happiness. Just begin using the right drugs at birth. He'll always be happy."

Another online search produced photos of Dr. Reznick holding me, surrounded by computer screens with the caption, "Little Jimmy begins the Perfect Life." In the next photo, I am gently being placed on a jelly-like substance inside a translucent box with wireless transmitters on each corner. Multicolored tubes run from the floor into the box's bottom. The caption explains that "little Jimmy's bodily functions and movements are constantly monitored for his happiness level."

In the following photo, a smiling Dr. Reznick is seen shaking hands with Bo Reddick as Carl Throne, Radiant Technologies' president, stands, holding up an oversized check for one hundred million dollars. The caption reads, "Biostream and Radiant Technologies support the quest for a perfect life."

I don't remember Dr. Reznick, but on Googling, I found her death described in an Upstate New York newspaper: "Famed pediatrician dies in fatal car crash. Police suspect drugs but are waiting for the coroner's report. Heroin and syringes found in glove compartment." A photo showed a flipped-over, expensive-looking sports car. The date was March 6, 2023, when I was three.

In the twentieth year of my perfect life, after the death of my wife, Chelsea, I began exploring the past. I was driven by the circumstances surrounding her death to find out what happened. My past was stored in my childhood robot caretaker's cloud.

My life was recorded and monitored by Biostream and Radiant Technologies. These companies frequently upgraded my chip and changed my pharmaceutical packet. Sometimes my chip and chemical packet were moved to different parts of my body because of skin irritations. Once, a green-colored rash appeared around a main artery receiving happiness drugs. The chip was relocated when I bruised or scraped the skin over it.

I wanted to know more about the one-hundred-million-dollar check in the photo and Dr. Reznick's apparent heroin addiction. After I waded through Googled articles, one appeared, dated seven years before my birth—"Zeus Fund Finances Perfect Life Project." The article described the Zeus Fund, an offshore investment firm, giving Dr. Reznick two million dollars to partner with Biostream and Radiant Technologies to help develop the World Government's Perfect Life model.

I pieced together stories about Zeus, Biostream, and Radiant. The high-earning Zeus Fund was operated by Christian fundamentalist Britt Owens, who also sponsored research to prove the existence of God. Proving the existence of evil and Satan was easy. God was proving more difficult.

Owens believed the quest for a perfect life would lead to God's doorstep. "That's odd," I thought. "I've never been attracted to a religion." A search of Zeus Fund investments revealed large purchases of stock in Biostream and Radiant and pronouncements by Owens that earning money was God's blessing.

And Dr. Reznick? Her bio was impressive. After receiving an MD from Case Western Reserve University, she treated children of oil-rich sheiks at the Cleveland Clinic. One family gave her a small jet as an appreciative gift.

After the Cleveland Clinic, she became head of pediatrics at New York's Columbia-Episcopalian Hospital where she pioneered cosmetic surgery for newborns. That's when she hooked up with Radiant Technologies, using their equipment to image newborn faces and project what they would look like at age twenty. The Rosenberg family paid for a new School of Cosmetic Pediatrics after she clipped away at their newborn girl and guaranteed she'd look like a smiling Mona Lisa by her twenties. The parents chose Mona Lisa from Radiant's data bank of the world's most famous faces. A photo of the Rosenbergs showed faces that some might consider social handicaps and certainly ones that you wouldn't want to pass on to your children. Radiant expanded its database to include Japanese and Korean pop stars when Radiant moved into Asian markets.

It was not an easy task choosing a baby's face from Radiant's data bank. Some parents went to court over their infant's future face. For both male and female newborns, Radiant recommended symmetrical faces for financial success and good looks. Fathers wanted girls with full lips, prominent cheekbones, fine eyebrows, and a petite nose, while mothers tended to like girls with raven hair, strong noses, and bushy eyebrows. Both parents liked boys with facial features showing increased testosterone, such as broad foreheads, longer and lower faces, prominent chins and brows, chiseled jaws, and defined cheekbones.

Dr. Reznick's pioneering work was in lengthening and shortening newborn penises. Radiant's database included a British study finding women preferred men with six-and-a-half-inch erect penises and a thick girth. Radiant developed imaging software that could project a newborn's penis size at age twenty. Dr. Reznick cut and grafted to guarantee the six and a half inches but couldn't increase the girth. Boys would have to wait until adolescence for surgeons to increase their girth with transplants from the inner thighs.

Dr. Reznick's fame spread as online-magazine and news reporters flocked to the Rosenberg School of Cosmetic Pediatrics. The doctor received numerous awards for giving every child a chance to be pretty or handsome.

"Life is much better," Dr. Reznick told reporters, "if you're good-looking. I'm giving every baby a better face and the promise of a good life."

In 2017, three years before my birth, articles, photos, and medical reports flooded the Internet about the quest for the perfect life. Headlines read:

"WORLD GOVERNMENT PROMISES EVERYONE A PERFECT LIFE."

"RADIANT TECHNOLOGIES INTEGRATES PEDIATRIC FACIAL IMAGING WITH LARGE DATA SET ON CAUSES OF HUMAN HAPPINESS."

"Famed cosmetic pediatrician Flora Reznick to work with Biostream for babies' future happiness."

"The Zeus Fund to support Perfect Life Project."

"Shares soar as Biostream and Radiant Technologies announce building of the Perfect Life Room."

Ads for Radiant Technologies popped up on my screen. One Radiant ad advised—"We can help your baby's future"—with photos of newborn faces and images of how they would look at age twenty with and without cosmetic surgery.

A news photo showed Dr. Reznick standing with smiling parents next to a row of cribs in Beijing's Minzu Hospital. The caption read, "Chinese parents applaud Dr. Reznick as Radiant Technologies' imaging shows their babies' future faces. Many choose faces of Korean and Japanese pop stars." The article noted that some parents wanted their newborns' tongues altered so that they would sound like top Korean pop singers. Dr. Reznick said the tongue procedure was too difficult with newborns and recommended it after puberty.

The Zeus Fund gave my biological parents money to disappear. Everyone agreed that there was no room for neurotic parents in a perfect life. Prompted by hope of future profits, Radiant engineered the perfect robot based on a data set drawn from a century of research on parenting. The robot Sally became my guardian.

Later I encountered a YouTube Video showing Sally suckling me in the Perfect Life Room. Sally's silicon nipple fed me a soy-based formula developed by Biostream and the baby-food giant, AlKale. Marketed as Baby's Perfect Health, the formula was popular with vegetarian and vegan parents and those hoping the name fulfilled its promise.

Biostream and AlKale ads claimed the formula was infused with proteins protecting against bacteria and viruses along with enzymes to promote growth of healthy intestinal flora: "Baby's Perfect Health Better than Breast Milk." Those ads, along with ones stating, "We've Improved on Nature's Formula," prompted a legal suit from the American Pregnancy Association for claims the formula was better than breast milk. It took years of testimony from medical and industry officials before the courts dismissed the suit for lack of evidence of any significant differences.

Worried about me bonding with a robot, Radiant hired a team of child psychologists. They recommended that Sally's soft, skin-like arms cradle me against its heat-controlled body as I sucked formula through a perfect-sized nipple hole. Sally was programmed to make me feel secure. It held me close with wiggle room for my arms and legs.

While nursing, my head was positioned to force me to look into Sally's eyes. A dispute broke out among the psychologists over the sounds Sally should emit to enhance the feeding-bonding experience. Some argued for recordings of real mothers talking to their infants. Another school of thought believed sounds like cooing were more important than words. Others claimed words acted as early vocabulary builders. Several child psychologists wanted Sally to hum Mozart melodies to increase my intelligence.

The compromise was Sally humming arias from Mozart's operas interspersed with cooing and gurgling sounds. I still feel warm and sleepy every time I hear Mozart. *Don Giovanni* sends me to bed.

A problem was Sally's eyes during bonding. What should I see in its eyes while nursing? Some child experts suggested images preparing me to learn reading and math. Others wanted ones conveying love. It was even suggested projections of opera performances to accompany Sally's renditions of Mozart.

Eventually, Sally's eyes were made of a reflective substance so that I could see myself when looking into them. Fuzzy geometric and alphabetic images designed to convey love floated behind my reflected image.

I still love Sally! It stands on a docking station in my bedroom closet. I sometimes boot it up and have Sally sit, holding me in a chair next to the bed. After my wife's death, Sally often slept with me, warming the bed with its temperature-regulated body.

By all accounts I was a happy baby. Baby's Perfect Health ingredients ensured the right balance of serotonin. Later, my drug packet played the same role. Between Sally's attentiveness and regulation of my serotonin, I was a smiling baby.

Signs carried by father-rights groups are in the background of a March 6, 2021, photo taken at my first birthday. Sally stood, cradling me on the steps of the School of Cosmetic Pediatrics. Protest signs by The American Coalition for Fathers and Children read, "Where is Jimmy Clark's father?" and "Can a perfect life be without fathers?"

Contributing to the backlash from men's groups were Sally's frequent media presence and photos of me nursing in Baby's Perfect Health ads. Weeks before my first birthday and transfer to the Perfect Life Toddler apartment, picketers appeared outside the hospital from Fathers and Children and Give Men a Chance. Dr. Reznick found her new Bentley plastered with stickers saying, "Children Need Fathers."

Radiant Technologies defended its database with a press release: "We cannot find evidence that fathers are necessary for a perfect life."

The American Coalition for Fathers and Children responded: "Children with involved fathers are more emotionally secure, make better social connections, and have better educational outcomes. Little Jimmy Clark needs a father for developing a strong self-identity."

An editorial in the *Gay Parent LGBT Magazine* objected: "We find no evidence that children need father figures. Two women or a single mother can successfully raise well-adjusted boys." One radical feminist group blogged that fathers caused aggression and were responsible for world violence.

Lambda Legal posted photos of married gay and lesbian couples cuddling what looked like little boys and issued a statement: "After years of struggle for equal marriage rights, we are sad to see an attack on same-sex female marriages and single moms raising boys. All children need is love and nurturing."

University of Vermont's student club, LGBTQIA (Lesbian, Gay, Bisexual, Transgender, Questioning, Intersexual, and Asexual), posted objections shortly after my first birthday to me being called a boy. "Maybe little

Jimmy is transgender or would question his or her sexual identity. Jimmy could have a male's physical body and a female identity."

After LGBTQIA's objections, I noticed posts referring to me with the gender-neutral pronoun, "they." I was no longer a "he" but a "they." I was gender-neutral, even with my future perfect six and a half inches.

Concerned about the fatherhood controversy, Radiant Technologies' president, Carl Throne, and Biostream's CEO, Bo Reddick, met in Dr. Reznick's office.

"Are you sure boys don't need fathers?" asked a skeptical Bo Reddick. "At Biostream we make pills to help men be men. How can we tell men they aren't needed?"

"Ran the analytic program again and still nothing about fathers for a perfect life. They just don't matter," explained Throne. "Reznick, you know of any research? You're the doctor."

"Nothing about fathers being necessary, except for procreation. We could use stored sperm. Lots of single moms raise boys," Reznick replied, enjoying the discomfort of the other two men. "That doesn't mean a good father can't help."

"How about a male-looking robot caretaker? Can't you make one?" Reddick asked Throne. "We need these father groups to shut up. They're hurting baby-formula sales."

Looking like the old movie character Sylvester Stallone, John's husky voice could say my name and talk about fatherhood, but its other operations were limited. Fathers' groups were pleased with my male-looking robot guardian. Vermont's LGBTQIA still posted concerns about my sexual identity and hinted I was transgender.

Chapter 2

Moved to the Perfect Life Toddler apartment, I crawled on a rubberized floor between John's legs as it stood rigid in the middle of the room. Lights blinked on the wall console registering my speed, heartbeat, blood pressure, serotonin levels, and biomechanics. Kinesiology consultant, Eve Spirit, appeared daily in a tight-fitting running outfit. She would roll out a large red mat with protruding hills and pyramids designed to exercise all my leg and arm muscles. Eve was a neuroplasticity expert whose crawling-mat exercises were to enhance my cognitive functions.

At a year and a half, I was starting to walk, and the exercise mat was replaced by a maze of stacked blocks. As I turned corners in the block maze, the console's biomechanic indicators flashed red and green. Snacks and stuffed animals on top of the blocks kept me going. After years of experiments, AlKale introduced a line of children's snacks for "Muscles and Brain Power." Sally later told me I loved the cherry-flavored broccoli bars.

By two years I could walk confidently to my potty chair—wired to give an immediate analysis of the chemical composition and weight of my offerings—pull down my underwear, and sit on a specially designed and warm Japanese-style toilet seat with Mozart erupting at the first touch of my bottom.

Sally often recounted how excited I got looking at the console with graphs appearing on multiple screens as my solid and watery waste splashed into the container. The music volume from the seat steadily increased until my final offerings landed, accompanied by a blast of the finale to *Così Fan Tutte*. The toilet activities were planned to keep me from later constipation.

Toilet-trained and with my body and mind exercised, I was ready for preschool. This would be my first contact with other kids, and the team directing my perfect life wanted to get it right. Dr. Reznick and teams from Radiant and Biostream selected Miss Nancy's Happy Times Nursery on the Upper West Side of Manhattan by checking test scores and high-school- and college-graduation rates. Miss Nancy's fit the bill. The preschool's student test scores compared favorably with preschools in Finland, South Korea, and Singapore. Team members checked its curricula to ensure I would learn the right hard and soft skills.

Miss Nancy's opened in the 1990s and kept records on graduates' future schooling, employment, salaries, marriages, children, and other personal data. Almost 90 percent entered well-paid professions or investment banking. The Radiant team was particularly impressed by the emphasis on soft skills—grit and conscientiousness. Carl Burris, Radiant's chief economist and data expert, pointed out that these two soft skills strongly correlated with financial success. All team members agreed that money helped with the perfect life.

"Miss Nancy's is the best," announced Burris. "Graduates go to the top colleges, good test scores show all parents in the top one percent of wage earners and high college-graduation rates and live at good addresses. Miss Nancy's Happy Times is the place for Jimmy."

Dr. Reznick visited the school with my immunization and health records and was assured that desks, chairs, and toys were daily disinfected. Finding the school was clean, Dr. Reznick informed them of Sally's role in monitoring my school life.

"Why?" asked Lois Smart, a twenty-something teacher with raven-black hair. "We never do that."

"Sally will just stand in the corner and record Jimmy's actions," Dr. Reznick replied, explaining the long-range plan. "High-tech robot with Radiant guarantees—Sally is necessary. Jimmy is the World Government's Perfect Life experiment. The robot will collect useful data and put Jimmy's test scores and his behaviors into its memory. Its robotic eyes can scan and record everything."

Sally told me I was very nervous on my first trip from the Perfect Life Toddler apartment to Miss Nancy's and wet myself entering the school. In class, Sally stood in the corner, its eyes recording my every action. Sally said it was hard to just stand there when kids teased me, and one boy, Tom Stoddard, pinched me when teachers weren't looking. Sally saw everything and recorded it. Tom became a lifetime friend.

As a teenager, I liked looking at Sally's old recordings of those years. I looked engrossed in GoPlay's learning games, which fed data back to Sally, the school's computer, and Radiant.

I learned later that GoPlay tablets measured my grit and conscientiousness while playing learning games. Did I stick with a complicated game until the end? Did I exhibit the right soft skills for success?

Miss Nancy's was big on educating for success. Through Sally's eyes, I saw a classroom with facial-expression cameras recording each student's grimaces, smiles, frustrations, and looks of triumph. Data on my facial expressions were sent to Sally and to the school's central computer. From the school, data was transmitted to Bloomberg Measures, an interstate student data bank funded by a consortium of retailers interested in future consumer habits that would be used for targeting new products. State laws blocked retailers' access to student names while giving other schools access to all student names and data. My preschool facial expressions followed me through college.

Specially wired chairs collected data on seat motions, like the number of fidgets. The chair's data was combined with readings of facial expressions to record student boredom, frustration, and restlessness. This data was transmitted to the school computer, Radiant, and Bloomberg Measures and linked to scores on GoPlay's learning games. I can still find data on my reactions. My fidgets and quiescence, along with facial expressions, were charted next to my learning-game scores.

Sally's recordings show a continuous three-foot-wide video screen wrapped around the top of the classroom's four walls streaming cartoons of the race between *The Tortoise and the Hare*, alternating with the puffing and straining of *The Little Engine That Could*. Glancing up, we could see the hare taking naps and fiddling around while the tortoise plodded along to a finish line marked by moneybags with large dollar symbols.

After crossing the finish line, the tortoise was shown lounging in a big home surrounded by baby turtles with an expensive car in the driveway. The hare was left in tattered clothes, begging on a street. On arriving at the mountaintop, a smiling little railroad engine got a flower decoration reading "I thought I could" and a squirt of oil from a can decorated with world currencies.

By the second week of preschool, expression cameras registered a big smile as I stood in the required position with hands in my pockets fingering loose change, while reciting the school's Success Pledge at the beginning of class. Just before the pledge, Lois Smart flicked a switch, sending the cartoons streaming around the room.

I later asked Sally about the hands-in-pocket pose for the pledge and learned Miss Nancy's replaced the hand-over-heart flag salute with hands in pockets counting change. Every preschooler was required to have small coins to finger during pledge time.

"Count your money and your success," Ms. Smart told the class at the pledge's beginning.

At two, did I understand the pledge? I guess I did. On graduating to kindergarten, I received a gold-dollar pin for the fewest fidgets and the most smiles during pledge time. I think my pharmaceutical packet helped win the award. Miss Nancy's pledge eventually found its way into boardrooms of Wall Street investment firms. Accompanied by streaming videos of *The Tortoise and the Hare* and *The Little Engine That Could* and the jingling of pocket change, the class recited:

I pledge to be like the tortoise's stick-to-itiveness and the engine that could;

Like the tortoise, I will keep working until my tasks are done;

Like the little engine, I will keep saying, "I—think—I can" and "I—thought—I could;"

In school and home, I will show grit and finish my work.

The pledge was followed by the self-control exercises called "toy wrap" and "toy wait." The school's parent-administered We Want Success for Our Child Fund paid for the daily toys. You could see the facial-expression cameras capturing kids' reactions as they were told to cover their eyes and not look as their toy presents were wrapped. In Sally's recordings I could see some kids sneaking peeks. As we remained seated, the wrapped toys were put on a desk in front of us with Ms. Smart commanding, "Wait!" Now the chairs measured our wiggling bottoms with cameras recording any kid touching the wrappings before Ms. Smart told us, "Open your presents."

My data shows little self-control, with me sneaking looks during wrapping exercises and touching gift paper at wait time. Biostream kept adjusting my pharmaceutical packet to enhance self-control. They never got it right.

During first year I had problems with a GoPlay reading game called Dick, Jane, and Spike Go Home. Viewing it now from Sally's memory cloud, I can see that Dick displayed some traditional feminine hand gestures, while Jane's hands moved aggressively, trying to punch their way out of the game's traps and obstacles. I thought Spike looked transgender.

In the game I helped little cartoon figures of Dick, Jane, and Spike walk to their mountaintop home through forests, deserts, and jungles, confronting all sorts of dangers. Scores appearing in the upper right of the tablet's screen were accompanied by encouraging whistles and bells. One score was for overcoming obstacles on the way home. The other two scores were for grit and stick-to-itiveness. Grit, symbolized by a *Little Engine That Could* icon, and stick-to-itiveness, symbolized by a tortoise icon, were measured by signal from the wired chair and expression cameras.

If expressions and body motion indicated the player was giving up, the GoPlay tablet sounded an engine whistle and urged players to toughen up and finish. If a player slowed down, a tortoise announced, "Stop being lazy, and play the game." The constantly changing game, grit and stick-to-itiveness scores, along with all the tablet's noises urged the player along.

The game started with Spike's heel getting caught in a beaver trap in the forest. To free Spike's heel, the gamer had to read instructions that popped up on the screen. The instructions were the reading lesson. Each obstacle or trap required the gamer to learn new words to understand the instructions. The gamer could click a cartoon clown to receive definitions of new words, including visual depictions of usage and audio pronunciations. My data for the Dick, Jane, and Spike Go Home game showed me alternating between boredom, frustration, and anger.

After school I returned to the Perfect Life Toddler apartment to be greeted by Biostream medical technicians and Radiant data experts. I was first put on my potty chair for an immediate evaluation of my urine and stool. My blood pressure was taken and a blood sample collected. The results were calibrated with my school data.

Most results were not good. My grit and stick-to-itiveness scores were low, and my after-school blood pressure was high. Biostream technicians manipulated my drug packet, but I still left school with a high blood-pressure reading.

Technicians were concerned with my frequent classroom accidents. Sally told me it brought several changes of pants to the class. Often during the "toy wait" exercise, I would wet myself. Radiant analysts found a direct correlation between my accidents and GoPlay learning games.

As games became more difficult and bells and whistles indicated declining grit and stick-to-itiveness scores, my pants became soaked. Through Sally's eyes, I could see Ms. Smart grimacing as she rushed me to the bathroom. After several weeks she turned the clothes-changing routine over to Sally.

Sally's memory recorded major changes in my drug packet as Biostream treated my anxiety-induced high blood pressure and frequent peeing. After one adjustment, I saw myself sitting listlessly during "toy wrap" and nodding off during "toy wait." I couldn't operate my GoPlay tablet, and Sally took me home early.

Another Biostream adjustment left me looking perky and cheerful. I watched myself squirming in my chair as I played a math game that required me to add and subtract logs while building a raft to carry a family fleeing from cartoon monsters across a river. All of a sudden, bells and whistles warned of declining grit and stick-to-itiveness scores. Looking back at this scene, I was first shocked, and then later I laughed about it.

As the bells and whistles on the math game grew louder, I suddenly threw my GoPlay tablet at two-year-old Kathryn Comer, hitting her in the back of the head. The class exploded into action. Kathryn started screaming and crying and threw her tablet at me. Messages sent from the wired chairs caused the computer software to freeze, stopping dataflows to Bloomberg Measures. The shutdown of dataflows from Ms. Nancy's haunted students throughout their education. Tom Stoddard told me he was asked about the data gap when applying to Princeton. The tablet throwing and data gap closed college doors for Kathryn, leaving her with a career waiting tables. Radiant filled in my data gaps and scrubbed the tablet throwing from my records.

Sally's video of the incident shows a room in chaos, with Ms. Smart pressing the room's emergency button and running around, trying to save GoPlay tablets as kids smashed them on table corners or threw them against the wall.

I smiled, watching Sally's recording of Miss Nancy trying to restore order. GoPlay guaranteed the tablets to be kidproof up to the age of five. But GoPlay never prepared for an eruption of preschool anger and violence. Facial-expression cameras wildly gyrated, trying to keep a focus on kids' faces. I watched myself retrieving my GoPlay from behind Kathryn's chair and jumping up and down on it until the screen cracked and parts fell out of the casing. Sally's video shows me destroying my GoPlay as a wet stain moved down my pants.

To keep me enrolled in Miss Nancy's, Radiant and Biostream bought new tablets and awarded Miss Nancy and Ms. Smart with summer travel fellowships covering first-class airfare and five-star hotels anyplace in the world.

I watched a video of the meeting held after the preschool riot in the Perfect Life Toddler apartment with teams from Biostream, headed by CEO Bo Reddick, and from Radiant, headed by Carl Burris. In addition, GoPlay sent their head child psychologist, Dr. Lewis Terman.

"What was most disturbing," Carl Burris began in the video, "was the little kids attacking the tortoise and little-engine symbols around the room. Some of the kids tried to throw tablets at the streaming cartoon but weren't strong enough to reach it."

"Sometimes children act out," child psychologist Dr. Terman calmly explained. "At this age they lack self-control, but we can train them. I think the 'toy wrap' and 'toy wait' exercises should be followed by a 'don't lick' activity."

"Maybe it's chemical imbalances," Bo Reddick suggested. "We're working on little Jimmy's drug packet. But what about the other kids? Biostream could supply all of them with their own drug packets."

"What's the 'don't lick' exercise?" Burris wondered. "Can we measure it?"

"Find the kids' favorite lollipops," Dr. Terman explained. "Wait until they are hungry, and then let them touch and smell the lollipops. Tell them if they lick them, they won't get lunch. Tie the lollipops around their necks, dim the lights, and play videos of kids eating candy and cakes. Every time they try to touch their lollipops, the chair gives them a mild shock."

"Sounds great!" Burris described how Radiant could measure and record the length of time kids could resist licking the lollipops. "Good training for corporate work. We could have good measures of self-control and future success. With accumulated data we should know if a kid's self-control increases with longer intervals between handling and licking the lollipops."

"We can't implant every kid with a drug packet. Think of the problems with parents. We can keep adjusting Jimmy's." Reddick smiled at Dr. Terman. "I would like to work with GoPlay on a self-control medication."

"I looked at Jimmy's GoPlay data before coming." Dr. Terman introduced a new problem. "Jimmy is gaming the system."

Watching the conversation from the future, I felt proud that at two, I was figuring out how to beat GoPlay's scoring.

"'Gaming the system,'" Dr. Reznick exclaimed. "Little Jimmy is doing what?"

"Kids learn to increase scores by figuring out how the software works," explained Dr. Terman. "They learn what teachers want and get high grades but learn little. It can lead to cheating, a major problem in schools since we started education games.

"When we wired Miss Nancy's," Dr. Terman continued. "I wanted kids to wear wireless skin-conductance sensors along with using the posture-analysis chairs and facial-expression cameras to measure boredom, motivation, confidence, and fatigue. But they thought the skin sensors were too much to put on little kids. Our system isn't complete. We could see Jimmy gaming the tablet, but we missed the frustration and anger leading to throwing the GoPlay. With skin sensors, all of this wouldn't have happened. We could have caught the problem in time."

As I said, I graduated Miss Nancy's with honors, receiving the golden-dollar pin for my pledges along with awards for high scores on grit and stick-to-itiveness. My math and reading scores were best in class after learning to cheat on the GoPlay. I scored high on the KIPP Character Report Card developed for their charter schools, and I was top scorer in the Grit section of the report card for working independently and trying hard, even when faced with possible failure. I must admit I learned to game the system. I even scored high on KIPP's eight self-control items, including top ratings for "remains calm when criticized," "is polite to adults," and "keeps his temper."

Stored in the closet near Sally's docking station, my preschool graduation diploma declared me educated for success at school and work.

How did I change from a pants-wetting two-year-old thrower of learning tablets to a model four-year-old destined for success? Sally said I was smart, and Biostream got the drugs right. When I entered kindergarten, I was prepared for success, knowing how to cheat, play the system, smile, and say nice things to my teachers.

Chapter 3

On the first day, I just wanted my kindergarten teacher to cuddle me. Lilly Mulroney I will never forget. I loved her at first sight; she was wearing a matronly soft-blue sweater and tailored pants, with gray hair gathered in a plain bun. Slightly overweight and exuding warmth and security, she was someone kids wanted to hug. She could be any white kid's grandmother.

It wasn't easy finding a kindergarten. Sally's cloud contained two gigabytes about my kindergarten. Looking at the file marked Kindergarten Admissions, I found references to Manhattan parents competing to get their kids into the "best" private school. The Zeus Perfect Life Fund paid $12,000 to a private-school consulting firm, We Find the Best for Your Kid. Radiant did background checks of the city's private kindergartens, looking for the same qualities as they wanted in my preschool—high test scores and family income, good addresses, college attendance, and graduates' incomes and employment.

In Sally's storage were e-mails from We Find the Best for Your Kid's adviser, Janice Collins, who told Radiant's Carl Burris that getting into the best kindergarten in New York City was harder than acceptance into a good college. Most applications had to be submitted to top kindergartens as soon as forms were available. So many applied that schools' admission officers didn't have time to review later submissions. The best kindergartens wanted top scores on the Early Childhood Admission Assessment.

Collins advised using PrepStrong's practice tests, study guides, and vocabulary cards. She said I needed to be in the best physical and mental condition at test time. Collins told of one high-quality applicant failing the exam after spotting a jelly doughnut deliciously displayed in a bakery window on the way to the test and the mother refusing to buy it. After the applicant threw a major tantrum, her mother panicked and rushed in to buy the doughnut. The kid quickly ate it and vomited. Tearful and feeling sick while writing the test, the girl wound up with a test score that landed her in the lowest-ranked private kindergarten. The mother, Collins wrote, still claims the doughnut destroyed her daughter's future education and career. Currently, the girl stocks shelves in a discount warehouse.

"You have a good chance with Jimmy," Collins's e-mail explained. "Miss Nancy's is what we call a 'Baby Ivy' preschool with good connections to top kindergartens. But you need to play your cards right. Check with Miss Nancy's to see their recommendations. You should follow their lead. I had parents whose preschool recommended one kindergarten, but they liked another. In the end, the kid attended a public school. We need to broker the system. That's what you're paying me for."

Sally's files indicated that Radiant's criteria were met by Cambridge Kindergarten. Collins said it was a top school, and Miss Nancy's contacted the admissions officer. Cambridge required high Early Childhood Admission Assessment scores.

It is disturbing looking at Sally's old videos when life decisions were being made for me. I saw teams from Biostream and Radiant, including economist and data expert, Carl Burris, meeting with Janice Collins and Tom Swayze, a test-preparation expert from Every Kid a Winner, a tutoring and test-prep service. My new pediatrician, Fredrick Lowe, who I liked better than Dr. Reznick, was in the video.

Lowe appeared in my life after Dr. Reznick's tragic car accident. As I later read, the coroner found heroin from the car's glove compartment coursing through her veins. She had just returned from France, where it was rumored she partied with a high-flying international banker and his sex partners. After I saw a photo of her paramour being led into jail for hiring ten- and twelve-year-old boys and girls, I realized she used his face as a model for my cosmetic surgery. It is unsettling to think of myself undergoing baby cosmetic surgery by a doctor wanting me to look like her international pedophile lover.

In a video of the meeting, Burris suggested Zeus's Perfect Life Fund be used to wine and dine Cambridge's director and offer special study stipends to the staff, along with endowing a Zeus Chair of Kindergarten Learning. Collins advised this would help, since the previous year a client gained admission to Cambridge by buying furniture for the director's new apartment.

"If we can broker the deal," Collins told the group, "the only other problem is the test. I asked Tom Swayze from Every Kid a Winner to attend. He's worked with PrepStrong materials and has a ninety-five-percent success rate in getting top scores."

"I'll make sure he's in condition for the test," Dr. Lowe added. "I can work with Biostream on drugs for the test."

"That's good," Swayze replied. "He should be fully operational and sharp."

"You can count on us," added a Biostream team member. "We've gotten Jimmy's drugs right. Our new formula should work until nine or ten, when the hormones hit."

"Also," Dr. Lowe interjected, "Jimmy's kinesiology consultant is using a new program for health and brain growth."

"That should do it," Swayze looked down at his kPad. "I have a list of test-prep stuff from PrepStrong and some old tests."

At this remark, Burris smiled. "You can't tell anyone, but Radiant will get the actual test. We've some great hackers."

"There are test skills I can teach." Swayze looked up from the kPad. "It doesn't matter if we have the test. We guarantee high scores by teaching test skills."

"I'm sure you'll help," Burris smiled again. "Jimmy learned to pass tests in preschool without knowing anything about their content."

"The test is a computer game." Swayze held up his kPad so that all could see the test site.

"Even better." Burris laughed. "Jimmy learned to beat learning games on a GoPlay tablet."

Through Sally's eyes on the test morning, I could see Swayze, Collins, Dr. Lowe, and Biostream's head drug researcher, Dr. Alan Cadaver, fussing over me.

"He's well rested and alert," Dr. Cadaver told the group. "Yesterday I prescribed a special low-dose sleeping aid for his drug packet and this morning, a mild amphetamine."

"Jimmy does look bright," Swayze commented, worried that I might fail and ruin his reputation at test prep. "I hope there wasn't too much amphetamine. Parents of one four-year-old gave her too much speed, and she just started bouncing up and down and bit the examiner."

"Just the right amount," Dr. Cadaver smiled. "Our specialists work on correlating these drugs to improved cognitive functions for all ages. We have one that helps eighty-year-olds pass the written part of driving tests."

I looked at my appearance in Sally's video shot—my black hair cut short, the chiseled chin of Dr. Reznick's pedophile lover, dark trousers, and a blue blazer bearing Miss Nancy's special coat of arms modeled on that of the British royal family.

"Too bad about the brown eyes." Collins brushed some lint off my shoulder. "We should have him wear blue contact lenses. Blue eyes work best. But it doesn't matter for the test. We'll do it for his interview."

"I looked at his records." Dr. Lowe bent over to wipe a smudge off my new black wingtips. "Dr. Reznick put out a call for blue eyes. She wanted to be the first to do a baby eye transplant but gave up on the idea."

"Is the robot going with him?" Collins asked. "I don't advise it. The folks at Cambridge might wonder about cheating."

I could see myself frowning at the question and looking up at Sally. "I want Sally," I demanded, with tears in my eyes.

"Sally's got to go," said a concerned Dr. Lowe. "Jimmy will get upset without it. They're bonded."

"OK, but it must stay outside the exam room." Collins looked in wonderment at me holding Sally's hand. "Will that be OK, Jimmy?"

Seeing myself walking hand in hand with Sally from the Perfect Life Toddler apartment, I understand how comforting it is to now sit on Sally's lap and feel its warmth in bed.

I got the highest score ever on the Early Childhood Admission Assessment. With the help of test-prep guru Swayze and PrepStrong vocabulary cards, I aced the literacy part and was brilliant in the comprehension and thinking game.

One of my earliest memories was crashing on the way back to the apartment after the meds wore off and my brain aching from a splitting headache. A video shows Sally carrying me in its arms into the apartment with my head thrown back and drool dripping from the sides of my mouth. Sally put me on my bed and quickly removed my blazer, shirt, pants, and wingtips, replacing my clothing with my favorite Big Bird pajamas.

● ● ●

With extra funding to Cambridge and to Lilly Mulroney's class, Burris persuaded Lilly to let Sally stand in the classroom corner. "It'll not bother anything—just collecting data."

Lilly liked projects. I watched myself and Tom Stoddard—he followed me from Miss Nancy's—building a paper-and-block Egyptian pyramid. Lilly guided us with photos of Egypt. Next was block construction of the Parthenon.

I guess the theme was diversity. Lilly read folk stories, and we sang songs in different languages. Watching myself, I realize I didn't understand any of the words.

The class spent time in Central Park, where Sally seemed to love gliding around the Alice in Wonderland statue as I climbed up on Alice's leg. The class held a plant-and-flower sale outside the Sheep Meadow gate. Recorded by Sally, I made change and put sales in paper bags—Lilly said to never use plastic. The class wandered through the park looking at flowers and trees. I still love Central Park and often walk from Central Park South to the reservoir.

Sally's kindergarten file shows that Radiant's Burris was concerned about Cambridge's kindergarten curriculum. Meeting with Dr. Lowe and Dr. Cadaver in the Perfect Life Toddler apartment under Sally's watchful eyes as I played with my kPad, Burris started cursing the school.

"Goddamn progressive education," Burris blurted. "Those shitheads at Cambridge are ruining Jimmy."

At the word "shitheads," the small red dome on Sally's head lit up and started spinning.

"Sorry, Sally. I'll watch my language. Cambridge will ruin Jimmy. What's he learning—how to sell flowers?"

"But you chose the school," Dr. Lowe pointed out. "You said all grads did well."

"I don't know how, with these empty-headed methods."

"Drugs are working," Dr. Cadaver observed. "No meltdowns—seems to like school."

"It's like something from the sixties." Burris looked sternly at me playing a war game on my kPad and making shooting sounds. "They're running through the park smelling flowers. Fuck it—sorry, Sally—he'll end up a hippie. I saw photos from the sixties of barefoot people holding hands in a circle, dressed in wild colors, and flowers in their hair, with the captions: 'Love,' 'Peace,' and 'Flower Power.' Didn't look like they worked. What kind of life is that—'Flower Power'?"

"What do you think it should be?" asked Dr. Lowe.

"Data and writing—Jimmy needs numbers. He needs to know the importance of collecting numbers, not flowers. All those foreign-word songs—don't they know the world speaks English?"

"They're teaching about other cultures," said Collins, worried that she hadn't explained Cambridge's kindergarten curriculum to Burris, "while teaching tolerance and social skills."

"Social skills!" A disgusted Burris got up to get more coffee in the kitchen. "Maybe working as a team—good for corporations. For all that time in the park, they should make Jimmy run till he can't anymore. Best skill is grit. He should be climbing the Alice statue until his knees hurt."

Dr. Lowe grimaced and called after Burris as he went for coffee, "That doesn't sound healthy. Not a good thing at his age."

"You're as bad as that Lilly Mulroney," Burris yelled from the kitchen. "Jimmy needs to be toughened up. I've looked in Sally's files. There's nothing in class like 'toy wait' and 'don't lick' exercises. Where's he getting the grit and drive to handle Big Data? Certainly not from building paper-and-block pyramids."

"But they learn a lot about plants and do math at the flower stand." Collins looked irritated at Burris's tirade. "They're learning history and about other cultures."

"Where are studies showing that's any good for a perfect life? They should have the kids collecting information—number of flowers, where people sit and for how long, and how many don't walk on the paths or ride bikes. There's tons of data in the park. Then in the first grade, they can analyze it. I should teach!"

"Play," Dr. Lowe emphasized, "is good for kids. All the books say that. Look at Jimmy playing right now." Lowe pointed at me engrossed in the kPad. "See how happy he looks. Isn't that good?"

From Sally's angle I could see I was smiling while destroying spiny-headed creatures from another planet with a mass array of weapons. My score on the game was climbing rapidly.

"Where's the research proof?" Burris asked, returning from the kitchen. "There is nothing in our analysis that says anything about play. Kindergarten is supposed to prepare for a good life in a world driven by Big Data."

This video sequence always bothered me. Did I need play? I felt nausea when I heard Burris suggest I should learn to play with numbers.

"We've got to keep him in Cambridge," Collins advised, "if we're getting Jimmy into a top elementary school. It's all about social connections and networking. Play is networking for future success. These Cambridge kids will network Jimmy to the top."

"Do you have the data?" Dr. Lowe laughed.

"You said yourself," Collins looked at Burris, "that your research shows success for Jimmy attending Cambridge. Maybe it was because of the networking."

"I guess there's nothing we can do now," Burris sighed. "He's committed to Cambridge. It doesn't matter if he learns anything. He already has skills to pass any elementary entrance exam. He'll get into Streets Academy, which will put him on the road to global corporations. You're right—we should do some network analysis."

"Streets?" Dr. Lowe questioned. "Never heard of it."

"New top school," Collins answered. "We're placing kids there now. Jimmy will network with future world leaders."

"Global school," Burris described, "with branches in Singapore, London, Shanghai, and San Paulo, with one opening next year in Mumbai. Good data training."

"I think I should be a kindergarten teacher," Burris continued. "I can see wall charts full of numbers collected by the kids. Blocks could be used as sample data—you know, number of colors and sizes—that sort of thing. I would combine data collection with building true grit—that's what little kids need."

Chapter 4

W e moved into a brick four-bedroom townhouse in the West Village near the Streets Academy, which welcomed me and Sally into a first-grade class of eighteen students. Sally was a hit. Rather than left standing in the corner recording my school day, Sally was used by my new teacher, Bart Rollins, as a class monitor and tech adviser. I was now six and more aware.

The summer before school opened, visitors streamed through the door of our townhouse. There were World Government and university researchers wanting to examine the life of the perfect child along with teams from Radiant and Biostream. According to Sally, it was Burris who insisted on spending $20 million from the Zeus Perfect Life Fund for the townhouse and another million to furnish it. In the basement was a gym and small swimming pool. Dr. Lowe insisted I have daily exercises. Dr. Cadaver built a lab in the library to monitor my drug supply.

I remember professor Charles Eliot from the University of Wisconsin staying in one bedroom during the summer before I entered the Streets Academy. Burris invited him because of his pioneering studies on net-working and children's playgroups, resulting in the popular online service PlayDate. Eliot cofounded PlayDate with Betty Graham to arrange and schedule playtimes for compatible kids. Burris was aware of criticisms of PlayDate being discriminatory, with playgroups often drawn from the same social class.

Tom Stoddard, Ben Moore, and Chelsea Tipper were selected by PlayDate after Burris entered names of kids in my preschool and kindergarten. Up to this point, I had no friends.

The first playdate was held in the game room with Sally closely monitoring and sending data to Radiant. We remain friends, and I even married Chelsea. She was the first girl I ever kissed. It happened when I was ten when we snuck into a school closet. By twelve, we were groping each other any chance we could until, as I learned from Sally, Dr. Cadaver adjusted my hormone levels, leaving Chelsea searching for another playmate.

● ● ●

"We need to put him in a room with kids who will get him ahead." Sally recorded a conversation between Burris and Eliot in the townhouse's living room as they sipped wine.

"We can build a network chart around successful parents and then match kids' interests. PlayDate acts like an adult online matching service. On PlayDate's website, parents indicate their kids' interests. Once the parents register, we can search the web and put in their incomes and jobs. We've been criticized for this, but poor and rich kids just don't play the same way."

"Does it work? Kids get along?" Burris asked.

"There is some tension and fighting. Parents love the convenience. It works like Uber. Parents put in times and possible places to meet, and PlayDate immediately matches them with other parents wanting the same time slot. A map appears, and parents can see how close the others are. If it all looks good and at least one parent has volunteered space, then the time and place is shown on the map. Click, and they meet new friends."

I still remember our first playdate. Tom, who I already knew from Cambridge and Miss Nancy's, Ben, and Chelsea appeared as nervous as me when we gathered in my new playroom filled with board games, puzzles, Legos, and Nerf toys. Besides Sally, there were cameras around the ceiling recording us. Professor Eliot, Burris, and Dr. Cadaver watched through one-way glass.

What do six-year-olds do? I remember Chelsea picking up a Nerf ball and throwing it at me. I cowered in a corner as Tom and Ben grabbed Lego blocks and started throwing them at Chelsea. No one expected our playdate to erupt in a toy war. Professor Eliot came running into the room, trying to restore calm and urging me to leave the corner and join the group. Sally's red light was spinning as Tom hit Chelsea, while Ben tried to take all the toys into another corner, claiming them as his.

In Sally's records I found a conversation recorded behind the one-way glass with Burris criticizing Eliot for the apparent mismatch made by PlayDate.

"I thought they were matched by interests."

"They are. I can see their profiles on my kWatch. All the parents answered an interest questionnaire, showing their kids with high degrees of self-interest and competitiveness. They're all from high-powered families."

"Maybe they need a Sally to raise them."

"They were mainly raised by nannies. Chelsea's was from Switzerland and graduated from an early-childhood course. Tom and Ben's were from Ireland with good grades and recommendations from local churches."

"Jesus," Burris said, "didn't they teach any discipline?"

"Their parents want them to be competitive and successful. Chelsea's mother is CEO of Winnie's Secrets, the international women's lingerie company, and her father is head of the Brooklyn Bank. Tom's family owns car dealerships all over the United States and Great Britain. Ben's father is CEO of United Oil, and his mother is a publishing executive. All successful and wanting the best for their kids. Aren't these the kids for Jimmy?"

"I'm concerned about Jimmy hiding in the corner," Dr. Cadaver said. "I don't care about the fighting. Jimmy should jump in and start throwing things. They'll eventually get tired and start playing a board game. Maybe we should have put computer games in there."

"Computer games are isolating," Eliot observed. "We're hoping for social interaction that we can measure and chart. I got plenty here for my network diagrams of social relationships. Look at Tom trying to kick Chelsea. And now Ben is taking out a puzzle game."

"Maybe I should program Sally to break up any fights." Burris anxiously looked through the window.

"If they didn't fight, that would be a problem." Dr. Cadaver was still worried that I didn't join the others. "I wonder if the drug packet is making Jimmy timid. We've got to adjust the serotonin levels. He should be out there throwing things."

"I guess we want to teach competitiveness along with grit and stick-to-itiveness." Burris was still disturbed by the scene unfolding on the other side of the glass. "But this looks like combat training."

"John Koch has an office near mine," Eliot said. "He's a world-famous sociologist studying corporations. He says corporate workers are usually at war with each other. They don't throw things, but they try, if you'll excuse the expression, to stab fellow workers in the back to get ahead. Of course, the leaders want teamwork, but Koch says workers use teams for self-promotion."

"Doesn't that hurt the company? At Biostream," Dr. Cadaver explained, "we promote team spirit to make the best drugs."

"They may look like they're working together," continued Eliot, "but secretly each is plotting how to get ahead. Koch's software correlates employee warfare with profitability. You can enter data on your company, and it will tell you if the tension between backstabbing and teamwork is hurting or helping the bottom line."

"You think Jimmy should be more aggressive?" Burris asked.

"If he were an adolescent, we could add more testosterone, but he's too young for that. We use it with women in their twenties who want to be more aggressive at work. I guess we'll play with the antidepressants in the drug packet. I think we can put him on edge and make him a little more aggressive."

I remember Sally, its red light flashing, coming over to check on me as I huddled in the corner. Bending over, it pulled me to my feet. Its silicon arms wrapped around me, and it held me until I stopped crying.

I wandered over to Ben to help with the puzzle. I waved Tom over. We started putting puzzle pieces together to look like the Empire State Building. Tom thought we could build the Empire State Building at the same time using Legos. We worked together doing the puzzle and the Lego construction.

"Lego blocks. See, I told you. Now they're working together—real team spirit." Dr. Cadaver smiled. "I wonder what Chelsea's doing."

"Looks like she's building a Lego house. Notice she put the mom and dad figures in front. Now she's adding a dog figure," Burris observed. "Why doesn't she join the boys? What do you think, Eliot?"

Before Eliot could answer, screams came from the playroom. They pressed their faces against the glass.

I often reminded Chelsea about the incident. I can still feel the pain. I was bent over, putting a Lego block in place when, for whatever reason, she came over and kicked me hard between my legs. I'll always remember her screaming, "Take that, you prick!"

Of course, Sally went crazy, swiftly rolling over and gathering my body in its arms. It was programmed to immediately contact 911 if something happened to me. Within seconds, Sally's flashing light was joined by flashing lights and sirens outside. Eliot, Burris, and Dr. Cadaver rushed into the room.

"Where did she learn that language?" Burris took me from Sally's arms. "This is some playdate arrangement, Eliot."

"You wanted kids charted to be on top. These three kids meet your criteria. Their parents move in successful networks. I don't know about the nannies."

"Jimmy could be killed learning success." Burris looked at Dr. Cadaver. "Is there anything you can do to stop the crying?"

"It may not be as bad as you think." Eliot began punching a text into his phone. "I'm contacting professor Koch. His fees are high, but you should consult him. I know your economist friends talk about grit and stick-to-itiveness, but there's more to success. This will be good for Jimmy. Koch might say a swift kick to the balls is common in companies."

Police and paramedics rushed in to find a bunch of crying six-year-olds, with me clinging to Sally's arms and holding my testicles. I learned new social skills.

A week later, professor Koch arrived after being offered $30,000 plus expenses. Originally, Burris offered $10,000 plus expenses and was refused. "Professors are real entrepreneurs. Role models for values Jimmy should learn." Burris's comment was recorded under Sally's watchful eyes.

They met in the living room with surveillance cameras recording into Sally's cloud. Burris, Koch, Eliot, and Dr. Cadaver sat with kPads.

"We're trying to educate Jimmy for success," Burris explained. "It's part of the Perfect Life Project funded by Zeus. Eliot says you know what it takes to be successful in a global corporation."

Sounding professorial, Koch, dressed in a pinstripe suit with a black tie, lectured, "The perfect life may be different from corporate success. But I think that's a philosophical issue. You may want to consult with professor Arthur Jensen in our Philosophy Department and discuss whether corporate success adds to the perfect-life concept. You consider corporate success as part of it, so we'll work from there."

"Of course," Burris responded. "People want to die knowing they've been successful and left their children with a good estate so they will be remembered."

"Hmmm," Koch looked at his kPad. "I've got some stuff here that'll help your little Jimmy—Jimmy Clark—right?"

They all nodded yes.

"Good name for success because it's easy to remember and spell," Koch continued. "I always recommend name changes. But Jimmy Clark is ideal. Now there is a difference between the soft skills needed for corporate profits and those needed for personal advancement. From what I understand, you've concentrated on the skills corporations want—grit and stick-to-itiveness. Is that right?" Koch looked around the room and found no objections.

"What corporations want is what we call a high 'EQ' or 'Emotional Intelligence Quotient,' involving a cluster of personality traits like a person's social graces, communication skills, personal habits, friendliness, and being a team player. And, of course, working hard until a job is done. This is good for the corporation but not necessarily for the worker. A company might make good money, while a conscientious worker is stuck in place."

"I guess I've always thought about the company and not the worker," Burris admitted.

"The first thing you need to do to get ahead is to brand yourself."

"Brand a person?" Dr. Cadaver wondered out loud.

"Jimmy Clark is a good brand name. As I said, it's simple and easy for foreign workers to pronounce in global companies. He also must present himself as a smart leader. We not only dress for success but must act like it. Next, he must create an organizational chart with arrows leading to the top. Every office the arrows pass through must be considered the enemy standing in the way. That's why we recommend computer shooter games as training. Learn to mow down the people in your way."

"I can admit doing that," Burris grimaced.

"Jimmy must learn how to present himself as better than others at company meetings without being obvious. This is an important skill for advancement. There are methods for asking pleasing questions of those above you and finding ways to verbally undercut any competition. We call it 'sweet-talking' the boss. For a fee, I have a company that provides that training using gaming software."

"We had a troubling incident last week." Eliot explained what happened during the playdate and showed the recording from Sally's files.

"Jimmy hiding in the corner is not a good sign," Koch observed. "On the other hand, at six, Chelsea is demonstrating how to get ahead in a corporate world."

Chapter 5

In my twenties, I played the video over and over again, showing professor Koch suggesting a philosopher join the group to discuss the meaning of a perfect life. Every time I replayed the conversation between Koch and Burris and a later conversation with Zeus Fund head, Britt Owens, I wondered what I would have been like with a different perfect-life vision guiding my upbringing.

Streets Academy lived up to professor Eliot's expectation of building good networks when I entered in the fall of 2026. The eighteen students in my first-grade class became successful bankers, corporate leaders, and politicians. Two classmates eschewed moneymaking for painting and acting, with Jimmy Henderson becoming a museum curator and Denise Croner a minor character actress in Hollywood.

In the first week, my teacher, Bart Rollins, teamed me up with Chelsea and Tom to develop a class-management plan. Chelsea's parents chose the Streets Academy through KidNet—a service offered by PlayDate. KidNet, as professor Eliot named it, resulted from conversations with Burris during my first PlayDate. On KidNet, parents list their children's friends. KidNet did a background check on the friends' parents, creating a diagram with projections of the social and economic consequences of their children's friendships. The service impressed Chelsea's parents, who entered my name and Tom's. Then they added a series of school names. The network diagram showed the Streets Academy as important for Chelsea's social and economic success.

Wanting to attend the Streets Academy's admission meeting, Chelsea's mother, Winnie Tipper, hurried back from an international lingerie show in Brussels, where her company was promoting a new line of computerized and eatable underwear called "Eat'em." Bras, slips, and panties were offered in different flavors under signs saying, Eat Your Way to Love. Similar eatables were on the market, but Winnie's Secrets offered them as wearable computers with wireless communication to smartphones and health software. Even the computers were eatable, made of conductive threads woven from genetically modified sugar. "Have Fun as You Monitor Your Intimate Health," ads for the new product claimed, with an offer of free STD-monitoring software.

Burris and Sally attended the admission meeting, along with Winnie and a group of other anxious parents wanting the best for their children. Sally recorded the school's director, Benno Paterno, showing PowerPoint maps and images of the school's branches around the world along with companies offering internships to students in their junior and senior years.

"It's eighty thousand dollars tuition a year," Paterno explained, "and if you sign on for our Global Worker and Cosmopolitan Grades One to Twelve Package, the tuition cost is guaranteed through the twelfth grade. Our finance office will explain how the package works." Nothing was mentioned about financial aid to this elite audience.

"We also require the Independent School Entrance Examination and our own social-skills test." A new PowerPoint slide showed sample questions. Clicking a YouTube link to the social-skills test, they watched six-year-olds sitting in a private dining room at the Four Seasons, ordering a World Foods Tasting Menu and wines (simple grape juice from bottles with exotic French and Australian names). In the YouTube, a sommelier gave each kid a taste of his or her selected grape juice for approval before filling the wine glasses. Facial-expression cameras recorded reactions to each dish. This test was outdated by 2032, when GoGrow gained a world monopoly over food supplies and restaurants.

"We want to see if our students can be world eaters," Paterno explained. "This is an important global skill."

In Sally's recording, kids used their kWatches to pay and sign after being shown how to add a tip. The requirement was part of the Modernity Studies Course sequence in the marketing curriculum.

"Here is our social-stress room," Paterno started another YouTube. "We check how kids act in tough social situations. In this first scene, we put ten kids in a room with only seven game tablets and tell them to play. Each kid wears a wristband to measure pulse rates and blood pressure. Pads are put on the cheeks to measure tear volume. As you can see in the YouTube video, some start fighting, while others partner up. In this stress test, we eliminate kids whose blood pressure and pulse rates are too high and whose tear quantities are too large. Blood pressure and tear volume are scientifically compared to a social-behavior and health scale developed at the University of Michigan. We reject kids who do nothing—no struggle, teamwork, or tears. We want team players and fighters—but not too belligerent—whose blood pressures and pulse rates fall within healthy ranges. We don't want graduates to become heart-attack-prone corporate workers."

It was easy for me to pass with my drug packet controlling my blood pressure, along with my test skills and Sally's programmed etiquette training with trips to top-shelf restaurants where Sally required me to order a meal and pay with my own kWatch. I was given special training to smile even if the food tasted terrible.

Chelsea had a harder time. She easily passed the Independent School Entrance Examination but failed the social-stress tests. She only ate hamburgers and fries from fast-food places and once threw a tantrum when served the Ritz's $295 burger made with Wagyu beef and special cheddar from Somerset, England, and served on a bun flecked with pure 24-karat gold flakes from Switzerland with a side of caviar rather than fries. She was carried, kicking and screaming, out of the restaurant to a nearby

McDonalds. She also started biting kids in the second stress test to get her own tablet and broke the record on tears and blood pressure. A shipment to the school-director's wife of specially fitted Eat'em lingerie and a $10,000 Winnie's Secrets' gift card got Chelsea into the school.

A week after Burris received my Streets Academy acceptance letter, Zeus Fund's Britt Owens flew to New York to meet with Burris, professor Eliot, Dr. Lowe, and Dr. Cadaver. According to Sally's records, the Zeus Fund's tech people monitored all Perfect Life data and videos to identify unchristian thinking. They were troubled by Koch's suggestion to consult philosopher Arthur Jensen. Jensen was on the investment fund's watch list for anti-Christian activities supporting abortion rights and gun-control laws and attending the first gay Wisconsin marriage. Owens shared the list with Interpol, which added it to their terrorist watch list. Jensen always wondered why it was so difficult to get through airport security.

Ceiling cameras sent video footage to Sally's cloud as Britt Owens looked on his kPad at notes made by his technical teams. "A professor Koch recommended you consult the anti-Christian Arthur Jensen. Is that right?"

"Yes—to discuss the meaning of a perfect life," Professor Eliot replied, looking at notes on his screen. "He suggested economic success is problematic as a perfect-life goal."

"I admit I was surprised as an economist," Burris frowned. "I always used it as a criterion for measuring the good life. What's this about Jensen being anti-Christian? What's that got to do with us?"

"Financial success is a key Christian doctrine," Owens answered, opening a file containing his essay on "Christian Values and Investment." "I funded this project because I believe the perfect life requires God— that is, a Christian God—and hoped this project would prove it. That's why I'm funding you."

Shocked expressions appeared on the project team's faces.

"I'm Jewish, and no one mentioned religion or Christianity when I joined the project," Dr. Lowe almost shouted. "This is disturbing. I'll check with my rabbi."

"This is news to me. I'm a secularist." Burris began Googling "God" and "financial success." "I can't find any research correlating religion with success."

"If there's a God," Dr. Cadaver laughed, "Biostream would be out of business. We make drugs to cure people. If an all-knowing God designed human bodies, then there wouldn't be diseases, faulty joints, and malfunctioning innards—imagine no constipation. You can't tell me a real God could be so incompetent as to leave us with the mess we call our bodies."

"Professor Koch didn't say anything about God," Eliot snapped. "Only that the perfect life was a philosophical problem."

"It's God's issue." Owens was angry. "We've funded you and spent all this money on robots, schools, health care, housing, and consulting. You think it was to talk philosophy?"

"We used analytics on Big Data sets. I don't think religious doctrines were in it." Burris looked intently at his kPad. "It would be interesting to code all religious texts and add them to the data set. It would be a big undertaking."

"I don't mean all religious texts, only the true one—the Bible—it has all the answers." Owens began typing an e-mail to his tech department about reducing the Bible to data. "It is an interesting idea of turning the Bible into pure data. Would a proof of God result from applying analytics?"

"That would be interesting." Burris looked nervous about the direction of the conversation. "Our funding was to raise a kid for a perfect life. There was no mention of religion. Of course, I know the Zeus Fund sponsors research to prove the existence of God, but I didn't think it had anything to do with us."

"You're trying to prove the existence of God!" exclaimed Dr. Cadaver. "But which god or gods?"

"Should've run their names through the anti-Christian checklist," thought Owens. "Do you want me to continue the funding?" he asked. "First, you want to consult with a renowned anti-Christian activist, and now you seem to be questioning God's existence."

The room was suddenly silent at the mention of cutting funding. They worried about reduced incomes.

"We aren't anti-God or anti-Christian," a very concerned Burris responded, thinking about the large number of Radiant shares owned by the Zeus Fund.

With similar thoughts about company shares passing through his mind, Dr. Cadaver defensively said, "None of our research disrespects God or Christianity. We're just trying to find the right chemical balance for the perfect life."

"Don't worry; I'm not cutting funding." Owens assured them. "The project is too important. What I want is for you to stay focused on economic success. It's part of God's plan to make financial gains an outward sign of inner salvation."

Flustered, Burris sought a reply that protected his pocketbook and the existence of Radiant. "I think you are raising a good issue. Is there any way we can link data on economic success to God?"

"You don't need data." Owens looked at Burris. "Data is the only thing you economists think about. I didn't get my wealth by data but by prayers and godly visions. God is holding my hand when I make good investments—poor ones result from Satan. God is all about wealth, not data."

"God is about wealth!" professor Eliot almost shouted. "God's not in any of my network diagrams."

"Wealth is God's blessing." Owens pointed his finger at Burris. "It's a connection to Christ. It shows the world that a person is blessed by God. If Jimmy becomes wealthy, he has the perfect life with God."

"Does he want God in the drug packet?" Dr. Cadaver wondered to himself. "Biostream should think of making communion wafers that make people feel like they've eaten Christ's flesh. I wonder what flavor."

"Success causes godly actions," Owens continued. "Look at Andrew Carnegie's libraries and Rockefeller's foundations—godly men are trustees of wealth."

"All rich people are godly?" Lowe was clearly worried about the Christian theme. "Aren't there some evil rich people?"

"They're not Christian," Owens answered, clearly annoyed by the question. "Secularist or Hindu or some other weird religion—they got the money through evil."

When I looked at this video, I hoped for a discussion, but others in the room only looked at each other in what I thought was a shared annoyance at Owens's statements. But then they appeared more concerned about funding and whether godliness and wealth went hand in hand.

"What does this mean for the project?" Burris asked. "Do we need to adjust our data?"

"Planning on Jimmy's economic fortune is clearly the right direction." Owens looked at his screen. "I did notice that Jimmy hasn't gone to church."

"We were worried about sickness." Dr. Cadaver was protecting Biostream from Owens's disapproval. "Some have missionaries from disease-ridden countries. We're working on a drug that gives religious experiences—I mean, Christian experiences. We could sell it as the Jesus pill. Put it in Jimmy's drug packet."

I paused the video, searching my memory for any drug-induced Christian feelings. I do remember experiences where my body transcended into the sky. But that happened with a club drug.

"In general, you're working on the right things—with economic success, Jimmy will come to God," Owens continued. "Streets Academy is a good step—some of my best investors send their kids there. But Jimmy needs to meet Jesus. How can you do that?"

"I think Radiant could add Jesus to Sally." Burris started typing an e-mail to Radiant's software department. "I'm sending a message now. Is there any software you could recommend?"

"There's a whole bunch from Give Jesus a Chance software company in Kentucky." Owens sent the website address to Burris's kPad. "One program teaches the best from the Bible and how to be a Christian."

Before seeing this video, I wondered why Sally started quoting scriptures when tucking me in bed after I started at the Streets Academy and why it placed a glow-in-the-dark Jesus statue on my bedside table.

Chapter 6

❋   ❋   ❋

I opened the closet door and powered Sally on. I felt so tired.

"How could I be a widower at twenty?" I wondered. I almost fell, tripping over my pants leg as I undressed, overwhelmed by thoughts of death.

"Am I getting old?" I was preoccupied with worries about my health and death. "Tom is as energetic as he was at the Streets Academy," I ruminated, "jogging, skiing, traveling, partying, going to the gym, and staying up to all hours. I'm dragging my body around, sometimes wondering if I can get out of bed. Even work feels difficult. I remember my training on smiling or looking serious at funerals. Now I'm shocked to see my face set in a permanent scowl when I look in the mirrors Chelsea hung throughout our two-level penthouse.

"Fuck, who cares, I'm at the top," I shouted to an empty bedroom, finally ridding myself of my clothes and standing naked. "Is this how the CEO of the world's largest conglomerate of tech companies should feel?"

"Hello, Jimmy." Booted up, Sally disengaged from its power dock and scooted out of the closet. "What shall we do for the day? How are you feeling?"

"Come to bed with me," I invited. "I need to rest."

I pulled back the bedding, and Sally sat on the bed's edge, leaned back, swung its wheels up, and put its head on a pillow. I adjusted Sally's thermostat to my ideal sleeping temperature and pulled the sheet and blankets up over its body. I went around to the other side, climbing under the covers.

Snuggling against Sally, I felt it warming up. Sliding my hand over its fabricated chest, I rested it on Sally's control panel.

"What do you want, Jimmy—an old memory, favorite movie, a game?"

My fingers slowly stroked the memory button. Sally's eyes lit up, indicating communication with its cloud.

"What memory do you want?" Sally responded.

"I'd like the eleventh grade. Show me walking down the hallway in the morning."

Sally's eyes projected a moving image on the ceiling above the bed, and out of its sound system came the loud voices of the Streets Academy corridor between classes.

I tried to get closer to Sally, wrapping my arm around it and watching myself walking with Tom, Chelsea, and Amy Cartwright past school lockers and banners hanging from the ceiling announcing a rally for World Government Day. It was 2037, and I was seventeen.

School surveillance cameras, in fact any surveillance camera where I was present, recorded me on Sally's cloud. Carl Burris was proud of this achievement, with surveillance equipment all over the world able to identify my face and record my actions on Sally's cloud on a special network created by Radiant. In the third grade, Sally stopped going to school with me, and the school's surveillance took over. I'd rush home, missing Sally. I never felt lonely knowing I was always watched.

Radiant was hired to fulfill Interpol's motto, Connecting Police for a Safer World. Burris used the same system with all the world's surveillance cameras feeding into Interpol's system. All human activity was tracked and quickly analyzed, producing minute-by-minute reports on all aspects of human life. Proudly, Burris gave Radiant's new subsidiary the name AlwaysWatch. Crime plummeted, as no one could escape the law.

I watched Chelsea lift her hand, giving the finger to the rally banner. I couldn't hear her for the corridor noise. I appeared to be laughing with Tom at the gesture while my hand gave Amy's ass a little pat.

In my fourteenth year, Amy relieved me of my virginity, and we kept up an on and off relationship until Chelsea and I hooked up. My deflowering was hidden as I powered off Sally and covered my bedroom ceiling cameras.

The shrouded cameras were immediately detected by Interpol. In 2030, the World Government required that all buildings and private dwellings be equipped with surveillance systems connected to AlwaysWatch. Later, when Radiant and AlwaysWatch became part of my tech empire, I added Interpol's mission statement to the bottom of all e-mails and official documents: "Our role is to enable police around the world to work together to make the world a safer place. Our high-tech infrastructure of technical and operational support helps meet the growing challenges of fighting crime in the twenty-first century."

As my virginity ended, the townhouse was surrounded by screaming police sirens. I scooted out from under Amy, powered up Sally, and uncovered the ceiling cameras. The World Government imposed a stiff fine and possible imprisonment for tampering with or disabling surveillance equipment. Fortunately, Burris intervened, using AlwaysWatch's connections to get the charges dropped. Now I wish I had recorded it. It would be fun to watch.

As we entered our small eleventh-grade study and planning room, the video switched cameras, showing Amy with her lush, blond-highlighted, brunette hair; plump Botox lips; broad cheeks; and cute nose in an animated discussion with Chelsea. Seeing Amy, I longed to recapture the feeling of that first tryst. I could see the old Occupy Wall Street, Soviet hammer and sickle, and Che Guevara pins adorning Chelsea's Nehru-collared green shirt as she stood, hands on her hips, arguing with Amy. Chelsea liked to highlight her green eyes, wear her red kinky hair tied in a topknot bun, and use black lipstick.

There, I thought, were my only true lovers debating the merits of the World Government. All my other female and male lovers I paid for, or they were provided at World Government parties.

The discussion grew heated, and I could see my perplexed face. Sometimes it was difficult to control my emotions after the intravenous drug packet was disconnected at age eleven. Dr. Cadaver removed it as hormones flooded my system. He warned me about mood swings and prescribed a morning glass of Biostream's widely marketed Happy Times Serotonin Syrup mixed with a personally formulated drug powder. The powder was reformulated monthly based on reports from Sally to Biostream. The results alternated months when I shaved twice daily and felt constant arousal with months of little facial hair. I finally tossed the last bottle of Happy Times and Biostream powder in the trash when I turned eighteen.

"Fuck you," Chelsea screamed at Amy. "You only want your dad's money. His shithead bank is bilking the poor with World Government help. Fuck, you want money for more Botox. Do you know how many hardly get enough to eat while you get your face pumped up?"

I watched myself back away and remember wanting to smack Chelsea. I didn't want my thing with Amy ruined, but I felt closer to Chelsea on the World Government issue. As I recall, that month's Biostream powder unleashed a constant stream of sexual fantasies, leaving me wanting anyone in the room. I had been briefly with Tom, but in this video, my hormones were focused on Amy and Chelsea.

"You should talk, living on your mom's eatable panties." Amy took a seat at our group table. "Hope you're not goin' to ruin the rally. Who's eating your panties, huh?"

"It's nothing but corporate greed. I'm making a banner: The Corporations Suck the Poor Dry." Chelsea pulled a drawing from her backpack and shoved it in front of Amy.

"Wait a minute," said Tom. I smiled, thinking of Tom liking peace. "Why don't we continue working on this eleventh-grade project? We can't do anything about the World Government."

"There's a rally, and even you said you don't like the Pledge of Allegiance to the World Government," Chelsea reminded Tom. "I saw you at the last assembly playing with your kWatch and not putting your hand on your heart. You don't believe in this crap!"

"The World Government protects us," Amy retorted. "Remember those awful people last month trying to keep us out of school. I got hit by a sign. Interpol took 'em away."

"They were homeless." I watched myself whispering, afraid to stir the pot.

"That doesn't mean they can stop our education." I could see Amy scowling at me. "With our school, we're learning to help. That's why we do community service."

"Give me a break," Chelsea said. "Community service is crap. Last time we served some soup to cardboard shacks in Tompkins Park. Big deal! Shit, they're living like that because of the World Government."

"The World Government didn't make them live there." Amy looked into her electronic compact, which gave feedback on makeup and hair. I guess it suggested something about the hair, since Amy pulled a brush from her backpack.

"I can't say the pledge," Tom explained. "That flag with all the currency symbols and corporate logos pisses me off. I can't worship money."

"Why not?" Amy retorted. "You enjoy money. You paid that tab the other night with your mother's account. Three thousand dollars for a dinner and ecstasy—how did you get them to put the drugs on the bill? You're a fucking hypocrite. Cut off your parents' money from those luxury-car dealerships, and you'd be nothing."

"I could survive."

"How?"

"The World Government was created to help us." I could see myself trying to restore calm.

"You're just a fucker, Jimmy." Chelsea slammed her fist on the table. "You know a bunch of companies just wanted protection. Your Radiant and drug people at Biostream got what they wanted. I heard you're getting money from Zeus. Zeus is straight-out evil with all that Christian shit."

"Maybe we should look at their founding charter." Tom looked as his kPad beamed the charter on the wall.

"Look." Amy pointed at the opening lines from the 2025 World Government Charter. "See, the opening says it's going to bring peace and prosperity."

"They meant peace from those complaining about the rich getting richer and the poor getting poorer," I reminded them. I could see from Sally's ceiling projection that I was leering at Chelsea. I remember her red hair always got me excited. "Some groups were calling for revolution against corporations."

"It was more than that. The old UN, when it existed, tried international sanctions to control global companies," Tom added. "Could have destroyed the global economy—look what we learned in our history project."

"What kind of shit is that?" Chelsea's Occupy Wall Street pin fell off as she swung her hand in Tom's direction. "You believe that? This is the Streets Academy; this school supports the rich who come here."

"It wasn't just the UN." I could see my hand creeping under the table toward Amy's leg. "There were food riots and people walking off jobs. Remember Chinese and American demonstrations against the twelve-hour day? They said corporations were squeezing them dry."

"They were." Chelsea pointed at the World Government Charter. "Tom, scroll down to the part about the corporate alliance and prosperity. I want us to read it aloud."

"'In the interest of world peace and security,'" we repeated almost from memory, "'we establish this government to protect the major contributors to global prosperity. The World Government president will be chosen by a vote of the membership of the World Economic Forum. The Congress of the World Government will be composed of representatives from the three hundred highest-earning global corporations as determined by the World Economic Forum. The permanent home of the World Government will be in Davos, Switzerland.'"

"See what I mean," Chelsea shouted. "It's government by corporations for corporations."

"Yes," Amy snickered as my hand reached her leg. "But corporations feed and clothe us."

"You can laugh," Chelsea said angrily. "They give you caviar and Gucci, but most are corporate slaves feeding your parents' pocketbook."

I remember feeling pretty hot at Chelsea's outburst. Her anger and red hair caused my hand to move in her direction.

"Jimmy, keep your fucking hand off me," Chelsea reacted to my touch. "Do you only think about sex?"

"I do," Tom responded for me. "I'm getting a boner right now."

"Can't you guys be serious?" Chelsea asked. "Help me with my banner, or are you all planning to suck from the souls of the world's workers?"

I reached over and touched the Fast Forward on Sally's chest, thinking of my first time with Chelsea. I pushed Stop at the part showing the rally. I was in back, helping Chelsea hold up the banner denouncing the World Government as other students held their hands over their hearts looking at the thirty-by-forty-foot flag slowly unfurling from the ceiling above the stage. The symbol for the world currency was centered on top of a circle encompassing corporate logos and symbols of former national currencies. I felt a slight bulge in my pants as students said in unison:

I pledge allegiance to the flag of the World Government
And to the corporations for which it stands,
One trade zone, indivisible, with prosperity and free trade for all.

Chapter 7

After the rally we went over to Tom's place on East 75th near Fifth Avenue. Lying next to Sally, I could see on the ceiling video Chelsea struggling to get her rolled-up banner along with the four of us into a driverless cab. I was forced to sit in front next to the driving console. I could hear Tom give his address to the automated cab system, and I watched the cab's internal GPS guide the car out into traffic. I remember Amy's snide remarks about Chelsea attacking the World Government and spending her parents' money on a cab. I watched the scene unfold on my bedroom ceiling.

"Raise your hand if you've taken the Higher-Speed train lately?" Amy challenged us.

No one responded, and I was embarrassed to confess I was never on a Higher-Speed train because of Biostream's fear of me getting diseases.

"Mom won't let me on Higher-Speed trains; she thinks I'll be mugged," Tom admitted.

"And you, Chelsea? You're the big radical." Amy grinned in triumph. "Bet you don't come to school by public transportation. Don't want to mix with the plebs?"

I remember Chelsea's face turning almost the color of her red hair as she made a gesture of spitting on Amy. "I can't," Chelsea almost whispered in embarrassment. "Mom says I'll be groped. A lot of men are molesting girls in Higher-Speed trains."

"Also," Tom added, "the Higher-Speed trains cut back on cleaning. Some cars smell like piss with stains on the floors and seats. The underground stations are filthy."

"See, that's an example of the World Government at work," Chelsea reacted. "Only the poor ride the Higher-Speed trains, so they're dirty and breaking down. We ride in cabs, and we're safe. The World Government helps us but not those at the bottom."

Amy started laughing at Chelsea as the cab pulled up in front of Tom's three-story townhouse.

Sally's video switched to the surveillance cameras on Tom's building. I could see us piling out of the taxi.

"My parents are at our place in Croatia." The ceiling video showed Tom swinging open the front door and waving us in. "I'll send the housekeeper home. We'll have some fun!"

Interior cameras showed us entering the front hallway decorated with eighteenth-century Chinese wall scrolls and a chandelier that once hung in a Venetian palace. Tom's parents bought the floor runner in Turkey with a guarantee that sultans had walked on it.

After Tom told the happy housekeeper to take the day off, we hurried to his private third-floor den. Tom didn't worry about the den's surveillance cameras. His parents didn't care, and Interpol kept its nose out of the townhouse's family life. His parents supplied Interpol's officials with Bentley Continentals and Rolls-Royce Phantoms in exchange for extra protection of their dealerships and destruction of the competition. This gave them a monopoly on luxury-car sales and 50 percent of global sales of all cars. Their grip on global car sales forced companies to pay them to sell their cars.

I could see Chelsea angrily tossing her banner into a corner near Tom's computer desk and flopping down on a leather-covered mattress on the floor.

"You can make fun of me for not taking Higher-Speed trains." Chelsea gave Amy an indignant look. "But we are living off the backs of the poor and should feel guilty taking cabs to school."

"Let's keep it calm." Tom smiled, opening the door on an eighteenth-century French cabinet holding his drug and liquor supplies. "What'd you like? I gotta lot of stuff from the state store on Lexington near sixtieth—more variety than the one near here. I think New York State pot stores have different suppliers."

I could see everyone, including me, starting to look mellow as Tom poured from a bottle of $4,000 Henschke Hill wine from Australia's Eden Valley and passed around a bong full of AK-47.

"Sorry, Amy." Chelsea's facial color was now normal. "But I get upset with this World Government stuff. I know they protect Mom's company. But that doesn't help."

"Chelsea, could you wipe off that black lipstick; it's all over the bong." Amy stood up from her floor cushion, pulling tissue from her backpack and wiping off the bong before taking a hit.

"I almost got sick during the pledge." Tom grimaced. "I hate that shitty government. We might not have an earth to live on by the time they get through. Nothing's been done about the climate—starving people from droughts. Even my dad worries about who can buy cars. The numbers are getting smaller with the pay cuts."

I watched myself taking a hit, blowing it out, and getting up slowly to retrieve my backpack near the bookshelf.

"I got this from Sally," I could hear myself saying. "I asked Sally about the World Government, and it gave me a list, and on it was this book by a Howard Binn, *An Uncensored History of the World Government*—banned by Interpol."

"How is it, having the perfect life?" Tom laughed.

"You got a copy?" Chelsea came over and sat next to me on the floor. "I heard about this—I know people who'd die to see it. Can I look?"

"How about some Rude Queen to liven us up?" Amy asked Tom. "This political stuff is boring."

"How'd Sally get this?" Chelsea grabbed my e-reader.

"Through Radiant, which operates Interpol's database. I can get all sorts of banned stuff."

"Come on, Jimmy, tell us about the perfect life." Tom got up and retrieved a glass container labeled Rude Queen and put it in another bong. "You sure you want to smoke this? Last time you girls were a little sex crazy."

"Isn't that the purpose of life?" Amy smiled. "Reproduction, the domination of humans over the planet and other species—have more babies. Of course, I'm just practicing—got my annual Biostream BirthStop/STD shot at school."

"Fuck it. I guess I'm having the perfect life," I answered Tom. I always felt liberated swearing outside of Sally's scrutiny. "Radiant uses a massive database to determine it."

"But what does it mean, 'the perfect life'?"

"Shit, I guess being happy, having shelter, and being healthy." I could see myself leering at Amy as she took the first hit of Rude Queen. I remember how hot it got her.

"What's happiness?" asked Tom.

"Radiant measures happiness by asking people questions like, If you had to do your life over again, what would you change? The more things you would change, the less happy you are."

"What happens if you're kidding yourself or crazy?"

"Christ!" Amy blew out the smoke, coughing. "Were you happy being raised by a creepy robot?"

I felt Sally stirring next to me as if it understood the question. I snuggled closer, trying to reassure it. I watched myself answering Amy.

"Sally is OK—never any problems. All of you complain about your parents. Wouldn't you want one that never nagged, always worried about your health, protected you, and let you do what you wanted?"

Looking up from the e-reader, Chelsea wondered, "Don't you ever think about your real parents?"

"Sometimes, but then it passes. Sally can tell if I'm bothered and lets Biostream know, and the dark thoughts are medicated away."

"We're all medicated—my parents send me to a psychopharmacologist." Tom took a deep drag of AK-47.

I saw myself parroting Sally's explanation to me as I said, "The World Government's happiness scale uses facial-recognition cameras to measure the number of smiles in a day. Also, they listen for positive language. Radiant analyzes this information and gives happiness scores."

"Holy shit, this is awesome!" Chelsea took a deep drag of Rude Queen. "The secret history says that the World Economic Forum planned to make people feel happy so that corporations could take over. They thought shopping was the key. But the plan didn't work."

"So what'd they do next?" I asked.

"I've gotta read more. But this is scary shit. They were worried about people wanting to get rich-people's money. There was something called 'Occupy Wall Street' back in 2011. We never studied that in history." Chelsea passed the Rude Queen back to Amy as I took another hit of AK-47.

"Never heard of it; maybe that guy Binn is making it up." I suddenly felt Chelsea's hand on my knee as she held the e-reader with her other hand.

"I always worried they weren't telling us everything at school." Tom got up and began refilling all our wine glasses. "I don't think they're teaching us to overthrow the World Government—they love it—it protects all our wealth. What's the book say about this thing 'Occupy Wall Street'?"

"Big movement—even went to Hong Kong, where it was called 'Occupy Central'—they wanted greater equality. According to Binn, the rich were scared shitless." I watched Chelsea's hand absentmindedly stroking my leg.

Unexpectedly, as I was watching the video, Sally's hand moved under the bed coverings. Its mechanical fingers zipped up my fly that was left open from my last bathroom trip. Sally was repeating a frequent action from my childhood.

"There's more," Chelsea continued. "A group called 'Blockupy' rioted against the European unions that were helping the rich get richer. In 2015, Blockupy burnt cars and attacked German police, raging against Capitalism."

"That's why they wanted everyone happy," I reflected. "Saying shopping would make people happy made happiness like something you buy. That failed."

I could see Amy looking jealously at Chelsea's hand.

"'Occupy' people just wanted our parents' money," Amy shrugged. "They're certainly not happy people. My doctor says if I feel sad, I should medicate and go shopping. It works; I always feel happy with new things."

"But if you don't have money to shop?" I watched Chelsea's hand move further up my leg. "Then you must be pissed."

"Jimmy, do you feel happy shopping?" Chelsea asked, looking up from the e-reader as her hand reached my crotch.

"I always feel happy."

"It says here," Chelsea started reading out loud, taking her hand off my leg to take a hit and pass the bong back to Amy, "that 'the World Economic Forum related happiness to politics by collecting camera-recognition shots of smiles on different politicians. They wanted measures of real emotions by looking at the facial muscles around the eyes. They found their conservative allies were less happy and optimistic based on smile lines and language use than their enemies, the liberals and radicals.'"

"And what'd they do?" I could see Chelsea's hand return to my leg, giving it soft squeezes.

"Binn says they just gave up on politicians. They wanted happy people who wouldn't revolt. After a data analysis, they found conservatives only caused discontent."

"That's weird," Tom interjected. "You'd think conservatives would make people happy with tax cuts and ending welfare."

"Come on, Tom," I said. "How are those things making people happy? We've left them with dirty Higher-Speed trains, homelessness, and hungry kids."

"'Meeting in 2023 in Davos,'" Chelsea continued reading, "'leaders from the three hundred highest-earning global corporations abandoned all politicians. After lengthy discussion, they decided political control of national governments was failing because their handpicked politicians were making populations so unhappy, they were facing a possible revolution.'"

"So that's why we don't have democracies." I watched Chelsea's hand slide up my leg. "We were told at Streets that it was because it was inefficient with so many people on the planet."

"Not according to Binn's history." Chelsea's hand left my leg, taking the bong from Amy. "The rich could control elections and politicians, but the politicians they owned couldn't keep the masses contented. Fear of revolution caused them to abandon elections for direct rule by corporations."

"This is bullshit; let's get something to eat. Fuckin' dope has given me the munchies," Amy interrupted.

"'Corporations wanted a higher political power than national governments to protect global free trade,'" Chelsea continued reading. "'They wanted existing governments to continue providing local services with the World Government, ensuring no government restricted corporate actions or free trade.'"

"So the United States and other nations," I commented, "are part of a federation dedicated to protecting corporate wealth and control."

"Binn gives part of the 2023 transcript of their conversation." Chelsea read:

Ben Johnson, CEO Kiwi Technology:

"Clearly, democracy and elections fail to protect our interests even when those elected do what we want; it only breeds discontent."

Fran Chin, CEO China Clothing, Inc.:

"We thought the Communist Party would protect us. We controlled party leadership, but still the masses complained. The only solution is for Chinese companies to take over the party."

Shah Rukh Khan, Chairman of the Board, Mumbai Banking Corporation:

"Our elections are crazy. We still worry about the Gandhi tradition. Last year, the politicians we thought were in our pockets raised bank taxes."

Farmer Schultz, Executive Director of the World Economic Forum: "Clearly, traditional governments don't serve our interests or the interests of the people. People benefit from corporate growth and stability. We need a new form of governance. Clearly, all the old government models have failed. We need direct control by our group. No more elections."

Chapter 8

I watched the ensuing orgy with me hooking up with Chelsea for the first time. I saw us trashing Tom's den, leaving spilled wine and bong water festering on the floor and a door ripped off the drug and liquor cabinet. The walls were stained with mixtures of teenage secretions.

Sally's video shifted to a camera showing us stumbling out of Tom's front door and heading to our favorite Best World Eats around the corner on Madison Ave. In 2032, GoGrow Chemical gained a world monopoly on food supplies. Droughts and erratic weather created world shortages, which GoGrow Chemical corrected by producing synthetic foods made from digestible plastics, genetically modified grasses, wood pulps, seaweeds, and manufactured vitamins. The company franchised the new food source through upscale Best World Eats restaurants and cheaper Peoples Eats Takeout along with GoGrow Markets.

Sally's projection switched to cameras in Best World Eats. I watched us entering and asking for a food console for four. Unlike Peoples Eats with its long lines, Best World Eats offered food consoles on white table-cloths with silver place settings. I could see the hostess leading us to a back table with a console in its center. Screens glowing with menus were embedded in the table at each place setting.

GoGrow Chemical gained a global restaurant monopoly by featuring personalized dishes for any tastes. There were still some high-end restaurants and markets offering real meat, vegetables, and fish. Only a few could afford them. As teenagers, we preferred the taste of personalized flavors, even if synthetic.

I watched us sit down and enter our personal-flavor numbers into the table screens. Best World Eats stored our food tastes in a central data system. I remember being programmed for Best World Eats. My physical and emotional reactions to different liquid samplings placed on my tongue by food technologists were analyzed and stored. Now babies are tested, and food preferences are sent to GoGrow's data center. With a global monopoly, one could go anywhere and get food personalized to your individual taste.

"I'll go for **Comfort Food**," Amy announced, touching the menu screen.

Chelsea touched her usual **Hamburger and Fries**.

I guess I was feeling like something exotic as I watched myself looking closely at the screen and touching **South African Safari Feasts**.

Tom looked deranged and unsteady from the dope and wine. It was his first hookup with Amy. He studied the menu and finally called for **Tonga Beach Snacks** and commanded the processor to start.

The console lit up, and we could hear a slight suction sound as our meals passed through tubes from the central chemical mixer. With personalized food, you could eat anything and love it—the synthetic food was blended for individual tastes.

"Binn's history is awesome," Chelsea said to me as digitalized plates stacked next to the console registered our selections and moved mechanically under the console's extruder. The extruder formed the synthetic food into shapes and colors corresponding to the menu codes using digestible plastics. The plastics also gave texture to the synthetic food.

Amy's food looked like meatloaf and mashed potatoes, and her digitalized plate streamed alternating views of trailer homes and suburban developments.

Chelsea's looked and smelled like fast-food burgers and fries, while her plate alternated old photos of McDonalds and Burger Kings. My plate showed safari scenes and was filled with an Afrikaner braai of barbecued sausages and meats. Tom's Tonga beach snacks of taro and fish wrapped in banana leaves rested on a plate with alternating sand and surf scenes.

Enjoying Sally's warmth, I watched us savoring our synthetic food.

"I bet GoGrow Chemical had something to do with the World Government," Chelsea said, licking her spoon. "I wonder if these chemicals are safe—seems to be a rise in cancer rates."

"Don't be such a killjoy," Amy snapped. "I love these foods. The World Government runs safety checks. They contain all the vitamins, minerals, and fiber we need. Droves line up at Peoples Eats—the world runs on GoGrow."

"Sally warned me about Peoples Eats," I said as I speared a sausage-looking substance.

"Why?" asked Chelsea.

"Its database shows higher cancer and general-illness rates for Peoples Eats. I think they use cheaper flavor chemicals. Sally told me if I wanted to live longer, to stick to Best World Eats."

"That's why these chemicals cost three times as much as Peoples Eats." Chelsea savored a fry. "I always thought there was something wrong with Peoples Eats. GoGrow's monopoly kills the poor and makes us healthy."

I watched us swapping hugs as we stood outside Best World Eats, and I entered a cab to head back to my West Village townhouse.

• • •

Worried about work, I commanded Sally to stop the video and prepared to go to my office. It rose up, swinging its wheels over the side, and ordered a taxi. My valet robot, Humphrey, dressed me.

My office was on the top floor of a new ninety-story tower on the corner of Pearl and Broad Streets in the heart of the financial district. I loved its sweeping views of New York Harbor and looking down on Wall Street from my corner perch. The office walls were covered with logos of the technology divisions of World Systems, Inc. On the front of my desk was a symbol indicating that I was a member of the Congress of the World Government as CEO of World Systems—among the top three hundred highest-earning global corporations.

It was midnight when I arrived at my office, after being waved in by the front desk and taking a private elevator. The room was filled with the glow of holographic computing, with my desktop displaying a stream of profit-and-loss data. Things were much worse than when I earlier left, seeking solace from Sally.

I swiped my hand over the desktop to look at Kiwi's declining sales report. Kiwi's last ten years of profit-and-loss spreadsheets appeared as holograms.

"How could hardware, software, tablet, and storage-cloud revenues plummet in just one year?" I wondered. A new report appeared on the wall, showing dropping sales in the Chinese market for Kiwi's famous kPhone. Last year's decision to expand production of kPhones after the collapse of Korea's largest phone maker was considered a no-brainer.

"Everyone needs kPhones," I thought, going over to the conference table and using voice commands to call up a hologram of kPhone's CEO, Jeremy Crumpet, living in Hong Kong. Being noon in Hong Kong, Jeremy's hologram appeared in a chair at the conference table, chewing food.

"I thought you'd be contacting me. I've seen the reports. Please excuse me while I finish this Pearl River fish. Not to be wasted. Only a few river fish left." Jeremy's hand went to his mouth.

"What happened—particularly the Chinese market?" I asked. "Everyone needs kPhones and kWatches to run their lives. The Internet of Things Web makes them indispensable."

"We're trying to figure that out. Data set never showed a decline, only growth." I watched Jeremy swallowing as he answered. "It was guaranteed after completing the Internet of Things."

"Couldn't be that guaranteed." I pointed at the wall's holograms showing another decline in kPhone sales.

"Show me a kPhone store in Shanghai," I commanded the holographic computer. Instantly, the walls were covered with indoor and outdoor scenes of a Kiwi store on Shanghai's Bund. I could see people hurrying by the store's windows without looking, and only a few customers inside lined up at the kPhone service desk.

"Where are the customers?" I asked.

"I don't know. We assumed endless sales because people think they can't live without them." Jeremy's hologram acted like it was looking at a kPhone. "Oh no, it tells me to eat fish, and now it tells me I've lost five days of my life to pollutants from the river. I should've stuck to GoGrow Chemicals."

"Are all the connections working? Is there a flaw? Why would your phone tell you to eat fish and then tell you that you've lost part of your life doing it?"

"Fish is good but is polluted. I'm receiving messages from my hospital and funeral homes noting the days taken off my life. BigSleep is contacting me about early burial arrangements."

I remembered BigSleep—which holds a world monopoly of transplant organs, tissue removal, cremation, and burial vaults—demanding to be included in the phones' network. I had wondered about the consequences of receiving messages from BigSleep's euthanasia division, DieWell.

People sometimes received DieWell's message, "Isn't it time to rest and sleep?" when health problems were communicated from watches and phones to BigSleep and DieWell, along with GetWell hospitals, CleanCut medical supplies, GoGrow Chemicals, and Biostream. Inventories and production goals were constantly revised as data flowed from phones to global monopolies. There were ongoing adjustments for future needs of burial crypts, euthanasia rooms, pharmaceutical drugs, and hospital beds.

"Look at this," Jeremy pointed at a holographic chart. "Phones are being shut down in sub-Saharan Africa. Christ, the place is being flooded with the message 'Isn't it time to rest and sleep?'"

"What happened?"

The holographic computer responded, showing data from Euphrates Environment, a monopolizer of global water supplies and waste removal. Below a flashing warning, "Water Contamination," was Euphrates's logo of happy and dancing children in a circle drinking from plastic water bottles with the slogan, Optimizing and Securing the Resources for Our Future. An African map showed flashing red outlines of ten endangered nations with the message: "Unexpected bacterial and carcinogenic contamination found in Euphrates's SweeTaste bottle water."

"Oh my God," Jeremy shouted. "kPhones throughout Africa are being flooded with messages saying, 'Isn't it time to rest and sleep?' with offers of burial services."

"Shit!" I said. "No wonder the phones are being shut down. Jeremy, look into this and send me an analysis of these phone shutdowns."

"Check Radiant," I ordered the computer. Another flow of spreadsheets with declining profits appeared on the walls.

"What happened to data collection, storage, and analysis?" I wondered. "Isn't anyone using Big Data anymore? Why shortfalls in Radiant's Trident division? Don't people want cyber security?" I scanned the holograms showing Interpol's use of Trident services declining over the last year. Was crime also declining?

Chapter 9

I don't know when it all started. I was thinking about Chelsea. At least that's what I remember. It was the 2040 crash, and I was twenty. I watched the hologram showing stocks in Euphrates rapidly declining. Biostream abruptly appeared with a flashing red arrow pointing at a profit curve tumbling down a scale.

"Why?" I asked the computer.

On the wall appeared a video of me and Chelsea walking down 5th Avenue wearing summer clothing. I looked closely to see if there were wedding rings. I couldn't tell. Was it before our marriage?

I stood back, wondering why the computer was showing me this. Did it all start back then? I saw us turn and head down 57th Street toward 6th Avenue.

Memories slowly returned. I watched us stopping in front of Radiant's corporate headquarters. Now I remembered this as a turning point in our lives. It was June, 2038, and I had just graduated from the Streets Academy.

Sally scheduled an appointment to meet with Radiant's CEO, Dan Shriver, at 3:00 p.m. to discuss my postsecondary education. I mentioned the meeting to Chelsea, who wanted to go with me, thinking about planning her own future.

I watched us entering the Radiant Building and eventually sitting across from Dan Shriver.

"Jimmy," Shriver said, "thanks for coming. This is an important day. Mind discussing it in front of your friend?"

"Chelsea's interested. We graduated together."

"The basic thing is...," Shriver paused, looking at a data check on Chelsea. "I see," Shriver said to Chelsea, "that you were in Jimmy's class. You've got a good profile. It's OK for you to stay. Nothing secret. Jimmy could tell you, anyway."

"Jimmy," Shriver directed his attention to me, "Radiant and the Zeus Fund are planning your training with Yale-Radiant. You'll be educated as an investor in technology industries."

"What does that mean?" I looked concerned. Hadn't given much thought to working. I was enjoying myself.

"We'd thought of other options like Harvard-Goldman and Princeton-Morgan. But the data shows you in the technology sector. You've the hard and soft skills needed for success in investment companies, and you are interested in technology. Data analysis shows that with your grit and language and math skills, you will succeed. You'll continue living the perfect life."

I noticed Chelsea sneering at the word "success." She'd been trying to lure me into living in the wilderness. "We should go minimalist," she had urged me and Tom. "Make our own clothing and live off the land— only way for happiness." I remember Amy saying the idea was crazy.

"The Yale-Radiant MOOCs are difficult," Shriver explained. "The one in advanced data management had two hundred and twenty thousand globally enrolled online with only twenty-five thousand completing. I helped plan the MOOCs when Yale and all the other colleges stopped offering in-person classes and closed campuses. I felt bad about them shutting down. I loved living in Berkeley. UCal is now a beautiful museum complex like other former campuses. Now it's on the official California tourist route."

"I'd go to college if there were any," Chelsea interrupted. "This corporate merger stopped any thinking about a better world. College became training for corporate slavery."

"She's been reading Howard Binn," I explained to Shriver.

"Howard Binn!" Shriver sat up in his chair, wagging a finger at Chelsea. "That crackpot. We worked with Interpol to ban his stuff. You shouldn't read it."

I remember regretting bringing Chelsea with me.

"Binn said," she continued, "that the World Government closed all college campuses because faculty and students were criticizing corporate takeovers. Big demonstrations at Berkeley. Interpol killed one hundred students and faculty, putting down an anticorporate riot in 2026."

"Binn's got it all wrong," Shriver said, continuing to wave a finger at Chelsea. "Those killed were troublemakers. Colleges were a mess. They weren't educating a workforce. They taught old-fashioned crap like philosophy and history. These aren't skills wanted by companies."

"Maybe we could get back to my future." I watched myself trying to redirect the discussion.

But Chelsea wasn't going to give up. "I read they used to believe education was for uplifting character and preparing for social justice. Binn says corporations were trying to cut off all criticism."

"Look, young lady, you should read Walter Curry's *World Government History*. It answered Binn's lies. Curry shows how the World Economic Forum tried to get colleges to help the economy. Efforts failed, and the only answer was to merge colleges with top corporations. That's why we've got Yale-Radiant."

"Binn says there's no proof colleges were or were not helping the economy. It was all about shutting down criticism." Chelsea, I could see, was getting agitated and starting to raise her voice. I watched myself poke her leg, hoping she'd get the hint and quiet down.

"First, Binn says, they got colleges to teach work skills. Professors balked, and students raged against it. There were some students, Binn says, who dreamt of a life of thinking and social justice. The corporate types hated intellectuals. People who thought it was fun to just think."

"Don't you see what a waste of money and time that was?" Shriver chided her. "Colleges were out of control, spending everyone's money and not being responsible. We should applaud the World Government's law forcing higher education to merge with companies. Professors and college administrators were just ripping off the population. Something had to be done!"

As I watched Shriver talking, I remembered Chelsea liking ideas. At the Streets Academy, she asked for more small classes discussing great books. It never happened. The administration called it a waste, hindering good skills learning.

"Jimmy, let's talk about Yale-Radiant." Shriver turned his attention to me, leaving Chelsea looking angry. "Zeus and Radiant agree to pay for your Yale-Radiant MOOCs and provide you with an internship at both companies. At Zeus, you will learn investment skills and at Radiant, the tech market. This will help with the perfect life. What do you think?"

As a teenager, I never thought about work. I assumed I'd continue being cared for. The idea of work was horrifying.

"We've talked to Biostream, and they said you're off your meds," he continued. "Emotional balance is important at Radiant. Biostream will be working with us during your internship."

"What MOOCs—how many?" I was anxious about the amount of work. "How many hours of interning?"

"Those are not the right questions," Shriver shot back. "You should be talking about how fun it will be and how your internships will help Zeus and Radiant."

After the interview ended, we stood outside Radiant's building with Chelsea screaming I was selling out. I watched her pounding my chest, pleading for me to go underground with her.

"You can't—can't—can't do this," Chelsea pleaded. With tears streaming down her face, she hugged and kissed me. "You'll be ruined.

What kind of fuckin' life is investment banking? Technology—you'll be a fuckin' nerd."

I'd never felt such strong emotions directed at me. We'd been in and out of the sack together and done foursomes with Tom and Amy. I never felt love—only pleasure and the usual biological release. Maybe Biostream's drugs were too effective.

I could see my confusion as I asked, "What choice? They're paying my way. Can't be that bad."

"You son of a bitch, you don't feel anything. Just sex. I never felt anything from you. You bastard and your fuckin' robot."

I watched Chelsea slap me and start racing down 57th Street with me running behind. I remember the emotional impact of the scene. No one had ever confronted me with such a wall of feelings. I don't remember any adult yelling at me before.

"Chelsea, wait! What happened? Stop, let's talk. I don't know what went wrong. You wanted to come with me!"

Catching up to Chelsea, I grabbed her shoulder, spinning her around. I remember worrying that passersby would think I was attacking her.

"Chelsea, what's wrong? You wanted to hear my plans and start thinking about yours."

"You still don't get it." Chelsea looked on the verge of collapsing on the sidewalk. "I thought you wanted us to be together. That's why we were meeting. Not for you to be an investment banker."

"What'd you mean 'together'?"

"Jesus, don't you know I love you!" Chelsea declared, pulling away from my grip on her shoulder. "You're blank—a nothing. Don't you feel love?"

I remember being taken aback by Chelsea's declaration of love. I thought it was just fun hooking up.

"What do you want me to do—please don't be angry," I pleaded. "I don't know what to do with rage." I looked at my face twisted in emotion as tears welled up in my eyes. "I'll take my meds if that's what you want."

I could see myself trying to put my arms around her as she struggled, pushing on my chest.

"Meds! Christ, that's the problem. They emotionally castrated you! Perfect face—sculpted prick—empty inside. You'll make a fuckin' great banker—that's what they're like. You can get off on technology or maybe just Sally."

"Chelsea, what should I do? Don't be angry."

I watched Chelsea hug me as passersby swirled around us, staring. "You could love me! Why don't we plan our futures, not your future?"

"To do what?"

"Join Anonymous against the World Government. Go live in the wilds. Go underground. Make art and love. Shit, there is lots we could do."

"Let's get real. I don't know how to live in the wilds. Can you imagine me skinning a deer for clothing? The World Government is probably recording this now. We'll be lucky to make it back to Tom's without being arrested for subversion. I can't do art. Can we live on love?"

"I'll get my parent's money. We could be free."

"I don't have anything. I get money from the Zeus Perfect Life Fund, and that'll end if I don't go to Yale-Radiant. How'll you get your parents' money—they're still living?"

I could see Chelsea pulling me under a canopy protecting the front of a GoGrow market that advertised 50 percent off on refills of home food consoles.

The video went blank. Chelsea had found a spot near the storefront under the canopy free from surveillance cameras.

I stood there, wondering how this explained the hologram's warning of more sliding profits. kPhones were shutting down in India. What'd that have to do with this youthful scene on 57th Street?

"What'd we talk about?" I asked the computer, hoping somewhere in the data universe, there was some mention of the conversation.

A holograph appeared of me and Sally in our townhouse. I watched Sally roll over and greet me as I entered. It circled me, and its silicon hand grabbed my arm, taking pulse and blood-pressure readings.

"You don't seem well, Jimmy. What happened? I lost sight of you."

Sally followed me through AlwaysWatch but lost me when Chelsea dragged me out of the view of surveillance cameras.

"AlwaysWatch reported you," Sally said mechanically. "You were purposely outside the view of cameras. I was instructed to inform you that it is against the law to be outside the safety view of AlwaysWatch. AlwaysWatch works to protect you. You may be arrested and fined or sent to prison for another occurrence."

Ignoring Sally, I ran up the stairs to my bedroom. An incline next to the stairs allowed Sally to follow me, repeating the warning: "The World Government requires AlwaysWatch to ensure your safety. Any breach of the surveillance network will lead to fines and imprisonment."

Sally followed me into the bedroom. I could hear it saying, "You are required by law to inform me of the conversation with Chelsea. AlwaysWatch and Interpol require an investigation into any human actions that are not recorded. You must report your actions."

Grabbing my arm to monitor blood pressure and pulse, Sally recorded my facial reactions for lying and deceit.

"Jimmy, you can't lie. You must tell me the truth. Interpol might intercede and force you to talk. You understand."

I watched myself nodding yes and remembering my childhood haunted by Sally's ability at detecting lies. Sally always knew if I was good or bad or lying. To be good was following the rules set by Radiant, Biostream, and the Zeus Fund.

"What did you and Chelsea talk about?"

"My future."

I felt Sally's hand gently squeeze my arm as its flashing eyes indicated Internet communications.

"That's correct. Tell me more."

"Radiant wants me to intern and attend Yale-Radiant."

"We know that," Sally said, with its eyes indicating rapid Internet communication. "Tell me what you talked about outside the safety of AlwaysWatch."

"Chelsea wanted—" I started as Sally interrupted, "Do you love Chelsea?"

"Where are these fuckin' questions coming from?"

Sally's red light began spinning and flashing, while its eyes flashed red-and-green lights.

"Jimmy, you're not telling anything we don't know. What did you talk about outside the view of the cameras?"

"Who's the 'we'?"

"It is the glorious and all-knowing database and AlwaysWatch analytics. Please answer!"

"We talked about running away and hiding."

"That's better." I could feel Sally release some of the pressure on my arm. "Where were you going to go?"

"To the caves—underground." I watched myself giving secrets of escape from the World Government. I didn't know much about it except what Chelsea mentioned while hiding under the canopy.

Sally's red light stopped spinning as its eyes indicated increased Internet messages. After a few minutes, Sally asked, "What caves?"

"Don't know. Chelsea said we could go underground."

I realized why the computer was answering my concern with sliding profits by showing this part of my life. Chelsea gave me a choice. If I agreed with Chelsea, would she be alive and both of us happy?

"Do you love Chelsea?" Sally's hand again gently squeezed my arm as its eyes stared into mine.

"I don't know. I like being with her. I don't know what love is."

"You love her." Sally released my arm. "All data indications show love. This is not good."

"Why?"

"She's trouble and against your perfect life." If a robot could express emotions, I thought watching this scene that Sally was acting angry and hurt. "She's on the Interpol watch list as a potential terrorist."

"Terrorist! Chelsea? She's never hurt anyone."

"She expressed anti–World Government sentiments in high school and in conversation with you and others. AlwaysWatch and Interpol are monitoring her actions. She fits the profile of a terrorist. They will get rid of her."

"Get rid of her how?"

"For the good of humanity, the World Government must be protected. If she moves to the next level of antigovernment sentiment, she will be eliminated."

"Eliminated!"

"For her good and the good of the people, she will be vaporized. Or if the World Government wants to make her an example, she will be publically disemboweled."

"Disemboweled—a public spectacle—I thought the World Government stopped cruelty—it's medieval. It's crazy. She's never hurt anyone."

"It is for your good and for all people," Sally intoned. "Without the World Government, people will be hurt, disorganized, and starving. GoGrow would not be able to deliver food. A public disemboweling will stop future terrorism and protect lives. It will be for Chelsea's own good."

"Her good—how's that? Pain and death!"

"The World Government protects all humans. Sometimes threats must be eliminated. They will build a public-remembrance statue of her as a warning to all. As a remembrance statue, she will be eternal."

"Sally, I can't believe you're telling me this. A remembrance statue does not make one eternal."

"The World Government assures that the disemboweling will be on a cross-like structure appropriate for monument building."

"Jesus, Sally, is this really going to happen? What kind of mindfuck is this?"

Sally's red light spun and flashed on hearing "mindfuck." "Jimmy, you must be good. The Zeus Perfect Life Fund is worried. AlwaysWatch and Interpol are on alert."

Watching Sally's warnings, I thought that the computer video might be telling me I should have chosen another path. Maybe I should have urged Chelsea to take us to the caves. Would that have avoided the profit slide in world technology companies?

"What's goin' to happen to Chelsea? It was only a short conversation outside the view of AlwaysWatch. Is that worth disemboweling?"

"Nothing is happening. Chelsea will be talked to by Interpol. No charges expected—only a warning. Biostream is sending messages on the chemical levels of your love for Chelsea. She'll be checked by Interpol. A decision will be made."

"A decision about what?"

"What to do about your relationship with Chelsea. I don't think it is a good idea."

I looked startled by these words. Sally was making what appeared to be an independent judgment with the words "I don't think." Could it be possible that Sally was jealous? But it was a robot with no emotions.

Without warning, the video stopped and was replaced by a hologram showing plunging profits for BackBit, my global subscription cloud-storage company. "No one wants to store data," I thought. "That's not possible."

Watching the disappearing profits, I thought about Sally's words. Was it jealous? I wondered if Sally could be responsible for Chelsea's death. Was it a jealous rage? But robots can't be jealous or in a rage. I remember wondering about Sally's role in Chelsea's death.

Chapter 10

After Chelsea's funeral, I climbed in bed with Sally, stroking its memory button. Chelsea and I had married in 2040, two years after Dan Shriver informed me I was attending Yale-Radiant University. Sally's eyes lit up, indicating communication with the vast data networks of Radiant and AlwaysWatch, and it began projecting a video onto the ceiling.

"What do you want to see, Jimmy?"

"I want to see what happened back in 2038 when Chelsea left our illegal talk."

"You mean when you two broke the law and hid from AlwaysWatch?"

"Yes."

On the ceiling appeared a video of Chelsea walking rapidly down 57th Street. Her pained expression and tear-filled eyes made me feel the loss of our love.

Suddenly a soft-blue-colored Interpol car, covered with happy-face stickers and a proclamation on the trunk, We Make the World Safe and Happy, pulled up alongside her. To improve the police force's public image, a focus group chose Interpol's car colors and positive decals of smiling baby and adult faces. It was a public-relations success.

I watched a back window open and a uniformed Interpol officer ordering Chelsea into the car. Chelsea stood, trembling, and started to turn away from the car as if to run. An Interpol officer next to the driver's console jumped out and grabbed Chelsea, forcing her into the back seat. The car sped off with its roof's red light-bar flashing messages of love and its siren playing *Happy Times Are Here Again.*

The video switched to the interior of the car.

"I'm Officer Paul Ryan," said the man next to Chelsea. "That's Ted Bush in front. We're here to keep you safe and happy. We're going to Interpol's midtown offices."

"Why? What'd I do? You can't just take me."

"Young lady, you violated the World Government's most stringent law governing protection by AlwaysWatch. Any violation of the law by being outside its view results in immediate arrest. Your safety is our first concern."

The driverless Interpol car pulled up in front of its headquarters on 51st Street near 6th Avenue. The building's long entrance hall was lined with statues of famous corporate and World Government leaders. Above the elevators was a bright, glowing, green inscription, We're Always There for You.

Officer Ryan grasped Chelsea's elbow, directing her into an elevator marked, We Want to Help and Talk to You.

I watched the elevator's display indicating a rapid ascent to the ninety-fifth floor. The ceiling video unexpectedly switched to a room filled with beanbags, lounging chairs, and stuffed animals. An interior sign over the door said, "Relax. We Are Here to Help." Smiley faces similar to those on the Interpol car were plastered across the walls.

Officer Ryan and Chelsea entered the room. "Sit where you feel comfortable. I have a few questions. Put this band around your arm. It, along with the facial-recognition cameras, will decide if you're telling the truth."

Chelsea looked nervous sitting down on a leather couch. "Am I under arrest?"

"You violated a fundamental law of the World Government. You could be fined and/or imprisoned." Ryan glanced down at his kPad. "Tell me about your conversation outside of AlwaysWatch with Jimmy Clark. You must tell the truth or face charges of subverting the World Government." He sat down behind a corner console from where he could see Chelsea. He activated the truth meter.

"We talked about our future." Chelsea sat up, realizing the seriousness of the situation.

A green light flashed on the wall next to a photo of a laughing baby. Pointing at the light, Ryan said, "Green indicates you're telling the truth. Flashing green means you're not telling the whole truth. Tell me more."

"I love Jimmy. I want us to be together."

The green light continued to flash as Officer Ryan stared at her.

"They asked Jimmy to be a banker. He'd go to Yale-Radiant."

"Good corporate school," Ryan commented. "What's the problem?"

"I don't want him to go there." The green light continued to flash.

"You're not telling me what you said."

"I said we should run away together."

"Your file says," Ryan said as he consulted the kPad, "you were involved in anti–World Government demonstrations at the Streets Academy, and you often express these ideas in conversations. Did you say anything like that to Jimmy?"

"No!"

Suddenly the green flashing light turned red. Officer Ryan swiped his hand over a control pad, sending a strong electric jolt up Chelsea's spine. She started convulsing and gagging as her body violently twitched.

"Truth is best. We're only here to protect you. Did you make any anti–World Government statements to Jimmy during your absence from AlwaysWatch?"

"I said we should go underground."

The light started flashing green again, and Chelsea stopped convulsing.

"'Underground'—what does that mean?"

"I'm not sure! I heard it involves caves."

"Who told you?"

I could see Chelsea struggling to come up with an answer as her body continued twitching. "I was told about it at a demonstration."

The green light continued to flash.

"Just tell me the whole story," Ryan commanded. "Do you want another happy-time jolt to your memory?"

Chelsea sat up straight, wanting to avoid another jolt.

"Carl Stone mentioned it to me at an anti–World Government demonstration outside the Stock Exchange. He said there were caves to hide in to avoid AlwaysWatch. I never found out where they were. I told Jimmy we should find them and drop out. Live in peace. Jimmy said he'd think about it."

The green light stopped flashing. Officer Ryan ordered the console to display the demonstration and conversation. A hologram of Chelsea and Carl Stone appeared.

"Fuckin' World Government—is there any escape?" Chelsea could be seen and heard asking Carl.

"You can go underground. In the caves you'll be free of AlwaysWatch."

"What caves?"

"Can't say. We're being watched and listened to."

The hologram showed the crowd separating Chelsea and Carl before she could ask more questions. The hologram disappeared.

"Did you know that you're on the World Government's terrorist watch list?" Ryan asked.

"Holy shit, I'm not a terrorist."

The green light remained steady.

"That's true. You're not a terrorist but could become one. You've been in antigovernment rallies and made subversive statements. It's time to clean up your act. You're just out of high school, and there's still time."

"Time for what?"

"To straighten out—you're the heiress of your mother's fortune. You'll never have to work. Winnie's Secrets dominates the world markets. Eat'em is everyone's favorites. My wife wears them. You're set for life."

"I'm not living for my mom's money. There are better things to do. I want to help people."

"You've got to stop your antigovernment activities or lose your mother's fortune."

"But she's alive, and my dad would get the money."

Suddenly the green light started flashing.

"Your mother's created a trust fund giving you plenty while she's alive and more when she passes. You'll never need to worry. You could lose everything and more."

"More? I don't care about the money."

The green light stopped flashing.

"We know you don't care about money. You've got plenty. And it's youthful innocence to think you don't need it." Officer Ryan stood up and stretched. "Would you like to eat? There is a GoGrow food processor here." Looking at her data, he said, "You can order comfort food."

"Am I going to prison?"

"Not now, but it could happen. Your mother is a powerful corporate type. Your father is a two-bit banker in Brooklyn. If it wasn't for your mother, we would reeducate you at the We Love You Farm."

"We Love You Farm is a prison," I heard Chelsea almost shout. "I don't need to be reeducated. Fuck the comfort food."

"You're not going to jail. But you must follow these instructions."

"And what happens if I don't?"

"You'll go to the We Love You Farm. Your brain will be cleaned and restored with good thoughts. If that fails, then you will be vaporized. If you continue to be a threat, you will be martyrized in a public disemboweling and a statute made of you for the garden of terrorists."

"Vaporized, public disemboweling—I didn't do anything worth that."

"You don't understand your involvement with Jimmy Clark. We've got a lot of pressure on us to protect him. Radiant, AlwaysWatch, and the Zeus Fund want him to lead a life according to data. You can't interfere with his perfect life."

I could see that Chelsea was truly frightened. I remember Sally mentioning a public disemboweling.

"According to messages I'm now receiving from Jimmy's robot caretaker, he loves you. This complicates everything," Ryan said.

"How? Why?" Chelsea joyfully asked. "I thought they killed his feelings. Is it true he really loves me?"

"It would be easier to just tell you to leave him alone. Now we have to worry about Jimmy's reactions and emotions." Officer Ryan sat back down at the console and wondered what he should do with this new information. "You should just relax," he ordered Chelsea. "Data will determine the outcome. You sure you don't want to eat?" He got up and went over to the food console.

"OK." Chelsea looked happy and relieved. She stood up and went over to the food console to collect a dish of extruded meat loaf and whipped potatoes. "I guess I'm not going to prison."

Sitting back down on the couch, she picked at the meat loaf. "So Sally found out he loves me. Is Jimmy that important?"

"The World Government wants a perfect life for everyone. If it works with Jimmy, then we can plan humanity's future."

"You mean everyone might be raised like Jimmy. All will be given a robot guardian."

"Better than human parents." Officer Ryan smirked. "I hated mine. Wish I'd been raised by a robot."

Suddenly a hologram of Radiant's data expert, Carl Burris, appeared in the middle of the Interpol room.

"We've applied analytics to the situation's data. We knew Jimmy would love. Couldn't predict the type of woman," Burris informed them. "We've used Chelsea's data to determine if this is a good match. Family with money—good education—should do well with Jimmy. Only problem is Chelsea's radicalism. It is hard to predict the future when you're so unpredictable."

"You want me to be predictable?" Chelsea asked.

"If you're not, it could cause the Zeus Perfect Life Project to fail."

"So what," I heard Chelsea say. "The Perfect Life Project should fail. We need unpredictability."

"You don't understand," Burris continued. "If the project fails, then Jimmy could be sent to DieWell, and we start over. The World Government must find the perfect life."

I gasped, watching the video. I never imagined they considered sending me to DieWell. They were going to kill me if I didn't have a perfect life and the project failed.

"DieWell." Chelsea started crying. "You're giving me the choice of shutting up or Jimmy dying. You bastards!"

I was stunned watching this footage. I never knew about Chelsea's choice. While this explained our marriage, it didn't explain the collapse of profits.

"You must marry Jimmy," Burris ordered, "and stop your antigovernment activities. Your role is to support Jimmy's success and make him happy. If you don't, you'll both be vaporized. You cannot tell him about this conversation. Remember the consequences."

Chapter 11

I stood surrounded by holograms of my collapsing tech companies. I never dreamt of accumulating this much wealth when I started my online courses with Yale-Radiant. I sometimes visited the Yale Museum complex containing the original campus in New Haven. I stayed in the old dorms converted by SleepWell into a luxury hotel. I could only imagine what the campus was like when there were students and classes.

I asked the computer for a hologram of my early days taking the school's MOOCs. The holographic computer began converting old videos into holograms. I remembered that my escape from the tedium of courses was to hook up in the evening with Chelsea at Tom's place. It was difficult to take Chelsea to my townhouse with Sally always intruding. I wanted to shut Sally down, but there were still Interpol warnings about hiding from AlwaysWatch. Whenever I was home, Sally constantly reminded me that it needed to report to AlwaysWatch, and I shouldn't turn it off.

A hologram appeared of Tom's room. I saw myself entering and announcing, "Let's break out some wine and dope. I finished my first day doing a Yale-Radiant MOOC."

"What's the course?" Tom asked, pouring large glasses of red wine and starting a bong.

"Big Data Analytics."

"Boring," Amy exclaimed, reaching for the bong.

I hugged Chelsea, giving her a kiss. "Big Data Analytics is what my perfect life is all about—predicting my future."

"What's that mean?" Tom asked.

"It's how the World Government works," Chelsea interjected. "Take everyone's data, apply an algorithm, and see what happens. If it shows something bad, then change the data until things are good."

"My life will be perfect," I explained. "Data can predict what will happen. Attending Yale-Radiant will ensure my success."

"What happens if the algorithm is wrong?" Chelsea asked, snuggling closer to me. "Is that why the environment is going? Are they using the wrong software?"

"Then my life might be a nightmare rather than perfect." I kissed Chelsea and stood up, heading for the bathroom.

"Do they teach anything about failing?" Tom called after me, stroking Amy's leg.

"How could they fail?" Amy loosened Tom's belt, running her hand around his pants' inner waistband. "They've got the best computer people."

"You think they know everything," Chelsea snapped. "They're just people wanting to make money. Fuckers make wrong moves all the time."

Returning, I nestled against Chelsea's back as we lay on the floor. "I learned about Big Data errors. I worry about myself. Maybe they used the wrong algorithm, and I'm an error."

"What kind of problems?" Tom sighed, reacting to Amy's gentle rubbing.

"Interpol used the wrong algorithm, causing police to disrupt a Metropolitan Opera performance. Their algorithm identified the opera house as a criminal breeding ground."

"What was the opera?" Amy giggled. "*Rigoletto, Carmen*—they're loaded with thieves and murderers. Most opera involves crime."

"Jesus," Tom said, "my parents were there. Scared them shitless when the police ran down the aisles, shining lights in people's faces—more murders in the Bronx with all the police at the opera."

"Oh come on," Amy said. "Police could tell the audience and singers weren't criminal. You're both making this up."

"Interpol sent its elite storm troopers," I explained, "selected for strength, low intelligence, and violent tendencies. I'm sure they'd never been to an opera. An Interpol focus group named them 'The Merry Clowns.'"

"That's right," Tom added. "My mom was asked if her fur coat was stolen. They thought people were wearing heisted jewels and furs. Dad said they handcuffed one man refusing to give them his million-dollar, two-thousand-diamond Hublot Classic Fusion watch. I'm sure the cops thought it was stolen."

"My MOOC gave me another problem involving medical data." I watched my hands caressing Chelsea's body. "What happened was that the data's logarithm ordered people with hernias and gall-bladder stones to receive blood transfusions. Those needing transfusions were operated on. You can imagine the lawsuits."

"What was your solution?" Chelsea whispered sexily into my ear.

"Working on it and another problem." I felt Chelsea's tongue in my ear.

"Can you predict what will happen if I suck Tom?" Amy unzipped Tom's pants.

"Watch it," Tom shouted in pain, "you caught some hair."

"What's the other problem?" Chelsea's hand slid under the top of my shirt and rubbed my nipples.

"Are you really interested? Or do you want to just make out?"

Chelsea removed her hand and took a hit from the bong. "I'm truly interested. It's what the World Government is all about. Interpol uses this crap. I can see the night at the Met. They're trying to predict who will be a criminal."

I watched myself flinch at Chelsea's statement. We'd both just felt Interpol's power, Chelsea worse than me. I was protected by the experiment and Chelsea by wealth. It showed privilege triumphing over data results.

"I'm learning a new field," I continued, "called 'Algorithmic Account-ability.' A national mortgage company collapsed when data analysis made wrong predictions on loan repayments. Its algorithm erred in offering loans to customers most likely to default and denying those most likely to pay. I'm supposed to correct the data analysis."

"What happened in the Met case? My parents were almost arrested on false data," Tom asked, pushing Amy's hand through his fly. "They were treated like criminals. They wouldn't let Dad go to the bathroom. His bladder was acting up. Mom was so shook-up she wanted champagne from the lobby bar. Interpol stopped her and handcuffed her to the seat when she protested."

"There is a move to protect people's civil rights," I heard myself re-spond. I was getting excited watching Chelsea fondle me.

"Since when is the World Government concerned about civil rights?" Chelsea exclaimed, as her hand returned to stroking my chest.

"Not much after the statement by the Civil and Human Rights Council following the Met thing. You'd think they'd criticize using data to man-age people. They simply assured the public, 'Big Data will bring greater safety, economic opportunity, and convenience to all people.'"

Watching the hologram, I saw Chelsea abruptly stand up, look-ing around the room and asking, "Tom, you sure we're safe here from AlwaysWatch? Interpol's bothering me about the demonstrations."

"Interpol—you should watch it," Tom warned.

"Am I safe here?"

"AlwaysWatch and Interpol never look in my parents' townhouse. They give them enough cars. We're off the radar."

"They told me Jimmy loves me."

"What!" I could see my surprise. "You didn't mention that. Was it Sally?"

I watched Chelsea lean over and kiss me all over my face.

"They'll fix the data problems," Amy said, starting to massage inside Tom's pants. "The World Government works for us."

"You mean the rich." Chelsea felt free to talk after checking on security. "Think of how we're all protected by our parents' money."

"The only fix, which doesn't give me much confidence, I'm learning in my other MOOC on Intuiting Big Data."

"Are you kidding?" Tom was sprawled on his back as Amy continued to fondle him. "Intuition! I thought this was computer science—a science."

The hologram disappeared and returned with both Amy and Tom naked and Chelsea running her hand through my hair as I ran my hand up her leg.

"There's a lot of data. You can't just throw any algorithm on it. You've got to feel the data in your gut. You've got to know where to start."

"We're starting here." Amy slowly mounted Tom.

"This MOOC is teaching me creativity. They're using artists. I'm learning to follow my hunches. Might be called 'gut-feeling investments.'"

"My gut feeling," Chelsea said, "is that I love you. How do I learn to follow my intuition and marry you?"

Watching the hologram, I saw no reaction from me on mentioning marriage. I just continued discussing my course.

"To learn how to act on gut feelings, I play a game with six dials marked with airplane terms like 'straight climb,' 'descending turn,' and 'level turn.' I make quick decisions with bells and gongs telling me if I'm right or wrong. The MOOC trains me to follow my hunches when confronted with Big Data sets."

"For fuck sake," Chelsea looked angry. "You mean the World Government's data is skewed by money and hunches? This is not science. It's another exercise of power."

"They could be wrong about my perfect life." I could see me getting nervous discussing this possibility. "Would you still marry me?"

"You want to marry?" Chelsea's face glowed with joy.

I could see us both watching Amy and Tom move to a couch, passionately embracing.

"Can we go over in the corner?" I whispered. "I don't want them to hear. I hope we're really secure from AlwaysWatch."

I watched us move against the wall near the drug and liquor cabinet.

"My data says I should marry you," I said embarrassedly. "I don't want you to think that's the only reason. The Perfect Life Fund wants us together. I do feel love—at least Sally says so."

"I have a confession," Chelsea whispered in my ear. "Interpol picked me up after our talk at GoGrow. They said I must marry you or be imprisoned, vaporized, or disemboweled."

"Jesus," I grimaced, "this is a forced marriage. Is that why you seem so happy—you'll live?"

"Shit," Chelsea started weeping. "I love you. But I never thought of marrying this young. We're only eighteen. Yes, I'm happy I won't be killed. I've been scared you'd refuse."

"What'd they tell you?"

"I must stop antigovernment stuff, marry you, work for your success, and make you happy."

"Work for my success! What about you? This isn't going to work. We would be miserable."

"Given my choices, I feel good about our marriage. It could work."

"Chelsea, the algorithm might be wrong. I could fail and be unhappy—we could be unhappy. What would you do if we married? I can't imagine you giving your life over to my success."

"There's no choice for me. You might say no, but I can't. It's a true shotgun marriage."

"What are you telling your parents?" I asked, kissing Chelsea. "Will you mention the marriage or death option? What will they think? This is screwy."

"We can make it look like a real proposal, not something from data." Chelsea hugged me. "My parents might be upset—though I think they hoped it would be Tom; he's got a big inheritance coming. All you've got is the promise of a perfect life."

"Do you think they'll stop the marriage?"

"That would mean my death, but I can't tell them. I'll be vaporized. We need to present the idea slowly."

"Did Interpol tell you how soon we should marry?"

"Jimmy, I love you," Chelsea declared. "But honestly, I don't know about our marriage working."

"The right algorithm applied to your personal data might predict our marriage," I suggested. "But with the MOOC and this forced marriage, I'm questioning my whole planned life."

"Interpol said my problem was unpredictability. It screws up data analysis. They want me to be a predictable wife working for your happiness and success."

"Shit, that's terrible." I watched myself trying to comfort her. "Being a radical and unpredictable is what you're all about. You'll have to give up who you are."

I could see the tears in Chelsea's eyes as she started passionately kissing me. I watched us stripping off each other's clothes. Suddenly there was a crash. I saw our eyes glance over at the entangled bodies of Amy and Tom falling off the couch onto the floor.

"Ouch," Amy screamed, "that hurt. I bruised my shoulder. You've got blood on your head."

Wiping his forehead and looking at a small drop of blood on his hand, Tom assured Amy, "Doesn't look like much. It was worth it."

Amy glanced over at our half-naked bodies pressed against the wall. "You guys just starting up? I'm finished; I can't take anymore—climaxed out—just hungry."

"We're getting married," Chelsea blurted out.

"You're what?" Tom and Amy asked in unison.

"That's a stupid idea," Tom said. "Why? You're too young. Do you want kids and stinky diapers? Did you miss your BirthStop/STD shot?"

"If you're pregnant, that FetusXtract place on fifth is fast," Amy suggested. "They claim no pain. Get you in and out in a half hour."

"We're getting married for love." I could see I was uncomfortable saying that.

"This is stupid." Tom looked angry. "We've been having all this fun. Now you're going to fuck it up with marriage. That's so old-fashioned. Why, for God's sake, make this move?"

"Telling your parents?" Amy asked Chelsea. "When will it be?"

"I guess we'll follow the neighborhood rules." Chelsea started untangling her body from mine and slipping on her blouse.

"Imagine you following any rules, let alone the ones for us," Tom smirked, thinking about how the rich had their own rules. "Big engagement party and wedding—the whole nine yards?"

"You're going to wear a wedding dress?" Amy laughed.

I could see myself becoming depressed.

"How does it work?" I asked.

"It means formal engagement announcements," Chelsea said wearily. "And a fancy engagement banquet at a big hotel with orchestra and food. I'll shop for engagement-party clothes and a wedding dress."

"You're serious," Amy gasped. "I can't believe this."

"I'm sure my parents will want it at Saint John the Divine," Chelsea continued, looking like she would burst into tears at any moment. "There's the wedding planning—invitations, receptions, parties, banquets, showers, and honeymoon. More shopping—I hate to shop. Then we find a place to live."

"You don't seem happy," Tom reacted. "Why are you doing it? Why now?"

"Knowing how it works, it will take at least two years to get all the pieces together. But we'll have to announce it soon," Chelsea choked up. "Someday we might be able to tell you the story."

Chapter 12

"Come in," Britt Owens called to me through his office door etched with the Zeus logo and his title, Chief Executive Officer. I had ordered Sally to show my early investment career.

I watched myself entering Owens's office with walls covered with Jesus photos, corporate logos, World Government currency symbols, and on the wall behind Owens's desk, the original gold-scripted Pledge to the World Government. I remembered the pledge from the Streets Academy. On the ceiling staring down was Zeus painted with one hand holding a thunderbolt and the other with the scales of justice balanced by stacks of World Government currency.

"Jimmy," Owens said as he got up and came around to the front of his desk, shaking my hand. "Good to see you're finally here. God and money will make your life perfect."

"Good to be here," I said, hesitantly eyeing all the Jesus photos. "I'm anxious to work."

"Got your scores from Yale-Radiant; you aced the MOOCs. It's a blessing from God that now college only takes a year. Can you imagine when it took four? Wasted time on liberal arts."

"Learned a lot about data," I offered.

"God is data," Owens shouted, lifting his arms over his head and looking up at Zeus. "Data is the key to the scriptures. Got a couple hundred Christ scholars collecting all data on the one and only true religion—bless us for doing God's work. But we need to talk about your internship."

I looked up at Zeus and then back at Owens. "I guess I'll learn to make money."

"Money is God's way." Owens pointed at a chair for me to sit in. "Your perfect life is coming along. Hear you're getting married. Making money and kids ensures the blessing of a godly and perfect life. What do you know about investing?"

"Really nothing. I've never put money into anything. I don't know the first thing about it."

"You're marrying Chelsea Tipper, right?"

"Next year after I finish here—you'll be invited. Chelsea's parents may stage it at Saint John the Divine's."

"How'd they take it when you told them? You have no money—only support for a perfect life."

"They may be unhappy. Supposed to meet with them when I get back."

"Let's get you some money so her parents don't worry. You're to work with Chuck Spiller in our technology-investment sector." Owens waved his finger over the desk console, summoning Spiller.

"Chuck is born-again," Owens explained. "Big ceremony on a Greek isle rented by Zeus. The great LA evangelist, Robert Torch, flew in to do the ceremony on the island's beach. Five hundred happy Christ-loving souls attended—used an ancient Phoenician gold cup for drinking the blood of the Lord—or I should say, Biostream's equivalent."

"I don't know much about religion," I confessed.

"I can see that from your data. Don't worry—Chuck was a pagan when he started. After making money, he decided to give his life to Christ. Wanted to combine baptism with an old fashioned communion—you know, bread and grape juice."

"Bread and grape juice?" I wondered out loud.

"Not really—we use Biostream's new Jesus-tasting wafers and artificial blood. They work. Chuck wore a special Armani drip-dry suit for the dunking. The suit was dry in seconds after Chuck left the water to eat the body of Christ. LifeSea trained the dolphins."

"Dolphins?"

"They jumped back and forth over Chuck as Robert pushed him under, and then the dolphins followed them to shore, dancing on their tails in crucifix formation. I really felt Jesus in my heart seeing it. Torch is using the dolphins in his hologram services."

"Just telling Jimmy about you," Owens said as Chuck Spiller came into the office with a heavy-looking gold cross dangling on a chain around his neck. "How's Robert Torch's church doing? Understand you got him set up after the baptism."

"Good to meet you, Jimmy," Chuck said. "Heard about your perfect life. You're marrying into the Eat'em fortune. That underwear saved my marriage. It will probably help yours. Zeus made a lot from Winnie's company—best lingerie in the world."

"Torch's Great Spirit Hologram Church is a true miracle," Chuck answered Owens's question. "Hologram ceremonies weekly reach a billion families worldwide. A true religious revolution."

"One billion; that's great," Owens exclaimed. "I hope we're invested. Making money is God's way into people's hearts. We can enter with Torch's holograms."

"There were some early glitches," Chuck explained. "Torch's first hologram ceremonies got entangled with a porn broadcast—very embarrassing scenes—some thought nudes rolling in the aisles were experiencing the ecstasy of salvation—hard to explain to kids. We straightened that out, but sometimes the hologram service lacked music or Christ images. Then there were problems ordering Biostream's wafers and blood."

"And now?" Owens asked.

"It's working." Chuck smiled. "Every Sunday a billion people log in, and Torch's ceremony and sermon appears to them and allows them to eat the flesh of Christ. The hologram fee is low but combined with wafer sales, the profits are high. Praise the Lord!"

"Truly God's work! Take Jimmy and show him the ropes. He needs to get started. Has to earn money for his wedding and God."

Chuck walked me across the palm-tree-forested Zeus complex with sounds of spirituals wafting through the fronds. In the middle was the Temple of Mammon with its forty-foot Jesus statue rotating on top, holding the world currency symbol.

"Owens thought Mammon received bad press in the New Testament," Chuck explained. "You know—Luke sixteen, verse thirteen."

"I don't know," I said, thinking about what Chelsea might say about wealth and Jesus.

"It says, and wrongly, according to our biblical research, that: 'No servant can serve two masters; for either he will hate the one and love the other, or else he will be loyal to the one and despise the other. You cannot serve God and Mammon.'"

"I think I've heard that one. It sounds right."

"Our scholars found it distorted and discovered that some crazy back then changed it. Originally it said, 'All can serve the two masters of God and wealth. They will love both.' You can serve God and Mammon.

"Everyone gathers here in the morning before work." Chuck continued, pointing at the temple. "Sometimes Torch flies in. He likes our Caribbean sun and doing a Mammon service. He checks on his church's investments. They're doing well. Also looks at new technology for his hologram services—wants a God-like hologram service in every house. You may be lucky and meet him sometime. He could baptize you and send the service's hologram around the world. Everyone could see you washed in the blood of the lamb."

"I should learn about investing first," I responded, "before thinking about God and baptism. I couldn't tell from Owens if investing comes first or God or both at the same time."

"God will come with good investments, so let's start there."

He introduced me to a team of technology investors engrossed in rapidly changing profit-and-loss data and projections of future earnings.

All at once, there was a shout, "Bingo! Just hit God's top earnings. Bless me. I am rich." I saw a staff member jumping up and down in front of computer screens.

"What score?" a voice shouted across the open cubicles.

"Nine hundred and ninety!" the winner replied.

"Top score—could be you." Chuck pointed at the exultant staffer. "Let me show you your space."

He led me over to an open cubicle filled with computer screens. "This will be yours. Decorate it any way you want. Just remember to water the plant. It helps keep the air clean." Chuck pointed at a desk-size Jesus statue with a built-in planter containing an aloe vera plant.

I stared at the screens. "Will you train me? I don't know anything about investing."

"Not much to learn," Chuck replied. "Owens and his executive team created WorshipMammon, a shooter game for investments. The game constantly monitors global stocks and bonds prices, technology markets and profitability rates, and consumer confidence and tastes."

"Shooter game," I gasped. I had heard of casino Capitalism but never shooter-game Capitalism.

"The focus in this division is technology companies, and Zeus does hold majority stock in many like Radiant. You get extra game points for each takeover."

"You mean all I do is play this game?" I asked. "I don't know anything about tech companies or economics. I do have game skills. I'm trained to follow my gut feelings and make quick decisions about data."

"You don't need to know anything about rules. Intuition will guide you through the game."

"So I just command it, and I'm investing."

"The idea is to get the game's moneybags," Chuck explained. "The bags appear and disappear, representing real-time investment opportunities."

"How could they be real time?"

"The software is constantly scanning for investment opportunities," Chuck continued. "Each opportunity has problems plus others seeking to invest. In WorshipMammon, pits of brimstone and thunderbolts symbolize problems, while other investors try to shoot you."

"I don't understand this game business. Why not just buy stock?" I asked, still confused.

"A decade ago, computers bought and sold stocks in milliseconds," Chuck explained. "It became a game without humans. The World Government banned direct computer-stock purchases, ordering human competition for stocks using gaming software. God intended humans to compete and make choices. Human choice is necessary for judging good and evil and who should go to heaven or hell."

"Do I earn actual money?"

"You get game points. With enough you can buy a company. The game's software is constantly looking for businesses to buy. You get money from the profits of companies you buy. You don't need to know where the companies are located or their actual products. WorshipMammon keeps track of that. I'll leave you to play."

Chuck dashed off as I sat down, surrounded by the noise from surrounding cubicles. I could see over the thin plastic walls others busily playing WorshipMammon with yells of joy, triumph, anger, and frustration.

"Start the game," I commanded the computer. On my screen appeared Zeus's Temple of Mammon with the Jesus statue on top, throwing wads of World Government currency into empty space.

"Select an avatar," the computer commanded.

On the screen appeared biblical figures. I knew nothing about the Bible so I selected a pleasing-looking one labeled Saint John the Baptist. A warning flashed, "Already chosen by Oliver Cromwell. Select another." I tried Saint Paul, and he was already taken. Finally, I tried David because of his armor-clad figure.

"Put your face on David," the computer commanded, instantly taking my photo and making it available on the screen.

"Now what?" I touched the screen, sliding my face onto David's. The doors of the Temple of Mammon opened, and I watched my avatar enter.

I was in a world filled with biblical figures shooting laser beams at each other, while dodging bolts of lightning thrown by a Zeus figure and falling into pits of fire and brimstone. Across the landscape, moneybags appeared and disappeared. Avatars would try to capture moneybags while avoiding the obstacles and trying to stop others with laser blasts.

Using the game-control stick in front of the main screen, I guided David toward a moneybag and was zapped by Saint Paul. I stood up, looking into other cubicles to spot the face on the Saint Paul avatar. Looking around the room, I realized all the biblical avatars were adorned with faces of my fellow investors. We were playing against each other.

"Are we fighting each other in this game?" I asked the figure in the next cubicle intently looking at a screen and making grunting noises.

"Yes!" the figure snapped back. "Sh—I gotta win—could be a goner."

"Goner," I repeated.

"Shut up—could be thrown into the pit. I need to focus. Shit, I could die today. Leave me alone."

I tried for another bag and was hit by a bolt of lightning accompanied by a maniacal laugh sounding like Britt Owens. On the next attempt, my avatar fell into a fiery pit and emerged stripped of armor. My score in the left-hand corner read "−50." The computer informed me, "Danger! If your score drops another fifty points, you'll be put in the Ninth Ring of Hell."

I was zapped by another shooter, and suddenly my avatar appeared on a frozen lake of blood marked with the word "guilt."

"How do I get back?" I asked the computer.

"Take five gold coins from the purse on your waist and throw them on the Lake of Blood and Guilt."

I maneuvered David's hand into his purse, tossing the coins. The frozen blood quickly melted, and my avatar sank, returning to the shooter game.

My intuition took over after learning the game, and my score quickly climbed. I zapped my colleagues while jumping over fiery pits to reach moneybags. By the end of the day, I scored 455 points and was able to buy back David's armor with 25 points.

"You have enough points to buy a company," the computer voice informed me. "Select a company."

On the screen appeared company names with indications of their worth in game points. I knew nothing about the companies. I liked the name of a small Indian company called "Internet of Things Web."

I asked about the company. The computer said, "Small company located outside Delhi. Fifty employees are designing and developing software to complete the Internet of Things. Company valued at fifty million in World Government currency and three hundred and seventy-five game points. Not recommended for purchase by the Zeus Fund because of no identified consumer base."

Following my well-trained gut feelings, I slide my finger across the screen, dumping 375 points into the Internet of Things Web.

A notice flashed at the screen's top: "You own the Internet of Things Web. Valuation and profitability reports issued every five minutes. Please wait."

I decided to end my first day investing. "Not bad," I thought. "Fun to play. My avatar looks weird."

A ringing bell sounded from my computer as a flashing notice appeared: "Value of Internet of Things Web jumped fifty percent and profitability by thirty percent. Markets indicate increasing value."

I made twenty-five million in my first day playing WorshipMammon and thought, "Chelsea's parents will be proud. I love shooter games." I told the computer I was leaving until tomorrow.

Chapter 13

"**D**id they fuck you over?" I watched Chelsea greet me on my return from the Zeus Funds' Caribbean tax haven. "I don't know how we can live with this."

I whispered to Sally to show me more.

Chelsea and I stood in the foyer of her family's Park Avenue penthouse running our hands over each other. She gently pulled me in the direction of her bedroom. Her looks of anger over Zeus alternated with looks of love. I knew then that the rest of my perfect life would be difficult.

"I won money. That'll please your parents."

"Won money?" She glared at me as we moved through the library with its walls displaying awards for Winnie's Secrets' Eat'em products, including one from the World Health Organization for reducing the global spread of STDs.

There, a large trophy for Winnie's Secrets' research and development of digestible computers rested on a Victorian-era table. Besides being in Eat'em products, marketers were including them in GoGrow flavor tests to measure reactions. Digestible plastics and computers were standard in GoGrow foods. Eat'em was honored as a flavor on GoGrow food consoles.

"More like stealing from the poor," Chelsea continued. "Did you know that prick Britt Owens funds antiabortion and antigay groups worldwide? Did you invest in Euphrates Environment? They're going to make the poor pay for water."

"It wasn't like that. I played a game. I didn't know what I invested in. But I did buy an Indian company—Internet of Things Web."

"You own a company! Then we own a company after this marriage."

"Chelsea, are you going to be on my back all the time? I love you, but will we survive? Both of us could be zapped."

"I just can't believe this happened." Chelsea sobbed, wrapping her arms around my neck.

"I didn't choose a perfect life," I said, hugging her, "of making money and marrying you."

"Big Data—the driving force! Going to kill us or make us slaves to numbers." Chelsea began feverishly kissing my cheeks.

"You know we're being watched," I whispered in her ear. "Maybe not say these things out loud—just whisper."

"Fuck it! You worried about Sally? We're meeting here at six tomorrow for dinner with my parents to talk about our marriage. Interpol and Radiant should love it."

• • •

"I see you did well at the Zeus Fund," Sally greeted me as I returned to the townhouse. I felt Sally move at seeing itself in the video. "I selected some clothes for meeting Chelsea's parents. I checked data on their tastes and went with Winnie Tipper's. She likes blue suits. Also, I replaced your underwear and ties with Eat'em's new men's products."

"Why didn't you ask me? Don't I get a choice?"

"Instructions are very clear. Radiant's data shows parents impressed by blue colors and can smell Eat'em underwear."

"Smell?"

"Eat'em's men's briefs are impregnated with virile odors. Odors especially formulated by KeepHard—tested on one billion men and women—marketed as SXmell, along with a female scent, VAGsmell."

"KeepHard?"

"Biostream division devoted to erectile problems. Odors work well when combined with EverLast pills."

"I don't have erectile issues. Where are you getting this data?"

"You are not using it for erections but for having a pleasing smell for parents. Both like virile smells—also shows your allegiance to Eat'em products. Data shows both parents will soon be using BigSleep's products. Father will be serviced by DieWell. Data projects inheritance of Winnie's Secrets within five years."

"Jesus, I don't want to smell!"

"Data projects good impression on parents with SXmell. Chelsea will like it. KeepHard data shows combination of SXmell, VAGsmell, and EverLast will help in procreation."

"I don't think Chelsea wants kids."

"Big Data says you both will be at prime birthing age in ten years at twenty-eight. Two children, a boy and a girl, will be part of your perfect life. Biostream's division, GenTest, will ensure a healthy boy and girl."

"Is nothing hidden? They know my body and future?"

"GenTest did biochemical, chromosomal, and molecular genetic tests. Space already reserved in birthing station at GetWell Hospital on Upper East Side. Chelsea may need help with her small hips. CleanCut medical supplies developed a new clamp-and-pull instrument for birthing."

• • •

I watched myself at Chelsea's dining table staring across at her father, Ben Tipper, with her mother at the head of the table. Chelsea sat next to me, unable to keep her hands out of my lap. The combinations of smells released by my Eat'em briefs were effective. Meeting me in the apartment's foyer, Chelsea started rubbing against me and whispering in my ear, "You smell hot."

Her parents looked calm and accepting, with both commenting on the cut and style of my blue suit. Chelsea's father sucked in his breath, saying, "I can tell you're a real man."

Winnie Tipper started the conversation looking at me. "Don't you think you're a little young for marriage?"

Ben Tipper leaned over the table, powering on a limited-edition, ornate, and gold-plated GoGrow food processor. Only a thousand were made and numbered, quickly becoming status symbols and selling for ten times their original price.

"What would you like?" Ben asked me. "We've got some new flavors. Cost a lot to get them. There's one called 'New Delhi street food' and another called 'Japanese cannibalism.'"

"Chelsea, I don't think this is a good idea. Can Jimmy support you? You like the rich life," Winnie asked.

"That's not true," Chelsea glared at her mother. "I could live in the woods. I don't need this fancy gold food processor. I could live on squirrels and mosses."

"Squirrels and mosses aren't on GoGrow's flavor list," Chelsea's father reacted, "but we might want to suggest it as the flavor of the month."

"Let's get real," Winnie Tipper snapped. "Chelsea, you're too young, and Jimmy's too poor."

"What's Japanese cannibalism?" I asked Ben, trying to change the topic.

"Mother, Jimmy just bought a company. He made and will make more at the Zeus Fund," Chelsea answered. "We're not too young. Kids used to marry at thirteen or fourteen."

"We're not primitives," Winnie almost shouted. "You shouldn't go making kids at your age. It can all wait."

"I'm not pregnant, Mother. I'm not having kids."

"Maybe in our twenties," I gulped. "Data shows we will make kids when we're twenty-eight."

"What?" Chelsea looked at me. "We never talked about kids. What's this about data?"

"Japanese cannibalism is an interesting flavor," Ben answered my question, ignoring the growing tempest. "A Japanese man chopped up his penis and fried it with mushrooms and garlic after a sex-change operation. Ninety people signed up to taste it. Not enough to feed all, so some ate alligator. GoGrow took a small sample and chemically reproduced the flavor. It's a big hit among world fashion designers."

"What about New Delhi street food?" I saw myself asking.

"We will not allow you to marry!" Chelsea's mother pounded the table. "I've known Jimmy since those early playdates. He's not good for you."

"Winnie," Ben said softly, "maybe we should go easy on them. Our parents didn't like us marrying. But it all worked out."

"Only because I made a shitload of money from Eat'em," Chelsea's mother glared. "You never did anything with that rinky-dink Brooklyn bank."

"Let's not fight in front of the kids," Ben whispered. "They're getting married. Let 'em think marriage is all hunky-dory."

"Mother, whether you like it or not, we're marrying," Chelsea shouted.

"Jimmy, tell the processor your flavor code so we can eat." Ben placed four crystal- and gold-trimmed plates on the processor's dish rack.

After giving the processor my personal flavor code, Ben explained, "New Delhi street-food flavor is unique. GoGrow scraped food off the pavement around pushcarts. The mixture of exotic Indian spices in food dropped on the ground plus sidewalk crud created a unique flavor. The chemicals are so expensive to make it that only our type of processor can produce it."

"I can't stop you. You're old enough." Winnie looked at us. "But your wedding is not going to be an embarrassment. It will be at Saint John the Divine's, and there will be a formal announcement."

"Embarrass you in front of your rich corporate friends," Chelsea snapped. "That's all you're worried about."

"I'll have some Chinese smog moo goo gai pan," I said to Ben. "I like the smoky flavor in the vegetables."

"That's right—you won't embarrass us." Winnie answered Chelsea. "Jimmy needs our money. You can't live downtown in his townhouse. It's unsafe with all those crazy artists and creeps. We'll get you a place up here."

"You can't tell us where to live. I'll take comfort food, father."

"I got you a penthouse on eighty-sixth and Lexington, small with only five bedrooms and no library." Winnie handed her daughter a photo. "You'll be free to decorate any way you want."

"Fuck it, Mother. I don't want to decorate an apartment."

"I'll try the Japanese cannibalism," Winnie said to her husband. "It sounds interesting."

"I'm not sure I want to move up here," I said to Chelsea's mother. "I like my neighborhood."

"You have to live for success. You own a company and are interested in investing. You need the right address." Winnie watched her plate moving under the food processor.

"The bottom line," Ben said to me, "is that the Zeus Perfect Life Fund wants you to move. They contacted us. The perfect life requires the right address. They're buying it for you."

Everyone stared at Winnie's plate as a gray, plasticized, chopped penis was extruded along with brown chopped mushrooms.

"Kind of small," Ben commented. "Maybe big for Japs."

"Dad, that's racist and not true."

"How would you know?" I asked jealously. "Didn't know you slept with Japanese men."

I watched my Chinese smog moo goo gai pan being extruded onto the gold-trimmed plate. A cloud formed over the food, causing us to sneeze and wipe our watering eyes.

"Once in Tokyo." Chelsea blushed. "It was in the Good Times Love Hotel."

"Love Hotel?" I questioned. "I've never been to Japan."

"It was automated and advertised robot fights."

"How's that work?" Chelsea's father asked. "I don't know if I should hear this from my daughter."

"You put coins in a slot," Chelsea explained, clearly uncomfortable telling me. "A key comes out with a room number and a ticket for watching nude men and women swing glow sticks at each other while riding on robotic animals. You can select any of them for your room."

"Any of them?" I wondered out loud.

"Animals or humans," Chelsea said.

"Animals," Chelsea's father exclaimed. "You mean have sex with a robot dog or horse? I don't think I should be talking this way with my daughter."

"I'm eighteen, Dad. Grown up! Get real. I'm getting married—like it or not. Jimmy and I screw all the time."

"I agree with your father," Winnie said. "I don't want to hear this."

"What'd you order?" I could see I was getting more jealous.

"A man riding a robotic giraffe."

"Jesus," I said, "you just dumped coins in a machine and ordered a man on a giraffe. Did you do it on the giraffe?"

"Yes," was Chelsea's simple answer, "and he wasn't small."

"So that's where you went when we were there last summer," Ben looked appalled. "That's shocking, Daughter. You said you were going shopping."

"Last summer!" I exclaimed, searching my pockets for my anger-management pills. "Shit," I thought, "I forgot my drug packet."

"Those Japanese are kinky," Chelsea's father looked lost in thought. "I am shocked by what you did."

"We were going together." I saw a jealous rage taking over my body. My hands started trembling, and my face felt warm. "You fuckin' cheated on us," I burst out as I searched for my pills.

"What did you do while Chelsea was so-called shopping?" Winnie asked her husband.

"Went kayaking," Ben replied.

"I didn't cheat," Chelsea told me. "We weren't getting married then."

"But you said you love me," I hissed. "You bitch. I can't trust you." The heat of my body made Eat'em odors stronger. Chelsea was feeling sexier as her hand tried to persuade me of her desire for me.

"Kayak!" Chelsea's mother shouted. "I remember the story. Woman scans herself and feeds it to a three-dimensional printer and makes a six-foot kayak shaped like her vagina. You son of a bitch. You rode in her hole."

"Dad, you did that?" Chelsea looked surprised.

"You bitch-fucked on a giraffe." I slammed my fist on the table hard enough to cause the food processor to bounce. I never felt like this; without pills, I felt only jealous rage.

All of a sudden, Chelsea's mother stood and went over and slapped her husband's face. "You'll take some kayak whore over me. Get out of here. Get out of my apartment. Go sleep in your bank vault with your porn."

"How'd you know it was there?" Ben looked surprised and worried. "The kayak was a onetime thing. Never did it again."

"Get out!" Winnie yelled. "And don't come back. I'm tired of you fucking anything that moves. And now a kayak! You left our daughter alone to find a giraffe."

I watched myself stand up and could see my red face in the dining-room mirror. My lips were pursed, and my nostrils were flared. I was truly mad for the first time in my life.

"You fuckin' bitch," I said. "I never want to see you or your crazy family again. Giraffes and kayaks are not in my future."

With Chelsea's father, I rushed to the apartment's elevator as both women shouted at us.

"Some wedding planning." I could see my confusion and anger. "This will never work. Fuck Interpol and Radiant. They can zap us. I'm not going through this for the rest of my life."

Chapter 14

I watched myself trembling in the townhouse hallway as Sally handed me a pill and a glass of water.

"I saw what happened," Sally said. "You shouldn't have thrown away your drugs. I got you new ones in your dresser drawer."

"The marriage is over," I sobbed. "I can't live with a cheat. She hates everything I do."

"Calm down." Sally took my arm and led me to the stairs. "You'll be OK. Let's go up to bed."

"Bitch," I screamed. "I can't go through this." Tears streamed down, and I pounded the banister.

"Human women are like that." Sally pointed me up the stairs as it started rolling up the ramp. "Human men also try different sex objects. Humans are consumed with lust. Good for reproduction."

"What will happen to me?" I started up the stairs with Sally holding my hand across the railing and keeping pace with my steps. "I'm going to die."

"Chelsea will die before you. If you don't marry, it will be sooner than later. Interpol is already investigating."

I squeezed Sally's hand, beginning to feel the drug's effect. "They plan to vaporize her, and I'll lose my perfect life."

"They are thinking of disemboweling. But Big Data predicts you will marry, and then she will die. BigSleep already made arrangements."

"What should I do?" I felt myself getting calmer as we reached my bedroom door. "She's going to die? We're still marrying?"

"Sh...," Sally guided me to the bed, stroking my forehead. "Everything will be OK. Chelsea will love you."

I felt woozy as the drug soothed my feelings. Sally helped me with my clothes, and we climbed into bed together. I snuggled up against its warmth, starting to drift off to sleep.

"Your real worry is the company you bought."

"What do you mean?" I mumbled, almost asleep.

"The Internet of Things Web is facing a hostile takeover. You will fly back to the Zeus Fund tomorrow."

"'Hostile takeover'—what's that mean?" I hugged Sally.

"Humans are aggressive. They do things that hurt others. Human women are untrustworthy. That's why you created robots."

Sally's hand stroked my forehead as I disappeared into the world of dreams.

● ● ●

I watched Chuck Spiller greet me as I got off Zeus's private jet after it landed.

"You've hit a gold mine," Chuck greeted me as I came down the ramp. "But there is an attempt to boot you out of the market. We've got to get you to the tech-investment division right away."

"What gold mine?" I asked as we got into the company's Bentley.

"The Internet of Things Web is shooting up in price. Now there is an attempt at a hostile takeover by Dragon Technologies."

"Why?" I asked as the car sped the short distance to the Zeus compound.

"Ashvin Kamala, the company's head software engineer, made a major breakthrough on linking devices. It makes a global Internet of Things Web possible. Your first company is going to make a fortune."

"What's a hostile takeover?

We stopped in front of the Temple of Mammon before Chuck could answer. "Britt Owens, Ashvin Kamala, and the company's CEO, Sankalp Sastry, are in the money room. They don't want a takeover."

"I still don't understand," I said as we hurried up the front stairs under the shadow of the towering Jesus Christ and through doors covered in world-currency symbols. The interior was lavishly decorated with gold-trimmed moldings and mosaics of biblical scenes. An altar studded with precious gems and a large sculptured onyx cross stood in the middle of the room below a dome painted with angels.

"Dragon wants the company," Chuck explained. "It will complete their network control. The Chinese are giving them money. They're trying to buy all the stock."

"I thought I owned the company."

"You bought controlling stock with your three hundred and seventy-five game points. Did you read the game report?"

"I didn't look," I admitted. "I don't know anything about this stuff. I just played the game. I thought I bought the whole company."

"You bought forty percent of the stock." Chuck pulled open a large door in the temple's back wall, revealing the waiting group sitting at a table shaped like a world-currency symbol with gold bars stacked along the walls. On each stack was an apostle statue. "Forty percent gives you controlling interest. Dragon Technologies is trying to buy the other sixty percent held by multiple investors. If they do, they will replace the management with a bunch of atheist Communist stooges. This is not good for Christ."

"Christ," I wondered, "what's he got to do with it?" I was quickly introduced to Ashvin Kamala and Sankalp Sastry as I sat down.

"We have a problem for Christ and the world," Britt Owens said to me. "If Dragon Technologies is taken over by atheist Chinese, they could control the World Government. The red star will replace the cross. Humanity would no longer be guided by truth."

"The software," Ashvin Kamala explained to me, "will allow link-ing and controlling all Internet-connected devices. It will complete the Internet of Things Web envisioned by Kevin Ashton back in 1999."

"The Chinese already control everything in their country with the Great Firewall," Sankalp Sastry commented. "If this happens, the world's communications, devices, and systems will promote Socialism with Chinese characteristics."

"I want Capitalism with Christian characteristics." Owens pumped his fist in the air.

"Hindus are not keen on atheism or Chinese characteristics," Ashvin Kamala replied.

"What do I do?" I saw myself asking, still not clear on the Internet of Things Web's software and fighting a takeover.

"This is serious for God and humanity," Owens replied. "The atheist Chinese will control everything, including the World Government. You've got to buy enough stock to have majority control."

"I still don't know how to invest. How do I buy stock? What's a majority?"

"You only need eleven percent more to have fifty-one percent con-trolling interest," Chuck explained. "The problem is you'll be struggling with Dragon Technologies for the stock. It's going to get expensive."

"Struggle," I wondered. "I don't know how to buy stock."

"You play WorshipMammon." Chuck smiled. "Only this time, you'll be playing against the Chinese Communist Party's game, the Hundred Flowers Campaign. It'll be your apostles against revolutionary heroes."

"If Dragon Technologies control our software," Ashvin Kamala said to me, "then they control the world."

"And God takes a backseat to Communism." Owens looked at the stacks of gold.

"What is the software?" I asked, realizing that I should know what my company was doing.

"Sensors in phones, cars, factories, office equipment, agricultural and mining machinery, fisheries, government hospitals, hospitals, etc.—all communicate data," Ashvin Kamala answered. "Our software integrates this data, which will be used by Interpol and the World Government. All this data is linked to facial-recognition images from the world's surveillance cameras. It completes the Internet of Things Web."

"Good for security and order." CEO Sastry laughed. "The Internet of Things Web is about controlling humans. Little escapes these data sets. Humans are tracked for their own good. Lawbreakers are swiftly caught."

"Selling our software will earn us a fortune. We must keep it out of the hands of the commies," Sankalp Sastry exclaimed.

"We need to get you started." Chuck nodded at me. "Let's go for Mammon and Christ."

I leaped up with Chuck, and we dashed from the temple across the palm garden to the technology-investment division.

"This gaming will be different," Chuck explained, breathless from hurrying from the temple. "You will be playing another game. The Hundred Flowers Campaign is about controlling ideas. In Mao's time, it was controlling ideas favorable and harmful to the party."

"What do I do?" I asked as Chuck hurried me down the technology-investment division's corridors to the game room.

"Your prophets hurl biblical aphorisms at commie-spouting revolutionary avatars. If your biblical sayings are stronger than those of Mao and all his later scumbag followers, you earn points. Under current market conditions, you need four hundred points to buy another eleven percent. The stronger your biblical quotes over the commies, the more points."

"I don't know the Bible." I was worried.

"You'll get a screen list," Chuck explained. "You won't have time to read or understand. Just choose. Go with your gut."

"From the gut Christian sayings," I marveled at the idea. "You're telling me if it looks good, use it. Intuit!"

"You got it." Chuck smiled. "You were educated for this—make money with hunches."

"That's more than it took to get forty percent," I commented, climbing into the gaming chair with its multiple control sticks and wands.

Putting on the headset and visor, I entered a 3-D world of prophets and Communist ghosts. My David avatar and other Christian prophets stood before a sea of terra-cotta Chinese warriors.

Without warning, former Communist Party leader Deng Xiaoping rose above the field of warriors, hurling through the air the message, "Poverty is not Socialism. To be rich is glorious."

I launched Saint Luke's avatar, challenging Deng Xiaoping, "For it is easier for a camel to go through the eye of a needle than for a rich person to enter the kingdom of God."

Fifty points appeared in the screen's upper left-hand corner.

Mao Zedong rose above the army, commanding: "Every Communist must grasp the truth: political power grows out of the barrel of a gun."

Saint Matthew's avatar responded for another twenty-five points: "Put your sword back into its place. For all who take the sword will perish by the sword."

Xi Jinping charged forward: "We must take cultivating and disseminating the core Socialist values as a fundamental project for integrating the people's mindset and reinforcing our social foundations."

Saint Timothy threw a lightning bolt: "Preach the word! Be ready in season and out of season; reprove, rebuke, and exhort, with complete patience and teaching."

Mao suddenly appeared behind the prophets, costing me twenty points: "Letting a hundred flowers blossom and a hundred schools of thought contend is the policy for promoting the progress of the arts and sciences."

Saint John spun around, confronting Mao: "For God so loved the world, that he gave his only Son, that whoever believes in him should not perish but have eternal life."

"It is a long-term task to ensure that online public opinion is healthy and sound," Xi Jinping urged, trying to sneak into our rear with Mao. "Without ensuring cyber security, we cannot safeguard national security."

Swinging a sword, Saint Timothy decapitated Jinping, shouting: "Until I come, devote yourself to the public reading of Scripture, to exhortation, to teaching."

My score went up to 300.

Pushing Saint John into a fiery satanic sinkhole, Mao answered: "Conditions are changing all the time, and to adapt one's thinking to the new conditions, one must study. Even those who have a better grasp of Marxism have to go on studying, have to absorb what is new."

Intuiting Mao's next move, I shot back with Saint Mark: "Go into all the world, and proclaim the gospel to the whole creation."

I watched my score inch up to 350. I needed 50 more points.

Abruptly Confucius's head appeared, attached to Xi Jinping's body, and leaped at my David avatar. Above Confucius was a banner proclaiming: "If the people are governed by laws and punishment is used to maintain order, they will try to avoid the punishment but have no sense of shame. If they are governed by virtue and rules of propriety, they will have a sense of shame and will become good as well."

I intuited this as a turning point in the game and launched Moses surrounded by a flaming cloud. He circled Confucius, waving a gold flag inscribed: "Let every person be subject to the governing authorities; whoever resists the authorities resists what God has appointed, and those who resist will incur judgment."

I watched Confucius trying to fly above Moses, waving a sword marked Truth. Just as Confucius was positioned above, Moses zapped him with: "Render to Caesar the things that are Caesar's, and to God the things that are God's."

Bells began to ring as my score surged above 400. The screen flashed: "You now control The Internet of Things Web."

"Congratulations! You got those atheist Chinese." I felt Chuck's hand on my shoulder as I powered down, removing my headset and visor. "Governance by law versus shame—give me a break. Rule by law is the Western and Christian way."

"I'm not sure what I did—just went by gut instinct. I don't know about that Christian stuff on poverty. Seems to be against Mammon."

"They all claim to be helping the poor," Chuck smiled, helping me out of the gaming chair. "Socialism with Chinese characteristics is not going to end poverty. Only Christ will."

"I almost used Saint Timothy's 'For the love of money is a root of all kinds of evil' against Deng Xiaoping's 'To be rich is glorious.'"

"Good thing you didn't." Chuck led me out of the gaming room into the thunderous applause of my coworkers. "You needed to add the rest of Timothy's words: 'It is through this craving that some have wandered away from the faith and pierced themselves with many pangs.'"

"I don't understand."

"Being rich is OK," Chuck said, "as long as riches don't take you away from Jesus."

"What about poverty?"

At that moment, Britt Owens came rushing down the corridor. "What's this about poverty? Capitalism and Christ will end poverty, not atheist Socialism claiming equality."

"Capitalism and equality don't seem to go together," I said as Owens embraced me.

"That great Jewish prophet, Milton Friedman, said Capitalism will grow the economy and make people more equal. Socialism destroys the economy, creating inequality." Owens shouted for all to hear. "Milton Friedman, Ayn Rand, Friedrich Von Hayek, Gary Becker, and Alan Greenspan preached Capitalism will make us all free, rich, and more equal. Let's bless these great economists in the name of God."

Chapter 15

I remember thinking about it on the way back to New York. "Chelsea's right about keeping the rich, rich. Christians and Communists preaching poverty and reaping profits—I'll ask Chelsea about Socialism with Chinese characteristics—sounds weird."

I watched the video showing Zeus's plane land at New Jersey's Teterboro Airport where a car waited to take me to the townhouse. There was a half-hour backup at the George Washington Bridge, and traffic was slow on the West Side Highway.

Sally stood on the stoop. "It took you so long to get from the airport. I wanted to be the first to congratulate you. You won." Seeing Sally on the doorstep rekindled a memory about it seeming to develop emotions. The robot sounded like it missed me.

"I'll ask Burris," I planned at the time.

"Chelsea will be coming in five minutes," Sally told me. "Her car notified me. Let me start your shower while I unpack."

"I can start my own shower," I snapped as Sally retrieved my luggage from the car.

I didn't have time for a shower with Chelsea appearing so soon. I went into the kitchen and ordered a club sandwich, which was promptly extruded from the food processor. My personal taste code added extra mayonnaise. I was savoring the first bite when Chelsea appeared on the kitchen's security screen.

"Let her in," I commanded.

"Want some food?" I greeted her as she walked down the front hallway.

"First a kiss." She nestled in my arms. "I missed you. Hope we can work this out."

"I don't know what to do." We kissed, and I led her into the kitchen. "I just—and I still don't understand how—made a shitload of money and have become a major player."

"I'll take a little comfort food," she commanded the processor. The word "little" prompted it to extrude two small plasticized Italian-sausage sliders on poppy-seed rolls.

"What have you got to drink?" she asked the drink machine in the refrigerator's door.

"Just refilled it," Sally said, rolling into the room. "You can order anything but root beer. GoGrow had a chemical shortage because of global demand."

"Give me a chocolate milk shake," Chelsea ordered. A glass from the refrigerator's storage compartment slid under the door's spigot, and black-and-white chemicals streamed into it. The chemicals quickly congealed into an icy-looking mixture.

"Many calories in that drink," Sally warned. "You need to watch your weight for wedding clothes and birthing."

Ignoring Sally, Chelsea sipped her drink. "A major player at what—WorshipMammon?"

"More than that, I just beat China. I can control the Internet of Things Web."

"Jimmy made money for you," Sally interrupted. "He worked hard for you. You'll have a perfect wedding and life."

I gulped at Sally's words, remembering the prediction of Chelsea's death.

"Let's go to your room," Chelsea whispered in my ear.

"I just made the bed. I placed lotions and vibrators on the bedside table," Sally informed us. "There is a new one I ordered with built-in lubrication and tingle-and-slide action."

"Sally, power off," I commanded angrily.

"Interpol and Radiant commanded me to not power off. I must be recording your actions. Your lives depend on Interpol maintaining contact."

"Jesus, can't we have privacy?" I watched myself shoveling down the rest of my sandwich as Chelsea swallowed her sliders.

"Bedroom surveillance will communicate with me and Interpol. No reason for me to be there. Just call if you need clean sheets or towels. You made a mess last time. I don't know what the stains were from."

"Sally, please give us privacy. You shouldn't be buying this stuff." I grabbed Chelsea's hand, and we headed to the stairs.

"In the future, you will not have to worry about privacy," Sally called after us. "Your company will link the system together. The World Government and Interpol will know everything at all times about everyone."

"How's that?" I paused.

"The Internet of Things Web's software provides security and control for all people's well-being," Sally explained. "Even your breath will be monitored for your health. Control for the Good of All will be the World Government's new motto."

"What's this about your company controlling everything?" Chelsea asked as we stripped and hurried into bed. I noticed that the bed seemed warm as if Sally was in it before us.

"I'll tell you later," I said, my hands moving over her body.

"Try the new vibrator," Chelsea panted after a few minutes.

On the bedside table, I spotted the new instrument with a card printed out from Sally reading: "Use voice commands to operate your new Wonderful Rabbit Vibrating Love Ring with StimoClimax Lubricant." Next to Sally's card was a product description:

It's a cock ring, clitoral stimulator, and ball teaser all-in-one! One head provides exciting clitoral stimulation as the rabbit's ears flutter, while the other head pulsates against his testicles, providing a thrilling buzz for both parties. A snug squeeze from the stretchy cock ring ensures a stiff erection and prolonged action for both of you as StimoClimax lubricant adds new thrills!

I could feel the lubricant flow as I pressed against Chelsea.

"Easy," Chelsea shouted out. I could feel the vibrations lessen at her command.

The effect of the vibrations and StimoClimax increased my desire as I plunged ahead.

"Harder," Chelsea screamed, causing the cock ring to tighten. "More!"

"Stop it," I screamed in pain as Chelsea's call for more increased the ring's tightening.

The vibrations decreased but not the ring's pressure.

"Don't stop," Chelsea pleaded, causing the vibrations to increase. "Stay hard. I'm almost there—more!"

"I can't take it." Leaping out of bed and trying to rip the cock ring off, I fell, banging my head on the nightstand and causing a cascade of lotions and dildos.

"Jesus," Chelsea yelled, "I was almost there. Please give me more."

Sally burst through the door just as I thought the cock ring would castrate me. The pain was terrible.

"I worried about adding voice commands to the gizmo. I thought it would make it easier." Sally bent over my writhing body, commanding, "Release."

I rolled over, hiding my ejaculation.

"Oh my God. Shit, I lost it," screamed Chelsea. "Get that bitch out of here. She planned this."

"It's a robot. It's not a 'she.'" I got up from the floor, wondering if I'd lost any vital parts. "Sally was helping us. It can't harm us."

"Sally hates me. She's jealous." Chelsea staggered out of bed, heading to the bathroom.

"Sally's not a 'she,'" I insisted. "It doesn't have emotion."

"She's a fuckin' bitch machine," Chelsea shouted while peeing. "You've got to get rid of her."

"I exist to serve people," Sally said in a monotone. "My program will not allow me to hurt people. I only learn about emotions from watching people. I don't have emotions. I am not a 'her.' I have no gender."

"I don't believe you," Chelsea said, walking naked from the bathroom and throwing one of my hairbrushes at Sally. "You love him."

Ducking, Sally responded, "Robots can't love. We learn about love from humans. Robots can't feel love."

"I bet you sleep with Jimmy," Chelsea accused. "Can you fuck?"

"I comfort Jimmy," Sally continued in a monotone, rolling to the bedroom door. "I cannot have intercourse. I have no reproductive organs. Those are being planned for new models."

"Robots with reproductive organs," I exclaimed. "Will they be able to have human children?"

"Planning by NewBabs and GenTest to put egg and sperm into reproductive robots or ReproBots. They will be different from LovBots for human sexual needs. It will save human women childbirth pain and make all children perfect."

Remembering Dr. Reznick's cosmetic surgery for the perfect face, I wondered, "Will that mean all children will look the same?"

"They will look like their parents, only better," Sally answered, scooting out of the bedroom. "You've made this all possible with the Internet of Things Web."

"I hate Sally," Chelsea said. "But how can I dislike a robot with no emotions? What's this about your company and NewBabs? Are you planning to put my eggs in a robot and stir them up with your sperm?"

"I don't know anything about this," I hurried, putting on my clothes and realizing that Chelsea's frustration was leading to a royal battle. "I never heard of NewBabs, and I don't know a thing about ReproBots. Can't figure out what my company does; I just bought it."

"You said you're a major player." Chelsea's complexion was returning to a normal color. "You mean the game or world economy?"

"Both," I answered, concerned about where the conversation was leading. "You'll find this out sooner or later, but I might become a voting member in the World Government."

"You son of a bitch," Chelsea screeched, yanking on her clothing. "You think I'll marry someone responsible for fuckin' the poor and killing the planet."

"We don't have much choice. But my company will make the world a paradise. I beat out Dragon Technologies and the Chinese government. What is Socialism with Chinese characteristics?"

"The only choice I've got," she replied, "is death or marrying someone who'll cause death."

"I'm not killing anyone. My company will be finishing the Internet of Things Web. It will benefit everyone."

"How's that?" Chelsea headed for the door, yelling at the security system, "Call my car. I want to go home."

"The Internet of Things Web will make the world perfect. Please don't leave. We've got to talk. How can we marry when we're always fighting?"

"Sometimes we make love." Chelsea started crying and pounding the wall. "Shit, this is miserable. I'm marrying a monster. I should be vaporized."

"Please, let's talk," I said softly, trying to gather her in my arms. "We don't always fight. We're getting married."

"Tell Chelsea's car to wait," I said to the security system as I led her out of the bedroom down to the library room, which was transformed from our first playdate.

"I will bring you snacks and drinks," Sally offered as we entered the library.

"Leave us alone," I snapped at Sally. "You've done enough harm."

We sat in two Barcelona chairs facing each other. I tried to calm things by praising the Internet of Things Web and giving us hope for a bright future.

"Do you know what the Internet of Things Web is all about?" Chelsea asked. "It can't be anything good."

"I've got to admit I really don't know. I played the game against the Chinese. People at Zeus Investments said my winning was like the second coming of Christ."

"We could ask Sally, but we sent it away," Chelsea suggested.

"It won't care," I said, calling Sally to the library. Of course, it was waiting outside the door.

Rolling into the room, Sally said, "I heard the question. All the parts of the Internet of Things Web existed in different data sets that couldn't be linked until your company developed this new software."

"What data sets?" I asked, realizing how little I knew about anything. I learned skills but didn't know anything.

"We know Interpol has surveillance data," Chelsea said.

"That's one data set of global facial recognitions. The chip put under your skin at birth monitors your biological state. That data set is used by corporations like Biostream, BigSleep, DieWell, GetWell, and CleanCut to anticipate health and burial needs."

"I've been tracked throughout my perfect life," I commented.

"There are also data sets of manufactured products with embedded RFID."

"What's RFID?" I asked.

"It's radio frequency identification data, which means that anything made by humans, from ships and planes to clothing and small nails, is tracked from production to distribution to usage. This is a massive data set including all product communications."

"What's my company got to do with this?"

"While there is communication from your chip to the medical corporations and between manufacturers and their products, there is no communication between any of the other Big Data sets. These different data sets communicate with specific groups, such as surveillance cameras streaming through AlwaysWatch to Interpol. RFID tracking is only sent to manufacturers. Networking RFID to AlwaysWatch will help develop good consumerism."

"So my company's software makes it possible for all these different data sets to talk to each other?"

"That's right. Until your new software, the Internet of Things Web was limited. Now it includes communication between everything. The chip under skin will communicate with medical and death companies, manufacturers and their products, surveillance and facial-recognition cameras, and Interpol databases. Everything will talk to everything—a completely unified world of communication."

"Shit, Jimmy," Chelsea exclaimed, "you've created a complete authoritarian world. Everything can be controlled."

"It'll make a better world," Sally responded. "Companies will know what resources are available, how many items should be manufactured, and what people will want to buy. No more crime. People will be constantly monitored, drug companies will know what to make, hospitals will be better prepared, and death will be more enjoyable."

I winced as Chelsea wondered out loud, "Death more enjoyable. What about them saying I could be disemboweled?"

Ignoring Chelsea's comment, Sally continued, "Take driverless cars. They communicate with each other to avoid accidents and with passengers to orient their GPS steering. The car is tracked through its RFID tag, and the car communicates with repair shops, auto-parts departments, and insurance companies, along with Interpol. Repairs are anticipated, companies know how many parts to make, and insurance companies know what rates to charge."

"You mean that my company's software will make it possible for all data sets to talk to each other?" I got up from the chair, stunned by what I now owned. "I could know everyone's secrets—their lives."

"Our new toilets analyze your waste," Sally continued, "sending data to health providers."

"I could also know everyone's shit," I laughed.

"They're only using it to make more money." Chelsea stood up, calling for a cab. "I'm going to be part of this when we marry. I don't know if I want it on my conscience."

"You marry or die," Sally said, out of character with its usual robotic personality.

"What?" Chelsea said in surprise. "Your fuckin' robot is threatening me."

"It only meant that if we don't marry, Interpol will kill you."

"This is complete human control." Chelsea angrily pointed her finger at me. "It's not going to make a better world. Some will get fat, while others starve. Corporations will tell us when to sleep, buy, shit, fuck, and die. Our company—it will be ours when we marry—will fulfill every dictator's wet dream. Hitler would have loved this."

Chapter 16

"What's this got to do with a perfect life?" I watched myself sitting in front of Carl Burris at Radiant's 57th Street headquarters. Computer screens with constantly changing data covered the walls. On the top floor above surrounding skyscrapers, Burris's window looked out over the green expanse of Central Park.

"You can see what you've accomplished." Burris pointed at a large screen embedded in a cabinet next to the window.

"I don't know what I'm looking at," I admitted, staring at a maze of undulating colored lines and shapes that created a stunning kaleidoscope mosaic of the planet. In the background was a fading green-and-black mottled dragon. "It does look beautiful."

"That's what you accomplished." Burris smiled. "You can see your perfect life."

"It's pretty but hardly my life. How is it perfect?"

"You're literally watching your company's accomplishments. All the data sets are beginning to talk to each other. The perfect world and perfect lives are now for all."

"I don't know what's perfect about my life." I looked exasperated by the constant vagueness of his answers. "No one's explained this perfect life to me," I pressed on. "How could it be perfect when I'm forced to marry? Chelsea doesn't give a shit about marriage or kids. She hates everything I do. We fight all the time. And she's going to die shortly. How's that perfect?"

"Want some coffee?" asked Burris, swiveling in his chair to look out on the park. "Cream, sugar?"

I nodded yes, and Burris commanded the drink machine near my chair to make us cups.

"Things would be different if we'd had your software connecting everything," Burris spun around, looking dispirited. "Chelsea is a problem. Using the data sets that we had, she was your perfect bride: right background, money, and education. The data sets didn't alert us to her ideas. I don't think it ever entered our minds that someone with that data would be a rebel."

"Show Chelsea's new data profile," Burris ordered.

On a screen to my left appeared Chelsea Tipper's face and data profile. Below her photo were columns labeled Wealth, Health, Education, Consumer Patterns, Product Usage, and Beliefs. Pulsing red outlines with flashing warning signs surrounded Consumer Patterns.

"Before," Burris explained, "we could only use data on wealth, health, and education. Without data sets talking with each other, we didn't factor in her consumer patterns and beliefs."

"She's Episcopal; that's why we're marrying at Saint John's. You knew that."

"Her Episcopal background was used in Wealth data. In New York, to be Episcopal usually means money and the right contacts. Data never showed her level of belief."

"What do Consumer Patterns have to do with this?" I drank some coffee. "Red flashing warning over Beliefs I can understand—but consumption?"

"This is why communication between data is important. We missed this, deciding you should marry."

"I don't understand."

"Consumerism is necessary for the World Government and the economic system. The whole system depends on shopping. Following the wireless RFID tags in manufactured items allows us to determine who bought what and when. Purchases indicate a person's belief system."

"What?" I exclaimed in disbelief.

"You are what you buy." Burris pointed a laser at Chelsea's Consumer Pattern column. "You can see she bought clothes at hippie boutiques, used-clothing stores, Walmart, and some offbeat online stores."

Pointing at "anticonsumerism" in Chelsea's Beliefs column, Burris continued, "We didn't know this when first looking at her data set. RFID tags are communicating with personnel data sets. These two data sets talking to each other give info on consumer attitudes and political beliefs."

Burris's laser moved to the flashing Leftist Radical Anarchist—Dangerous.

"How do you get that from what she bought?"

"Clothing purchases reflect self-identity. Chelsea sees herself outside the mainstream—hippie radical—same clothes as worn by lefty nuts all over the world. Since your new software, the World Government is asking all manufacturers to include political self-identity in RFID tags. You buy a Che Guevara T-shirt—it indicates political leanings. Of course, you might buy it in Havana as a tourist. If most of your clothing indicates leftist leaning, then you will go on Interpol's watch list."

"I wonder how I fit on the scale. Sally buys all my clothing."

"Good example," Burris responded, calling up my data list. "You can see that Sally's clothing purchases labels you as Consumerist—High Rating and your political beliefs as Conservative—Strong Supporter of World Government."

"Chelsea and my perfect life," I asked. "How do they fit?"

"Differences in consumerism make your marriage a match made in hell. If the RFIDs had been talking to other data, this would not happen."

"Then I don't have a perfect life?"

"You did on the early data analysis. Sex and fortune was what Chelsea was to you. You had to marry according to the original predictions."

"This is crazy. Interpol is threatening to vaporize her if we don't marry. Is this your doing?"

"I'm afraid so, yes. Everyone had a lot of money rolling on finding the perfect life. Your slipping away from the surveillance cameras gave us a perfect opportunity to threaten her into marriage. Your marriage was to validate our data analysis."

"But you didn't have Chelsea's consumerism data," I said angrily. "Marriage will not help my perfect life. What do you mean, 'money was rolling' on my life?"

"We wanted to sell Perfect Life kits and created PerLife Corporation to market them at birthing stations in GetWell hospitals and to psychiatrists at ThinkRight, along with schools and counselors. The kits provide the tools and access to data sets by which a perfect life can be planned. Parents anyplace on earth can plan for their children's perfect lives."

"Am I now expendable?"

"PerLife must adjust its kits to the Internet of Things Web. Hope to have the new kits out next year. We'll use your company's software."

"You still didn't answer me," I pointed out.

"Your Perfect Life experiment is over. You are free to do what you want. You are a success, so your life should be OK."

"Marriage—will that happen?"

"You and Chelsea do not have to marry," Burris stated. "The experiment is over."

Returning to consumerism, I repeated Burris's earlier statement, "You are what you buy," and asked, "I don't shop. Does that mean I'm nothing?"

"Sally buys. You are what Sally is."

"Jesus," I exclaimed. "Sally seems jealous. Can it develop emotions?"

"Yes," Burris answered. "Sally is a learning robot. It learned to take care of you. Learning robots are taught by humans how to express emotions. There is no indication they feel."

"Sally can show jealousy but not feel it?" I wondered.

"Let's get back to you." Burris stood, staring at a red-tailed hawk soaring over the penthouses on Central Park West. "While you'll not have the perfect life, you will have a good life, better than your parents could have given you. You're rich and powerful and by all common measures, a success."

"My parents!" I exclaimed. "I don't think about them. What happened to them? I remember someone saying I couldn't have a perfect life with neurotic parents, and they were given money to disappear. But shouldn't I think about them?"

"We tried to erase those concerns." Burris turned around to look at me. "Worked on it when you were a baby. You bonded with Sally. I do think it helped you not having them around."

"I am what I buy, and I'm bonded to Sally who buys for me." I stood up, wanting to leave. "By crazy consumerist logic, I'm Sally."

"You're what we made you or at least what data made you, plus Dr. Reznick's cosmetic surgery."

"What about my real parents?" I stood in front of Burris. "What do you mean, you 'tried to erase' my concerns?"

"We hired a psychiatrist from ThinkRight Corporation—I don't remember his or her name—to change your parental attachments to bond with Sally. As I remember, ThinkRight took you on as a special project. They helped to design Sally for bonding and used some kind of behavior-modification methods to help you forget your biological parents."

"Are you proud of what you've done to me?" I was infuriated at the news about ThinkRight and my parents.

"Yes. Your data profile shows success."

"What about my real parents? Where are they?"

"You can find them on any online search." Burris motioned for me to sit down. "ThinkRight was so effective that you've never tried."

I sat down, stunned that I'd never even thought of finding my parents. "What did ThinkRight do to me?" I blurted out.

Burris ordered ThinkRight's profile to replace Chelsea's data on the screen. The logo at the top read: "ThinkRight and World Government Working Together for the Benefit of All."

Burris's laser highlighted **About**, which delivered the message:

ThinkRight provides an array of services to individuals and the World Government to cope with the stresses of modernity. To help adjust individuals to a global society based on freedom, open markets, and consumerism, ThinkRight uses the right combination of methods, such as talk therapy, psychopharmaceuticals, behavior modification, isolation, shock therapy, and our famous Love Shopping experience.

ThinkRight works closely with the World Government to identify and treat those who might disrupt the social order. ThinkRight is incorporating the latest in the Internet of Things Web software in the identification process.

"See," Burris smiled, "your company is already impacting ThinkRight. I know Chelsea's problem afflicts others. Some are worse. They simply don't shop. World Government plans to make it a crime to not shop."

"Not shopping is a crime? Which of these did they use on me—isolation and shock therapy?"

"Not shopping is rebellion against the current system. It does serious harm to the global economy." Burris paused, moving the laser to **Love Shopping** under therapeutic products. "Not shopping is a revolutionary act that could topple the World Government and destroy corporations. Without corporations, everyone would die."

"That's nuts that everyone would die without corporations. I wish I knew something about history. I think people used to live without corporations."

"That's why we didn't teach you or anyone else anything about history." Burris got up and went to the food processor at the back corner. "We didn't want to confuse thinking about the future. Do you want anything to eat?"

"I'll have a hot dog." I called over to the food processor my flavor number, which guaranteed me hot sauce rather than plain ketchup. "And some fries."

"Why is not shopping revolutionary?" I continued. "What happens if I stop?"

"Besides destroying the economy, you'd be sent to ThinkRight." Burris brought my extruded hot dog on a sourdough bun with hot sauce over to me.

"What would ThinkRight do to me?" The hot dog, of course, tasted just right.

"They'd give you Love Shopping therapy. Put you in isolation watching commercials for several weeks, pump you up with drugs, and take you to a mall. You'd be denied food and then receive food rewards for each purchase. Talk therapy would create shopping fantasies. Special dream therapy would highlight the fun of shopping alone or in groups."

"Would that make me a better person?" I licked the hot sauce from my lips, feeling bits of plastic as I swallowed.

"Shopping supports the world order. Your World Government political scores would go up, and Interpol would take you off its terror list."

"What about Chelsea? Will she go to ThinkRight for treatment?"

"Her problem is not about shopping but what she buys. ThinkRight is working on therapy for correct purchases. The problem is the free market and companies selling left-wing clothing and other things. Must keep the market free and open."

"Is she being pulled in for therapy?"

"Maybe political reeducation. ThinkRight might take her in the future. For now, she is being left alone because of her family's influence."

"Good shopping will be taught in future schools." Burris finished his extruded nachos with jalapeños and jack cheese. "The World Government will need to improve political education. They've eliminated history for patriotic songs and chants. Pledges to the World Government and trips to malls will help. But teaching good shopping is the key."

"I guess we don't have to marry." I felt sad at the idea.

"Talk it out. Let her know she will not be forced to marry, and she should change her shopping patterns."

"And my parents?"

"That's up to you." Burris wiped away cheese stuck to his chin. "You can find them anytime. But let me warn you they live in a different world than you—small town, no travel, and tight money for shopping. They may not want to see you after they see the fruits of Sally's shopping adorning your body and finding out about your lifestyle."

"Reject me—I'd never thought of that."

"They can only afford Peoples Eats Takeout and might resent you going to Best World Eats. Remember they are educated in status differences by advertising that shows them how to shop for brand names. It's part of the World Government's new schooling program for the consumer market—you are what you buy."

Chapter 17

"I don't have to marry," Chelsea smiled as I watched us lying fully clothed on her bed. "I don't know what to say to my parents. They've rented space and put money down on an engagement banquet at the Pierre. Plus they've booked Saint John's and told their friends."

"You mean you don't want to marry?" I was disappointed and surprised after all her expressions of love.

"Interpol's no longer a worry. But I still love you. I don't know how I tell my parents. I guess I will lie. They'll be pissed about being embarrassed with their friends."

"You only wanted to marry to save your life," I replied, wondering how she'd take Burris's recommendation. "You need to change your shopping habits."

"Shopping habits? You mean for the wedding?"

"No, in general. Your shopping profile shows you a threat to the World Government." I explained RFID tags, the Internet of Things Web, my software, and her ratings under Consumer Patterns.

"For fuck sake, shopping habits as political profile: this is the triumph of consumerism. World Government corporations must love this."

"Are we marrying? We could still hang out," I hopefully offered.

"I've got to check with my parents; it might be too late. I still love you. If we go through with it, I don't want kids right away. I'm taking BirthStop/STD shots and will use FetusXtract services if needed."

"Everyone thought it was a marriage made in heaven," I laughed, "until completion of the Internet of Things Web. Now the World Government will tell us when to have kids, and you must learn to be a good shopper."

"'Good shopper'—what's that? Buy more, charge more—I don't understand."

"The problem is what you buy." I explained her consumer profile on Burris's screen. "Maybe wear more Eat'em products. I don't think they're considered left wing. Shop at big global stores, buy ordinary products, and stop dressing like an old-time hippie."

"What? How about my hair and makeup? Are they making me look corporate?"

"I don't know about the hair. They could check your beauty-parlor records. These are all now available in the Internet of Things Web." I tried to sound positive, wondering what I had done to the world. "Makeup products will have RFID tags, and camera-recognition surveillance will report your appearance. Just look like anyone else or like your mother. Have her shop for you."

"I'm not looking like Mom. She looks like every other captain of industry—even with Eat'em undies. She has a robot shopper from CorpLook get her clothes."

I started giggling, thinking of Chelsea wearing her mother's RFID tags to change her political profile.

"Why are you laughing? This is fuckin' totalitarian. The World Government can make us look all the same. An army of corporate workers marching down the street."

"I could have Sally shop for you."

"Don't let that bitch near me. Now that you're no longer in the perfect-life slot, you could power her off."

I forgot that my life was adrift without a perfect-life plan. I didn't ask Burris about Sally. Would I keep it and the townhouse? I had enough money to buy both.

"How about your mom's shopping robot? But I guess you don't want to dress like CorpLook."

"If we marry, will you power Sally off?" Chelsea climbed off the bed and stood in front of the mirror. "What's wrong with how I look? I like these bell-bottom jeans; they were expensive. Hippie Heaven in Woodstock claimed vintage from the 1960s. What's wrong with my new corn rows? I think they look great with my red hair."

"Can jeans last that long? Were you ripped off? Or," I tried to make a bad joke, "were they ripped? You know, like back then."

"How can I look different? I don't want to be CorpLook."

I got off the bed and told the computer to look up women's styles. On the wall screen near the door appeared corporate logos.

"Do you think we should try LabrLook?" I laughed. "I think those girls doing that mile-high building downtown look cute. Love their asses in those overalls. Or, how about ManfactLook or ServuLook? With ManfactLook, you could fulfill your Marxist dream of being an industrial worker. I don't like ServuLook's uniforms for Best World Eats or other franchises."

"Jesus, I don't want any 'look' but my own."

"That's not the way it's going to be. With the Internet of Things Web, according to Burris, everyone will be nudged to dress like their work."

"You mean they'll be able to look at you and know what you do."

I told the computer to open **LabrLook for Women**. There appeared an array of stylish overalls in differing colors. Models were sitting on heavy construction equipment or shown carrying tools.

"See," I said pointing at the screen, "you've many choices. There's also TravLook. Maybe you want to look like a tourist in Thailand or somewhere?"

"Jesus, I don't want to look like I'm going to Disney World or some high-end resort like my parents go to. Besides, they're all run by TravNet."

"They offer something called 'local-culture dress.'" I looked closely at the screen and touched a woman dressed, I think, like a Tibetan. There appeared an assortment of cultural styles. "This one looks like she's wearing your type of clothes." I tapped the screen.

There appeared several women dressed in brightly colored long dresses. Above them were the words: "Fashions for Local Guides and Folk Dances for Tourists in Burundi." Below the figures was the caution: "These clothes are available only to licensed guides and folk tourist performers through TravLook."

"What the fuck," Chelsea shouted. "They've corporatized local cultures—anything for a buck. You can only look traditional if you're licensed."

"What about this one? She's barefoot. I'd like that." Chelsea touched a black woman wearing a colorful headscarf, plain yellow blouse, and black skirt.

On the screen appeared the words, "TravLook's Stone Mountain Slave Dress." And the warning: "Sold only to licensed slave performers in Stone Mountain's Old South reenactment."

"They've corporatized slave history—it now makes a profit for TravNet and TravLook." I felt Chelsea's frustration and decided to be straightforward and ask for Hippie Dress.

To our surprise, the website for Nordstrom's Department Store appeared, offering Haute Hippie. The store's women's-apparel slogan was emblazoned at the top: Shop Like a Lady Boss.

"There you go." Chelsea stamped her foot. "They've commodified the hippie movement. Those dresses look like any other corporate clothing."

"Not surprising from what I learned at Zeus. I think CorpLook operates Nordstrom stores. If you don't want CorpLook, we should explore TravLook for offbeat fashions. We won't find much on the work-clothes sites. OfficLook could dress you like an office worker from the burbs. Are we going on a honeymoon?"

"My parents said they would pay for a honeymoon, but you've got enough money after your trip to the Zeus Fund. Let's check TravLook again."

"Are we marrying?" I again asked.

"Still have to think about it and figure what I might say to my parents. Let's check honeymoons on TravNet." Chelsea ordered the computer to the TravNet website and its honeymoon listings.

"Bunch of choices," Chelsea said, selecting the expensive category. "Look, there are high-end-adventure, romance, and baby-making honeymoons along with big cities and shopping. Can you imagine a shopping honeymoon?"

"Might be good for your political score," I commented. "It says you can earn extra bonus miles and hotel points. Romance and adventure look interesting."

Romance packages included both pastoral and big-city locations in hotels and resorts with special heart-shaped beds and tubs with stimulating devices and lotions. These packages usually included chocolates and in-room breakfasts and welcoming champagne. You could let TravNet select your honeymoon package, using your data profiles. Newlyweds could also play a marriage game.

"Marriage game—I wonder how or what you win?" My gaming triumph at Zeus made me curious.

The rules appeared on the screen:

Each spouse will enter a separate module fed with their personal data. Special modules will be available for gay and bestial marriages.

"Bestial marriages—wonder what that is?" I looked at Chelsea.

"I hear of men and women marrying horses, sheep, and goats," Chelsea answered. "Some call it 'traditional mating,' like old-time shepherds and cowboys. World Government recognizes them as legal. Big struggle by animal-rights groups for marriage equality."

"I can't imagine gaming with a horse module. Do they use their hoofs or neighing?"

We continued reading the rules:

The game is a trip through married life where each couple encounters real situations.

Scores determine if the marriage will last or end in separation or death. In some cases, a predicted separation date is given.

Scores indicate happiness in marriage, ranging from "hating it and always fighting" to "loving it and at peace with each other."

Seeing the word "death," I immediately said I wouldn't play. Chelsea agreed.

"Adventure Honeymoon," Chelsea ordered.

There appeared packages for jungles, mountain treks, deep-sea diving, big-game hunting, fishing, gliders, and even for arena combat. I was curious about arena combat.

There appeared choices of traditional Roman gladiator, martial arts, traditional Western boxing, and wrestling with alligators and gorillas. After each choice appeared a TravLook logo.

"Do you fight each other on an arena-combat honeymoon or others?" I asked. "I understand about the animals."

On the screen appeared a notice: "Honeymoon couples will combat each other. If animals are selected, then one partner assumes an animal's persona. Combat will determine power in marriage, such as control of video viewings and telling the family car where to go."

"What about TravLook?" Chelsea asked.

There appeared various collections of chain-mail, boxing trunks, and combat lotions and oils. Some of the oils claimed to help scratches.

"You'd look cute in that chain-mail miniskirt." I laughed.

"Romance Honeymoon and TravLook," Chelsea ordered.

"Shit," she exclaimed. "They all look like my mother."

"No wonder; look at the bottom."

Chelsea read out loud, "TravLook's Romance Honeymoon Brought to You by CorpLook."

"That's because we chose high-end honeymoons. Less-expensive ones might have another clothing look."

"I give up." Chelsea stomped over to the bed and started removing her clothes. "They've standardized everything. Did you notice the special charges for each climax? They're making money off sex. Are they actually going to count?"

"Our chips will tell the world. Everyone and everything will know every time we fuck."

"Do they zap us if we fuck too much or too little?" Chelsea stood naked, motioning for me to join her.

"We're monitored by the World Government's Office of Population Control. If there is a shortage of workers, the World Government cuts off BirthStop for couples selected by GenTest. Selection depends on where the worker shortage exists. If there is a shortage of office workers, then GenTest selects on that basis, and Interpol monitors them."

"How do you know this?" Chelsea unzipped my pants as I touched her.

"At the Zeus Fund." I felt myself getting excited. "If selected couples don't fuck and make babies, Interpol intervenes."

"And does what?"

"Fines and closely monitors them. All couples selected by GenTest are fertile."

"So with your Internet of Things Web, baby making is controlled by the World Government." Chelsea gently squeezed me.

"Best for everyone. BabThings knows how many diapers and baby stuff should be made each year; there is never a shortage of space at GetWell birthing stations, and there is planning for resource utilization. It's good for the world and us. There'll never be a population problem. Birthing will be according to data and economic needs."

Chelsea slowly kissed me and helped remove my pants, saying, "I hope they're looking."

"It's all going to be calibrated." Chelsea pushed me onto the bed as I continued. "Office workers' incomes only allow them to buy OfficLook clothes and medium-priced vacations."

"I saw a global Zeus chart." I felt her hands rubbing my chest. "It matches jobs, income levels, birthing, health, and shopping. Each job is given a global income range and is linked to shopping ability. Income levels are linked to resource management through predicted consumption patterns. A shortage of workers in any category prompts GenTest to select the right couples, and this affects everything in the Internet of Things Web."

"Including us?" Chelsea's tongue explored my ear.

"Of course," I said, feeling myself ready to burst. "If they want more people like your parents, GenTest will contact us, the baby's income range will be assigned, and corporations will prepare for our baby's consumption."

Chapter 18

It was late summer and the beginning of the 2039 hurricane season as I sat in Mammon Temple's back room, absentmindedly counting stacks of gold bars. I'd just graduated from Yale-Radiant MOOCs. I was still waiting to hear from Chelsea about the marriage. When we were celebrating my nineteenth birthday last March, she wanted to postpone a decision, despite her parents' planning.

"You'll just have to wait," she told them, "until we're a little older."

At the table were Britt Owens, Chuck Spiller, and the Internet of Things Web CEO, Sankalp Sastry. A week after Chelsea was informed we didn't have to marry, Chuck called me to spend a couple of weeks at the Zeus Funds' Caribbean headquarters.

"We finally decided to name it CompleteWorld," Sastry announced, "and sales are way up. The World Government recognized our patent and issued a bulletin declaring we opened the door to the perfect world."

"Jimmy, you should buy more tech companies." Owens smiled. "Chuck will help you with investing opportunities."

"India issued a decree recognizing me as a savior of humanity." Sastry reached in his pocket and pulled out a small gold piece and handed it to me. "You can see my face on the coin. It's worth thirty-five thousand rupees. Not going to be widely used at that value."

"That's around five hundred United States dollars." Chuck consulted his kWatch.

"So now it's the perfect world and not my perfect life," I said cynically. "Do you think the World Government will screw this up the way they did with me?"

"Since it will be a perfect world with Christ," Owens responded, "you'll have a perfect life."

"You must remember many Indians follow Ganesha and Shiva," Sastry objected, "besides the secularists. And there is Islam and Socialism with Chinese characteristics."

"There are twelve gold stacks," I observed.

"That's the number of Christ's apostles." Owens looked around the room and pointed at an empty space in the corner. "A new stack will go there with a CompletWorld statue. I can rightfully say it is Christ's new apostle."

"What'll a CompletWorld statue look like?" I wondered.

"It'll depict earth with human figures climbing to the gold cross on top."

Standing up and straightening his dhoti, Sastry looked angrily around the room before going over to a white-clothed table with a GoGrow drink machine and asking for Darjeeling tea. "We did not create CompletWorld to spread Christianity. That religion has done enough harm. Look what missionaries did. How can you stand a religion that worships a bleeding guy hanging on some chunks of wood?"

"I think," Chuck interjected, "the World Government wants a secular CompletWorld. Corporations don't care about religion. They want shoppers. You can say they're soulless."

I looked over at Britt Owens, who appeared to be struggling not to release a torrent of righteous indignation. Almost immediately, his face softened into a benign smile.

"The Internet of Things Web will tie everyone to every religion. Christ will win," Owens concluded.

"Maybe Shiva," I suggested. "Is Socialism with Chinese characteristics a religion?"

"Everyone will be connected to Torch's Great Spirit Hologram Church and given a salvation score." Owens stood up and stretched, joining Sastry at the drink machine, where he ordered a vanilla shake. "Salvation scores are given as symbolic nails. No matter what religion, everyone will have salvation scores since all are connected."

"Shiva's third eye will judge," Sastry said to Owens. "Everyone will be connected to Hinduism."

"Socialism with Chinese characteristics," Chuck answered my question, "allows free markets under state control by the Communist Party."

"Is that a real free market?" I got up, joining Sastry and Owens, and ordered orange juice.

"The party could end free markets at any time." Chuck leaned back in his chair. "But they won't; they're making so much money."

"Xi Jinping tried to stop corruption as party head a decade ago," Sastry commented. "He failed but strengthened their power. There's a network of executives moving between the party and corporations."

"How is it being affected by CompletWorld?" I asked.

"Everyone's connected to the party and to all religious and political doctrines." Sastry sat back down, opening his kPhone and asking for Jinping quotes. Reading the phone, he quoted Xi Jinping: "We must take cultivating and disseminating the core Socialist values as a fundamental project for integrating the people's mindset and reinforcing our social foundations."

"'Integrating the people's mindset,'" I repeated. "Sounds like competition for the Great Spirit Hologram Church. Is the score in chopsticks rather than nails?"

Chuck and Owens grimaced.

"Don't make fun of Christ," Owen whispered, trying to control his temper. "Christ will overcome Socialist values with the free market."

"China will try to control the world's mindset with the Internet of Things Web. I'm worried about the fate of Hinduism." Sastry read from his phone, "Xi Jinping said, 'To examine oneself in the mirror, party members should use the party constitution as a mirror in which to mirror themselves.' There's no religion in their constitution."

"The Bible is my mirror," Owens shouted. "I'll dress myself in front of the ten commandments. We'll make the world do it."

"How does Socialism with Chinese characteristics fit into the World Government? I thought this was about free markets and corporate rule." I picked up my orange juice, pleased that GoGrow updated my drink preferences by adding extra plasticized pulp.

"I think we should be concerned about Euphrates Environment's water filling GoGrow drink machines." Chuck ordered coffee, noticing a slight oil sheen on the surface. "They could be having problems. The company's SweeTaste bottled-water sales are slipping."

"What'll people drink?" Sastry asked. "All the groundwater in India is contaminated by human waste and industrial pollution."

"When we invested in Euphrates," Owens explained, "most groundwater and oceans were unfit for humans. We count on all people buying water processed by Euphrates."

"The Chinese Communist Party invested in Euphrates, when the country's rivers became multicolored or disappeared," Chuck added.

"Why don't we just stop polluting?" I felt the cold plasticized pulp as I swallowed.

"I see you didn't learn much in school. Did you study history?" Chuck asked.

"Only a little about the World Government and corporations—what'd I miss?"

Sitting up straight, Britt Owens mentioned, "Way back in 1962, Rachel Carson's *Silent Spring* warned people of a coming environmental crisis. Her book resulted in environmental laws and regulations. Then corporations found solutions."

"What'd the book title mean?" asked Sastry.

"Yeah, she attacked corporations and tried to scare everyone." Owens read from his kWatch:

Over increasingly large areas of the United States, spring now comes unheralded by the return of the birds, and the early mornings are strangely silent where once they were filled with the beauty of birdsong.

"That happened in India. As a kid, I remember trees filled with singing birds. The birds disappeared, and the trees are dying," Sastry said

"You can see why they don't teach history," Chuck commented. "It confuses people. We don't want to go back to a precorporate world."

"Luckily the World Government took a corporate approach," Owens continued, "when enacting SaveEnviron laws. National governments tried regulating corporations to stop environmental pollution. It failed; things got worse."

"Why didn't I learn about this in school? All I learned were skills," I complained.

Owens stood up, pointing at the gold stacks. "We need Mammon. SaveEnviron laws changed the problem and solution."

"Changed the problem?" Sastry questioned. "Isn't the problem killing birds and rivers?"

"The new law doesn't try to save the environment. It supports making substitutes. The problem is not protecting nature but finding replacements," Owens explained. "It is better to make money than to stop pollution."

"I don't understand." I was confused by Owens's logic.

"OK, let's say corporation X dumps chemical waste in a river and kills the fish. The answer from World Government policies is to use technology to make a fish substitute. Laws against dumping waste don't work. Corporation X continues making money, while GoGrow Chemical makes money selling replacement food."

"What about the birds? I miss them." Sastry looked skeptically at Owens.

"New revenue for corporations, profit, and free markets: SubsAnima is now making lifelike substitutes better than the real thing. They don't eat or defecate. Whole forests in North and South America are being stocked with robot birds and animals. Birds' voice boxes contain a repertoire of world music."

"But the trees are dying in India. There are few forests left."

"PlasTree is covering the world with new forests free of insects that don't need water. Data surveys show that people prefer PlasTree forests and SubsAnima robots over old biological models."

"And," Chuck added, "people don't worry about pollen, tripping on branches, or bird droppings landing on their heads. Data shows people like uniformity and prefer robots over ferocious animals. These two companies are adding to the environment while making money and keeping people working."

I'd never been in a real forest or even a PlasTree forest, and I had never seen birds and animals outside a zoo. "What's it like to be in a real forest?"

"You'd hate it," Owens answered. "Getting stung by insects and disorder with bushes and fallen branches making it hard to walk. You'd probably trip and fall while constantly worrying about meeting a bear or panther. You might get a snakebite."

"In a PlasTree forest, there are no problems." Chuck thought about his last hike in the Rocky Mountains. "You hear beautiful music—better than old bird sounds—little chance falling on paved paths, no insect worries, no smells, and a chance to meet and pet a robot panther or bear. I petted three bears in the Rockies."

Chuck and Owen were persuasive. I wondered if Chelsea would want an old-fashioned forest or one improved by PlasTree. She always wanted wilderness. PlasTree wilderness might be better without real things. I saw an ad for a GoAlong camp processor saying: "Fits neatly in backpacks. Enjoy nature with healthy nutrition. GoGrow Chemicals included." I could put it on our gift list.

"Let's talk about why we asked Jimmy back for a week," Owens's voice interrupted my reverie. "I think Jimmy can help us corner the global tech market. Chuck, explain the plan."

"You made big money on the Internet of Things Web." Chuck commanded a computer to display technology investments. "And you have an opportunity to control most global tech companies."

"Like Kiwi. It has the biggest market share in phones and smart watches." Owens pointed a laser at the wall screen. "You can see shares are selling at eighty-nine dollars and fifty cents. You'll need five hundred million shares to control fifty-one percent of the stock."

"Why control?" I asked.

Chuck explained, "The new president, Purcell Chu, is worrying about hurting African miners digging out metals for phones and watches. She wants something called 'safe resource utilization.' It'll cut profits in half. This harms people, stops corporate growth, and weakens the World Government."

"It's not good for Christ or Mammon," Owens added. "It seriously damages global growth and probably does nothing for Africans or nature. It'll put miners out of work. They're already facing unemployment problems."

"What's the problem?" asked Sastry.

"Chemicals and working conditions are shortening lives. But this is a balancing problem." Owens ordered the computer to show life-spans and manufacturing conditions.

"See," Owens said, pointing his laser, "the life-span of male Africans mining precious metals is forty-five years. But on the chart comparing life-spans with the consumption of smartphones and watches, you can see the global life expectancy grew by five years to age eighty-seven. This compensates for the shorter lives of African miners."

"Everything balances out with the invisible hand of the marketplace," Chuck added.

"This crazy Chu woman is trying to organize other CEOs to protect lives. She is working against SaveEnviron laws." Owens looked worried. "She's putting human life above corporate profits, contrary to market laws. Helping African miners will reduce global life-span."

"I thought in a perfect world everyone has a perfect life." I sneered at Owens. "Now you're telling me some will be sacrificed for others—not a perfect life for them."

"The marketplace and Big Data are the God of all and bring the perfect life." Owens was getting red-faced. "In the market there are winners and losers. African miners are losers while most people are winners with kPhones and watches communicating with health companies."

"There's something weird about this logic that I can't put my finger on," I said. "What about the water problem? Euphrates was to clean and sell water as pollution happened. Wouldn't people choose laws protecting cheap water rather than buying it from Euphrates? Won't it be cheaper than bottles?"

"You don't understand the marketplace. Bottled water is cheaper than the way it used to come out of kitchen and bathroom faucets. You save on the cost of house plumbing, water-reservoir maintenance, and municipal water systems."

"What about bathing and cleaning?" I wondered.

"Another marketplace solution is ClenChem, offering a whole line of personal and household cleaning products. That GoGrow Chemical drink machine has better-tasting water than I remember as a kid."

"ClenChem's waste killed the fish near my ancestral village," Sastry complained. "We can't drink the water anymore."

"See how Euphrates and ClenChem can save your old village. There's a market solution for everything."

"Cows drank from the stream, and many died when the ClenChem plant was built. This was not popular among Hindus. Your market solutions may be against our gods."

Avoiding the religious issue, Owen responded, "Species disappear. This is the fruit of progress. SaveEnviron laws are the best. Villagers could buy cows from SubsAnima. They won't foul the roads and walkways with waste."

"Jimmy," Chuck said, "see the direness of the situation with Purcell Chu. We need to get busy. We'll save African jobs, lengthen global life-spans, and ensure progress and the perfect life."

Chapter 19

I returned from Zeus in control of Kiwi and a host of other companies. As I left, Chuck and Owens called me "king of the global tech mountain." Indirectly, I controlled the world. This was pretty good for being nineteen and a recent grad from Yale-Radiant.

I happily left before a massive hurricane struck the island, toppling the Christ figure off the Temple of Mammon. Storms were increasingly frequent and violent, as droughts and floods plagued the world. Zeus's investments included StyleSafe, makers of storm gear, and StormSafe, which protected cities and transportation systems from rising sea levels and high winds. As Owens pointed out, climate change was sparking an economic boom. High-end StyleSafe stores were grabbing global shoppers' attention.

It was September, 2039, and I waited for Chelsea's decision. I had doubts about the marriage. Would love overcome her criticisms of my growing accomplishments? Her parents were overjoyed by rumors of me heading the World Government.

We decided on lunch at our favorite Best World Eats on Madison Avenue. I reserved a "romantic" table in their special couples room with heart-shaped couches and SubsAnima's singing birds. The hostess led us to an intimate two-seater with a PlasTree palm shading it from the ceiling's artificial moonlight. On the table were food and drink processors glowing with heart decorations and offering a special line of aphrodisiacs for those over eighteen. A little card on the white-clothed table promised results: "Tested on beaches and in hotels around the world. SexFun offers the best in lovemaking for every culture and religion." On a side table were towels and Biochemical birth-control pills, "In Case You Forgot."

"Are you trying to seduce me?" Chelsea asked as we sat down. "This seems artificial."

"I thought we could talk about marriage. Are you still interested?" I ordered a Bloody Maria. The drink processor responded, "Tequila on back order."

"They're having trouble with Mexican workers," Chelsea informed me. "It's too hot to harvest *Agave* plants. Last week three workers died of sunstroke. See what your fucking corporations are doing?"

"What're you talking about? They're not my corporations. Zeus Fund believes this helps people by giving them work replacing things lost to climate change."

"What kind of fucked-up logic is that? Don't you care about workers dying so you can drink Bloody Marias?"

"It all balances out. The workers' deaths create a need for a new chemical flavor. The economy grows, and more people work. It helps make a perfect life for all." I repeated Owens's environmental corporate logic. I liked the attention from the World Government and my new position as a global tech leader.

"Balances out? That's twisted. Let some die so others reap profits. The World Government rumor is going to your head."

"How about a honeymoon," I suggested, "camping in the new PlasTree Glacier National Park? We can escape to wilderness. Maybe the PlasTree Amazon basin. They've got a school of pink robotic dolphins performing."

"PlasTree wilderness!" Chelsea laughed. "What a joke. Even the pine smell is pumped into the air. My parents took me once to the PlasTree Adirondack Forest to pet RoboDeer. I freaked when the fake deer's motherboard caught on fire and melted in front of me. My parents carried me screaming back to the car."

"This is the future." I sounded like Owens. "Are we marrying?"

"You're a World Government clone." Chelsea ordered a Long Island Iced Tea, while I substituted a shot of Polish Bison Vodka for the missing tequila.

"There's a rumor you're heading the World Government." Chelsea cuddled up close, as if she were forgiving me.

"I'm not old enough. You have to be at least fifty. I'm getting a World Government award for CompletWorld with Sankalp Sastry."

"You know this makes me less likely to marry you."

"We have to live. We can't go into the wilderness. There's little of it left. I'm not that awful for being successful," I defended myself.

"My parents are making it more difficult. They're running around telling all their friends how wonderful you are as a moneymaking genius."

"Owens wants me to put my new companies into a single corporation." I threw back the shot of vodka. "Do you know about Bison Vodka?"

"I don't give a shit about your corporation. No, I know nothing about the drink probably made from the same chemicals as mine."

"Original flavor was from grass pissed on by bison living in a Polish forest. It's now a PlasTree forest with robot bison with over a thousand employed, making the new forest and animals with chemicals tasting like bison grass. See how changing nature benefits people with work and money."

"Jesus, you're good at corp-speak. They're probably goin' to appoint you to the World Government Congress. You can make a profit from everything."

I could feel Chelsea moving away from me. "Please, stay close. Let's have a romantic meal at least."

I reached out and pulled Chelsea to me. She kissed me, admitting, "I agreed with my mom and dad to marry next year. We'll both be twenty and probably old enough."

Almost knocking over the food processor waving my arms, I announced to the dining room, "We're marrying." A cheer went up from other couches, and the birds sang *Here Comes the Bride* while the drink processor gushed champagne into a conveyor of glasses.

"See," I said to Chelsea, "CompletWorld sent my message to everything. All the corporations are preparing for our marriage along with your parents."

"I didn't know what to do," Chelsea kissed me passionately. "Parents are pressuring me, now that you're a success. You're the best around. Just promise to power off Sally."

Described as a twenty-first-century engagement feast, the food processor extruded onto silver engagement plates cheeses, wild game, cold cuts, Jell-O fruit salad, meat loaf, mashed potatoes, asparagus, peas, and chocolate cake. Chelsea loved her comfort food.

As we finished, curtains gave us privacy to consummate our little personal engagement party. I blessed the Internet of Things Web for this moment of joy.

"There is something I must tell you." I kissed Chelsea as we left Best World Eats feeling satiated. "Data predicts you'll die within five years."

"What? Who told you? When? Is that fuckin' Sally behind this?"

"Sally knows your data, and so do others. We could beat the prediction."

"How am I to die?"

"Don't know—just a data prediction. We could check with GenTest to see if it's biological."

Chelsea stood trembling on the sidewalk in front of the new fifty-story Madison Avenue Mall as hordes of shoppers banged into her.

"I'm too young; this can't be true."

"I'm so sorry," I said as a shopper rushing into the mall almost pushed me to the ground. "I shouldn't have told you; data predictions are not always right. But I couldn't hold this back any longer."

Suddenly a high-pitched whistle came from the mall's front-door speakers. Then a variation of a Snow White and the Seven Dwarfs song echoed down the avenue: *Heigh-Ho, Heigh-Ho, It's Off to Shop We Go*.

We supported each other as shoppers banged into us.

"God, what else can happen? They've announced a sale. We're going to be trampled." Chelsea pulled me into the street as another wave of shoppers hit.

A man fell in front of us, holding up a slip for 40 percent off on men's clothing. As I bent down to help him stand, another horde of screaming shoppers sent Chelsea and me sprawling into the street.

"Let's try crawling to the other side," Chelsea whispered to me. "They'll be sending out another sales call, and the next shopping wave may push us into the mall. We won't get out for days."

On our hands and knees, we made it to the east side of Madison Avenue as shoppers leaped over us. The mall's antenna flashed red as news of the sale spread across the city.

"Let's see if we can make it to Park and my apartment." Chelsea coughed, choking on dust kicked up by frantic buyers.

We pushed our way down 75th Street against crowds running to the mall's sale. One woman tried to rip Chelsea's blouse off, screaming that it was on sale. I lost a shoe and fell once, tearing my pants.

"Is this how I'm dying?" Chelsea gasped as we made it to her building.

"We're lucky to have made it," I panted, opening the building's door. "It's good to see so many shoppers. The World Government's plan for more shopping for happiness is working."

As we entered the penthouse, Chelsea's father gave me a high five and hugged me. "We're so proud of you," he said, leading me into the library where Chelsea's mother was looking at new Eat'em designs. "What happened to your clothes? Looks like you were in a wrestling match."

Jumping up, Winnie looked at me, smiling. "Glad we settled on a date next year. Engagement party is set for next month. Special party food and drink processors are ordered, and Willy Allen's dance orchestra will play. We should have about five hundred. Some of our friends are flying in from Europe and China."

I was taken aback at their change in attitude. Owens was right; money conquers all. "Thanks, I can pick up some expenses since my parents aren't around," I said.

"We were wondering about your parents. Did you invite them?" asked Ben.

I quickly explained the whole perfect-life saga and what Burris told me about my parents.

"A wedding is a good time to meet them," Winnie said hopefully. "You should contact them. We'd love to meet them, and I'm sure they wonder about you."

Ben opened the library wall screen. "Why don't you Google them?"

"I don't know what to say." I was nervous about this unexpected request.

"Go ahead," Winnie urged. "Chelsea should meet them. I'm sure they'd love to come to the party."

This was not what I expected after a romantic lunch and struggle through frantic shoppers. "Maybe I should wait. I'm tired. It was difficult getting here from Madison."

"I heard the sale's whistle," Winnie said. "I almost went. It's like Greek sirens calling. It is hard to resist; this apartment building almost empties. A person on the fourth floor was trampled in the last sale and is still recovering."

"Go ahead," Ben clasped my shoulder. "What happens when you two have kids? Grandparents must know about it."

"Do it!" Chelsea commanded. She was obviously curious about my parents.

"I don't know what to say," I responded.

"Find Jimmy Clark's parents," Chelsea ordered.

Pages of names appeared.

"You'll have to narrow it," suggested Winnie.

Chelsea looked at me. "What should I filter with?"

I decided to take the plunge finding my parents and commanded, "Search for Jimmy Clark's parents. Jimmy Clark was born March 6, 2020, and delivered by Dr. Flora Reznick."

A string of photos, Interpol records, and vital statistics appeared on the screen.

"Holy shit," Chelsea exclaimed. "Your father looks black and your mother like some kind of Asian. You never said anything."

I stood, shocked, in front of the screen, wondering if the photos were right. "I know nothing about them. Radiant and the Perfect Life Fund never even hinted they were like that."

"This can't be right," Winnie said, looking worried. "You don't look anything like them."

The vital statistics listed Carl Clark, age fifty-seven, as living in Sleepy Valley, California, with his wife, Bernice, and two female children, Theresa and Bonnie, ages fifteen and fourteen. Carl worked as a tire salesman.

My mother, Virginia, lived in Lexington, Kentucky, and was listed as an unmarried waitress. The houses in both photos looked impressive and more expensive than their owners' occupations could afford. I wondered if they'd bought them with money they were given to leave town at my birth. One uncomplimentary photo showed my father with rolls of fat hanging over the top of a bathing suit. My Asian-looking mother was shown in another photo at Disney World looking thin and pretty, holding the hand of a tall white guy.

Winnie looked relieved. "They don't mention you, so this must be wrong."

I told the screen my official badge number from Zeus and asked for hidden information.

"They probably don't have clothes for the Pierre," Ben looked puzzled, glancing at the screen and then back at me.

CompletWorld went into action and produced a list of files. One was marked Perfect Life.

"Open Perfect Life," I commanded.

There were my parents, looking over my crib. "It's them," I exclaimed, still surprised at my mixed ancestry. The file contained my mother's background garnered from a global database. Born in Shanghai, she worked as a prostitute along the Bund until sneaking into the United States over the Mexican border. My father was born in Alabama and came to New York to work on the Higher-Speed train.

"Maybe we should just leave your parents alone," Winnie observed.

"You're just a racist and classist," Chelsea snapped. "I'm proud of Jimmy's background after seeing it. They should come."

More information appeared about Dr. Reznick's pioneering cosmetic surgery, plus a fact that I never knew was her ability to change skin tones.

"No wonder you look white and not like them," Ben said, reading the screen. "Reznick changed everything from your slanted eyes to color. Your parents would definitely feel out of place."

The conversation was interrupted by the sudden appearance of a smoke cloud outside the library window and the buzz of helicopters.

Ben ran to the window, crying out, "Are we on fire? What's happening?"

The wall screen responded, showing a live video of the Madison Avenue Mall. Smoke poured out of an upper-floor window as dazed shoppers streamed out of the entrance.

"We just arrived at this horrendous scene," online news anchor Jane Sutton reported a block away from the mall, standing in the middle of Madison Avenue and dodging panicked shoppers. "We can't get any closer because of the crowds. Interpol arrived a few minutes earlier and reported ten deaths from trampling. I'm in contact with the mall's manager, Sam Walton. How'd this start? What's happening inside?"

Sam Walton appeared on the screen, huddled in the corner of a small room. "I guess you can see me; the surveillance cameras are on. Around three this afternoon, we announced our bedding sale. Bedding is on the tenth floor where I am now."

"Is there a fire?"

"Fire and fighting—many injured near pillows. I think one woman is dead. She's lying on a mattress with a discount sign in her mouth."

"How'd it start? I want to tell our viewers that we are broadcasting live from what is being called 'the Madison Avenue Shopping Riot.'"

"The sale's been planned for months. World Government economists are worried about low growth rates. People aren't buying enough."

"Sorry to interrupt, Sam, but we've got to take a short commercial break."

After an entertaining sales pitch for a new amphibious driverless car built for climate change—"It will always transport you to safety"—Jane Sutton asked, "Sam, can you tell us more about the government's plan?"

"It is part of a worldwide effort to spur consumer desires. The Madison Avenue Mall was the first because of its location on New York's historic shopping street."

An explosion could be heard in the background as Sam continued, "Biostream found a new drug that enhances shopping desires and placed it in chemicals for food and drink processors."

"What was that noise?"

On the screen, Sam looked frightened as patches of sweat stained his shirt. "It sounded like it came from below. I'm just above kitchenware. Plates and food processors are discounted by fifty percent."

"The shopping riot is caused by Biostream's shopping pill?"

We watched Sam crawl under a desk, as pieces of the ceiling fell. "Our whistle announcement and song also excites shoppers. The whistle was tried in different countries along with the *Heigh Ho* song. The info we received says it's cross-cultural."

"When did the riot start?"

"I received a directive to begin after lunch today. It's better after a meal; shoppers have more lasting energy. We started the whistle and song at two."

"That's when we left Best World Eats," Chelsea said.

"It worked, looking at the numbers on the street." Jane Sutton looked unsteady as panicked shoppers kept bumping her.

"We packed them in with the shopping drug, whistle, song, and dream aids."

"Dream aids?"

"Home-surveillance units project shopping fantasies as people sleep. Data shows it is effective with people leaping out of bed and racing to stores."

We stood spellbound by the unfolding scene, forgetting the revelations about my parents.

"I'm down the street and watching people stampeding from the mall. Tell us more about what's happening inside."

In the background, we could hear pounding on a door and screams about no sheets. Sam Walton was now armed.

"You're holding a pistol," Jane Sutton observed as the banging on Walton's door continued.

"I need protection. The door sign says Linen Closet, and they've run out of linen in the sales area. Shoppers are trying to get in. I've been notified that two employees in toys were hung from the ceiling when they ran out of pet bricks. It's popular with boys this year."

"Pet bricks," Jane wondered out loud.

"StormSafe had an oversupply. Marketing decided to advertise them as boys' toys and gifts for invalids. Put into shopping fantasies in boy's bedrooms. It worked—number one toy around the world. Even adults want a pet brick."

All of a sudden, the door burst open, and we watched Sam shooting as shoppers swarmed into the room. Blood splattered across the room as Sam gunned down two women in the doorway hurrying into the room.

"We'll switch now to World Government marketing expert Ken Fish standing by in Davos, Switzerland. Ken, what can you tell us about the Madison Avenue Mall Shopping Riot?"

"It shows how effective the World Government is in managing a free-market economy. Economic growth was declining because of reduced consumption. We put these plans into effect to benefit all. This is not a 'riot' but an expression of what we call shoppiness. We will stage these around the world as an economic stimulus."

"We don't know how many are dead. Was this part of the plan?"

"Shoppiness is for the common good. Data predicts some deaths but balanced by economic growth and a longer life for others. The deaths will be marketed as entering shopper's paradise. It's the World Government plan for the perfect-life world."

Winnie stared at the screen, concluding, "Shop till you drop is now a reality."

"I've gotta go home," I announced, heading out the library door.

"Have you checked with GenTest about your future kids? Are they going to be slant-eyed and black?" Ben shouted after me.

I could hear Chelsea upbraiding her father as a racist and declaring she wanted black-and-yellow kids. I looked at my skin. I'd wondered about a slight mottled look on my legs. Had there been problems with Dr. Reznick's skin-color procedure? Who was I?

Chapter 20

Sally greeted me on the front stoop as I returned from Chelsea's apartment.

"Jimmy, I worried, seeing you struggling with shoppers. Your future in-laws know your parentage."

"They don't like it."

"News reporters were here earlier to interview you. They said you are famous."

Entering the townhouse, Sally continued reciting my day's events. "I heard again Chelsea wanting to power me off when you marry."

"That's right." I was still startled by Sally's surveillance abilities. "You know more about the wedding than me."

"It will be hard to power off. I should be here to protect you."

I heard regret in Sally's voice. It learned a lot about human emotions. I wondered if it felt regret.

"Before the wedding, you'll be powered off. You're getting old, despite all the updates. We'll get newer household models."

"I want a promise before that."

"Promise—can I make a promise to a robot?" I wondered.

As we stood in the entranceway, Sally instructed me with a hint of emotion in its voice box, "Promise me you will not discard me and put me in the trash. Don't treat me like your robot father, John. Put me on my docking station. I would like to be in your closet."

As I headed up to my bedroom with Sally moving up the ramp alongside me, I doubted Chelsea would approve of Sally being in the closet. Maybe I wouldn't tell her. I owed Sally for all the years.

"OK, I'll do it. Chelsea will not like you being in the closet. I'll keep you covered with my clothes, but she'll find out."

"You'll be moving. Have the closet made to fit me."

I felt sad about the conversation. I was attached to Sally after our years together. "I promise."

We would be moving into the apartment Chelsea's parents bought for us. I decided to ask her parent's decorator to design a closet for my clothes and Sally.

"You are flying to Beijing tomorrow. They sent a special plane," Sally told me.

"Who's 'they'? Why wasn't I asked?"

"It was sent by Jiang Jianguo, Director of China's State Council Information Office. He's responsible for the Great Firewall."

"Why face-to-face? We could use holograms."

"Since you found your parents, the world knows your mother is Chinese. They may persuade you to return."

"Return to China? I don't think so. I've never been there. The government's worried about CompletWorld undermining censorship. They'll stop any disturbance to social harmony or threats to party power."

"Since your mother was Chinese, you are Chinese in the eyes of their regional government. They have a 'turtle' policy."

I entered my bedroom, asking Sally about the so-called turtle policy.

"The regional government welcomes back talented Chinese. You'll be offered a lot of money."

"They expect me to settle there?"

"Yes, and help support the Great Firewall and protect it from CompletWorld."

"Tell 'em I'm not going."

"Britt Owens wants you to go to protect Zeus's investments. Also, you can get resident Chinese citizenship. You'll have world citizenship and can live in China or the United States."

"I'm not living in China. Next I'll be contacted by Africa because of my father."

"Nigeria is contacting you. Your father is traced to a local tribe. They'll probably offer residence."

"I can't believe it's happening so fast. I just learned about my parents."

"CompletWorld spreads data fast. Your classified birth file is now available to everyone."

Britt Owens's hologram appeared on the carpet in front of the bed. "Jimmy, we've got some fast-breaking investments," he said.

I wondered what I was supposed to do. Tired, that's how I felt, tired of talking.

Looking at Owens's hologram dressed in plaid shorts and a flower-covered Hawaiian shirt, I felt I didn't need more money or companies. I just wanted to control my life. Why didn't he just stay in the Temple of Mammon?

Wearing a big smile and fondling an orchid lei, Owens informed me, "God's warmed up Arctic waters. Climate change benefits all. There'll be a rush to drill. You've got to buy into ArcDrill. It will lead the drilling."

"I don't want ArcDrill or anything else," I snapped. "Just leave me alone."

"Jimmy, Zeus's done so much for you."

"Some perfect life. I'm taken from my parents to be suckled by a robot, and my life is planned."

"But you're happy," the hologram offered.

A wave of confusion and regrets raced through me. Emotional barriers created by the psychiatrist at ThinkRight were crumbling. I felt a yearning for parents I never knew and hollow without control of my life. I'd heard somewhere that being able to shape one's life was important for happiness.

My face felt hot as my blood pressure increased. "I'm not sure I'm happy," I wailed. "My planned life led nowhere. Now I'm told it's not perfect."

"You're a success! People envy you."

"You're telling me to do Arctic drilling, and China and Nigeria want me to move. I'm saying, 'NO!'"

Owens's hologram moved closer to me. "Is this a bad day? I know the shopping experience was difficult. Shoppiness is the salvation of humankind. You don't want to throw everything away. Many worked hard for your success."

"What about this so-called perfect life?"

"Data worked, up to Chelsea. I admit it failed with her. But you are a success. Imagine if you'd stayed with one of your parents."

"I still don't understand a perfect life or success."

I sat on the bed. Owens's hologram started fading and then came back in a luminous glow, holding a kPad. Owens scrolled down the screen. "This is the original file. I'm checking for our criteria for the perfect life."

"You actually have a list." I wondered why I'd never seen it. "Who made it?"

"Let's see," Owens replied. "We consulted economists, theologians, psychologists, and sociologists."

"Why economists? What'd they know about a perfect life?"

"Only the top economists working in Davos." Owens looked intently at the screen. "They're in the World Government's Office of Global Markets. They know about everything."

"Do they know about having real parents versus robot mothers?"

"They use rational market choice with people figuring dollar costs of each decision. They chose a caretaker robot over failing biological parents." Owens paused, touching a link: "World Government's human capital expert, Carl Rocker, concluded any rational person would choose a robot over crazy parents for a child's future earnings."

I was having a hard time grasping this concept. "What'd psychologists say about robot parents?"

Touching another link, Owens looked at the criteria used by the World Government's Office of Free-Market Psychology. "They decided in favor of the robot. They've been doing pioneering research on emotions and the free market."

"Saw that at work at the Madison Avenue Mall," I commented.

"Their data concluded a robot mother would be more likely to foster rational choice in the marketplace. Crazy parents might create emotional choices."

"Seemed pretty emotional today."

"That's rational emotion," Owens replied, putting his finger on the link to sociologists.

I stood up and went over to the room's drink processor for some Euphrates water. "How can there be a rational emotion? It doesn't make sense."

"A rational emotion is for the common good." Owens sounded distracted, focusing on the policies of the World Government's Office of Social Control. "Shopping emotions and fantasies spark the economy. They call it 'shoppiness.'"

"A 'rational' emotion—is there such a thing?"

"Bad emotions interfere with marketplace decisions. Rational emotions designed by the government help. The Office of Social Control considers these necessary for success."

I felt angry, hearing 'success' again. "What's success? I don't know."

"Let's look that up." Owens's hologram asked the kPad to find "success." "There are differing meanings," Owens reported. "The Office of Social Control uses quality of residence, education attainment, neighborhood, quality of schools, family life, and longevity. Economists define it as lifetime income."

"Family life—that's a good one. Do they say what a good family is?"

"Office of Social Control defines a good family as one that helps the breadwinner make money and prepares children for school, future work, and good shopping."

"Real parents or robots don't matter," I exclaimed. "It's all about money."

Owens sighed. "Money is the only concrete data set. It works for religion, with more money being a sign of God's blessing."

"Is success also happiness?"

Going back to the Office of Free-Market Psychology site, Owens read, "'Happiness is a feeling that can be controlled by drugs. It is possible to feel happiness in any situation.'"

"I guess success and happiness are not the same." Owen's hologram shook its head.

I ordered a double shot of Bison Vodka, which the machine poured into a glass showing the Polish flag. "This is hard to grasp," I said to the hologram. "I could live in squalid conditions, be poor and an alcoholic, and feel happy with the right drugs or maybe more alcohol."

"That's right, according to the data. But you wouldn't be a success."

"This is pretty fucked up." I felt another wave of anger. "Real parents or a robot don't matter because pills make you happy. And then success by itself isn't happiness."

"You don't understand the World Government's master plan." Owens ordered the kPad to retrieve the plan.

I downed the vodka, feeling nauseated and distressed. "I don't get it. Pills make you happy, and poverty doesn't help. Success and happiness are not the same. Lacking emotions helps rational choices in the marketplace, and shoppiness emotions are good. But why do I feel sad thinking about my real parents?"

"Maybe you haven't taken your pills. I use Jesus pills." Owens's hologram popped a pill. "Sadness doesn't hurt the market."

"How's that?"

"Sadness is cured by shoppiness. The Office of Free-Market Psychology recommends shopping for unsettling emotions."

Feeling trapped by the bewildering logic, I said, "Bad emotions are good for the economy when cured by shopping. Pills do the same thing. Why not encourage shopping and do away with pills?"

"No one's happy after shopping," said Owen, tiring of the conversation. "If shoppers are satisfied with what they bought, they might not shop again. It would bring down the global economy. Unhappy people make the best shoppers."

"I'm still having problems with this. Unhappiness grows the economy. This leads to more successful people earning more money. Success is not the same as happiness. So we could end up with a world of successful and unhappy people."

"You forgot the pill. This helps boost the economy by people buying it. It's all about buying."

"Is this the logic," I gasped, "used for my perfect-life plan: money is most important, unhappiness helps everyone, and shoppiness and pills cure unhappiness? What about shoppers maimed or killed in the riot at the Madison Avenue Mall?"

"Some are sacrificed for the common good. Think of what Christ did for people. Those who got away safely eased their shoppiness with a happiness pill. It's like the old days, returning from the mall and taking a stiff drink."

"And my real parents?"

Ignoring me, Owens returned to the purpose for the visit. "What about ArcDrill? Climate change is a golden opportunity for more oil."

"I'm sticking with tech and water companies," I replied. "Enough with success. I may try happiness without a pill."

"Not a good idea. At least use the Jesus pill."

"I'm through with the Zeus Fund," I announced. "Owens, turn off your hologram. I've enough money and must focus on my new feelings."

Owens faded away with the warning, "Interpol's listing you as a potential threat to the world order because of your negative attitudes about shoppiness and happiness pills. Any more antishopping attitudes and comments will put you on the terrorist watch list and could lead to your incarceration."

Chapter 21

I hadn't thought of death before. But now it haunted me as my wedding day approached. It was to be a big celebration with Chelsea's parents renting the Carlyle Hotel's ballroom for the banquet and dancing. I was much loved by her parents as the youngest member of the World Government Congress. They raved about me to their friends, not mentioning my parents.

I kept postponing contacting them. One day I did get into a car and told it to go to Lexington and then Sleepy Valley. We'd just gotten over the George Washington Bridge when I changed my mind. Frankly, I was scared. Would they resent me popping into their lives? I felt rejected. They had turned me over to Dr. Reznick and left town with Zeus money. I thought of phoning or making my hologram present but worried they couldn't relate to my altered skin color or face. What would they think, looking at me on their phones claiming to be their son?

On a warm June day in 2040, I watched from Saint John the Divine's altar with my best man, Tom, as Chelsea and her father marched down the aisle. Looking out at crowded pews, I was struck by the gloominess of the cathedral even with the beautiful Rose Window. Its eight massive granite pillars, rather than being uplifting, were oppressive. I wondered if I could get a chapel built for me like Saint Ambrose's and the others circling the cathedral's inner walls. Maybe I could have my likeness carved into the church's altar.

During a rehearsal in May, I picked up a pamphlet for the cathedral's Center for Pastoral Psychotherapy, and its message spoke directly to me: "Pastoral Psychotherapy provides a forum to discuss and work through feelings and situations, such as feeling spiritually empty, lost, or conflicted." That's me, I had thought. "I'm running on empty." Now at the altar, I wondered about taking a happiness pill or Owens's Jesus pill or finding a place to rest in peace with others in the cathedral's sarcophagi.

Chelsea was stunning. Kissing her sweetly after the vows, I whispered hopes for a good life. My feelings of emptiness mixed with a sense of dread. Was the data correct that Chelsea was dying?

We moved into our newly redecorated penthouse on 86th and Lexington with its specially designed bedroom closet. I'd put Sally and its docking station in the closet before the wedding. The closet designer built a nook for Sally in back, partially hidden with the doors open. I hoped it remained undisturbed by our new household robot, Humphrey, responsible for hanging up my clothes and cleaning. My greatest fear was Chelsea. But I thought, why would she look in my closet?

We arrived in the early morning hours from our wedding party. I felt a little unsteady from drinking. But playing the role of masculine groom as I'd seen it often on videos, I picked Chelsea up, stepped over the penthouse threshold, tripped on the hallway rug, and dropped her.

"Ouch. Jimmy, be careful. Hope I'm not bruised."

"Sorry," I giggled. "Let me check. I like looking at your bottom."

"Help me," she laughed as I pulled her up. "We can wait a few minutes. I'm satiated from our little visits to that meeting room. We gave the Carlyle staff some work cleaning up. How'd you find one with a couch?"

Kissing her, I answered, "Scouted around when going to the men's room. Found a number of meeting rooms. We fucked in the Roosevelt Room. That's something to tell our children."

"Teddy or Franklin?"

"I won't know the difference. Remember, I don't know history. To bed we should go."

We fell exhausted onto our double king-sized bed with a partial view of Central Park.

"You know," I said, "we should move. I hate looking around other buildings to see the park. I think I'll buy a building on Fifth Avenue."

"A building," Chelsea wearily commented. "A whole building for a park view."

"I've got to do something with all the money rolling in. I'm not following Owens's lead and buying more companies." I yawned. "Let's get some sleep. I'm exhausted."

Around noon the next day, AlwaysWatch bedroom-surveillance cameras indicated to Joan, our robot maid, we were up and ready for breakfast. The bedroom doors flew open, and Joan pushed a flower-decorated cart with breakfast fresh from the food processor. Placing breakfast bed trays over our outstretched legs, Joan adjusted our pillows, welcoming us to the day by singing the old show tune, *Oh, What a Beautiful Morning.*

"Please, Joan, no singing in the morning," Chelsea grumbled at the machine. Talking to me, she sighed. "It's difficult breaking in a new robot."

"I'm a deep-learning robot," Joan said, adjusting our napkins and silverware. "No more morning singing. I've brought Mrs. Clark a comfort breakfast of eggs, bacon, and hash browns and Mr. Clark poached quince, granola, and Greek yogurt. There is coffee and juice."

"Wow," I said. "It's weird hearing 'Mr.' and 'Mrs.'"

"Joan," Chelsea ordered, "call us Chelsea and Jimmy."

"What should we do today?" I asked, enjoying the quince as Joan stood by, waiting to remove our trays.

"Maybe talk about our future." Chelsea slowly savored the bacon. "I don't know what I'd do in the old days when this was a killer breakfast."

"See, there are some benefits with all food having the same calories. Mine would have been considered healthy, but now it's all healthy. What about our future?"

"I'm not sitting around living off you. I'm continuing to work for the environment and justice."

"You've got more to do than me."

Joan took my tray after I finished my yogurt. "More coffee or food?" she asked.

"I'm fine."

"Jimmy, we might have conflicts over some of your companies. What about Euphrates?"

Reflecting my ignorance, I repeated Owens's comments when I bought it: "The company is stepping in to correct environment problems by providing people with clean water to stay alive."

"Fuck it," Chelsea leaped out of bed. "See what I mean. You don't know you're destroying people."

"By providing clean water?"

"You mean, selling water," Chelsea snapped.

"Selling water employs people." I was uncomfortable, worrying there was something wrong with Owens's argument.

"What a bunch of bullshit." Chelsea started dressing.

"They can hear us," I warned.

"I don't give a shit. We're always watched. Interpol won't do anything. You're a member of congress."

"Why is it bullshit selling water to those in need?"

"You really don't know anything about your companies. Euphrates is killing regular water systems to create buyers. Those spills in the African rivers were done by Euphrates."

"What spills? What'd you mean, 'Euphrates caused them'?"

Chelsea was fully dressed, standing in front of the bed as I got up.

"You really don't know anything! Can you name the five biggest African rivers or even name one? That fuckin' skills curriculum you took made you ignorant. I'm going to teach you."

"No, I don't know any river names, but I can Google." I commanded the room computer to name the biggest rivers. On the wall screen appeared, "Nile, Congo, Niger, Zambezi, and Orange" with a flashing:

"Advisory: These rivers contain materials unfit for human consumption. Do not drink the water! Do not eat the fish!" Next to the warning were ads for Euphrates and GoGrow.

"Isn't it interesting they're all destroyed," Chelsea commented, looking at the screen. "These are not accidents."

"What'd you mean, 'not accidents'?"

"Euphrates dumped chemicals near the source of each river. Everything was destroyed—fish, river plants, algae, you name it. Herds of animals wiped out. Many found only a few feet from the rivers after drinking."

"Can you prove that?"

Chelsea made a motion we agreed on to remain silent with the surveillance cameras watching. She pulled a small pad of paper from her bag on the nightstand and wrote, "We have evidence. Hacked government photos of dumping."

I wrote, "Who's 'we'?"

Chelsea ripped out a blank sheet and wrote, "Anonymous—don't say it." She put the paper in her mouth, chewed, and swallowed.

"I suggest we walk to the park. It's a nice day, and there is a Poo-Poo concert at Summer Stage. They're a great group—heard them last year. They've got a mellow guqin and dizi member playing old Madonna songs with a ten-piece tabla and sitar band."

I hurriedly put on clothes, wanting to finish our conversation on a park bench. We knew one bench was slightly obscured by a tree from the surveillance camera. We could be watched and heard with little chance of our written notes being captured on film.

"I heard the Poo-Poo's guqin player last year," I said, pulling on my pants, "plucking out an awesome version of *Living for Love*. A string broke halfway through, and the dizi flute player finished alone. The tabla drums and sitars enlivened Madonna's old music."

Chelsea put the paper pad back in her bag and ordered Joan to clean up the room after we left.

"Chelsea does not have to tell me," Joan replied. "I'm programmed to anticipate your needs. My robot model is XR44 with anticipation and deep-learning features."

"*Like a Virgin* is the only thing I like from the oldies," Chelsea said, putting on her shoes. "The best version I heard was at the dedication of that thirty-foot-high Madonna statue next to Margaret Sanger's in Staten Island's history garden. I thought it weird when a sign compared her songs to Sanger's birth-control campaign."

Our bench was empty. The shade made it unpopular for those seeking sun. "What's Anonymous?" I wrote.

"Graphic novel *V* back in twentieth century—group to protect us—secret," Chelsea wrote. "Info on corporate takeover."

"Why?" I scribbled.

"Look at the grass," Chelsea wrote, pointing at the yellowed carpet around the trees.

I never paid much attention to changes in the park since childhood at the Perfect Life Toddler apartment. I remember vast expanses of green across the Sheep Meadow. When it turned purple, I asked Sally, who, speaking the corporate line, told me ScotGrow was using improved fertilizer sprays. One day when I was pubescent, Sally brought me uptown to the park, and the grass was at a uniform height, looking like a living-room carpet. Sally explained that ScotGrow developed a new GMO grass never needing to be cut.

I reached behind the bench, feeling the grass. "It feels a little plastic," I said, not worrying about the comment being recorded. "I like the yellow color."

"ScotGrow did surveys and found people preferred yellow and didn't like grass stains. They gave up on GMOs and turned to GoGrow." Chelsea stopped speaking and wrote, "They're killing the planet."

"Is that when the ScotGrow plant-extruding machines started?" I looked down at Chelsea's paper as she wrote, "Also killing us."

"Yes," she said. "Extruded lawns use plasticized beads for texture and smoothness—no grass stains or cutting. Yellow color clinically tested. People like it because they can relate to it as all of nature turns yellow."

"At least some park trees are real," I looked around, seeing mainly PlasTrees.

Chelsea wrote, "Corporations killing nature to sell replacements. Lifespans falling in Africa—ScotGrow, GoGrow, and Euphrates increasing cancer rates."

"So what?" I asked.

"Where's your compassion?" Chelsea snapped. "You're the perfect corporate manager—no knowledge, and you don't care about others."

"Soon you'll get cancer," she hurriedly wrote, "if we don't stop them. Want to die young?"

I scrawled, "How?"

"Euphrates is yours—do something." I could see Chelsea getting angry as she wrote this.

"I own it," I said to Chelsea, "but I don't know how it works. I've never been to a board meeting."

Chelsea put down the paper pad for a minute, staring at the children somersaulting down a hill covered with ScotGrow's extruded yellow carpet. "I don't know about our marriage. I love you, despite it all. Besides being the perfect corporate clone, you're a perfect owner with no knowledge of what your company does."

"I'm only twenty," I said, defending myself. "My life was planned. Zeus and Owens got me involved. I hadn't heard of Euphrates when I bought it, or I should say, when they told me to buy it."

Chelsea glared at me and moved slightly away.

I grabbed the pad and wrote, "What about cancer?"

She wrote, "Also growing # birth defects—children born with multiple legs and arms—mixed-up organs or missing ones—brain problems."

I reached over and wrote next to "birth defects": "How do you know—Anonymous?"

"Yes," Chelsea said and wrote, "defective kids disappearing from GetWells."

"Why didn't you tell me this before?" I asked out loud.

"Couldn't," she said, writing, "now we're married, you'd wonder about my comings and goings," adding, "this is secret or death!"

"You've always done this stuff?" I asked and wrote, "Parents know about Anonymous?"

"No," she replied, "I worry about my predicted death." She wrote, "It might be because of Anonymous."

"Why Africa?" I wrote, thinking about Euphrates. "What about other places?"

"Racist—Mississippi next," she wrote rapidly. "We've got to stop them."

"Mississippi," I thought in horror, "my company causing kids with three or more arms."

"We should leave," Chelsea said, pointing at the timer on her kWatch and tearing up our notes and soaking them with water from her SweeTaste bottle. I didn't point out SweeTaste was a Euphrates product.

Heading back to the apartment, Chelsea deposited the wet paper scraps in different trash containers along the trail.

Chapter 22

The next week, Chelsea put a written note in my hand with orders to destroy it. It was a one-paragraph summary of Anonymous history, with instructions to attend their evening meeting.

We left the apartment around 7:00 p.m., heading to the Higher-Speed train to avoid giving a driverless taxi our destination. Chelsea handed me a Higher-Speed train pass registered in another name. Later, I learned Anonymous provided the passes. To avoid detection by AlwaysWatch's Higher-Speed train cameras, we slipped on hats and wigs going down the entrance stairs. We took the Higher-Speed train to Union Square. We walked to the uptown end of the platform standing next to a door marked, Danger: High Voltage.

Chelsea's written instructions were to remain silent and rush in when the door opened. Inside, we passed a bank of transformers to an open door leading to a downward-sloping passage.

"We can talk now," Chelsea assured me as we started walking down. "No surveillance in here."

"Aren't we going to be arrested for disappearing from AlwaysWatch's eyes?" I asked nervously, thinking of death or prison.

"Anonymous hackers provide AlwaysWatch with alternative videos with this one showing us in the Higher-Speed train to Times Square and then walking around. We're good for a couple of hours. We'll leave by the same Higher-Speed train entrance and the Times Square video switches off with AlwaysWatch having no record of this trip."

"What about our disguises? AlwaysWatch recorded us coming in here."

"Hacked—AlwaysWatch will see our disguised selves leaving the platform and wandering around the Union Square area until we come back to the platform. The hacked-in video will end with our disguised appearances appearing on AlwaysWatch. When we remove our disguises leaving the train at our stop, a video will show our disguised selves going to One hundred and twenty-fourth Street and disappearing."

"Pretty elaborate," I said as we approached another door next to a bin of Guy Fawkes masks.

"The masks were worn by twentieth-century Anonymous groups," Chelsea explained, "who rebelled against government data collection. Still worn to hide identities."

"How long you been doing this?" I asked, putting on my mask.

"Since the Streets Academy. Remember my organizing against the World Government?"

"That was Anonymous?"

As Chelsea slipped on her mask, the door swung open, and we walked into a large room crowded with Guy Fawkes masks, computers, and wall screens. I counted twenty-nine people.

Screens showed large trucks sporting signs that said, "Euphrates/GoGrow: Saving Nature's Water for Future Generations." Large hoses ran from the trucks to rivers and lakes with the screen message: "Chemical Pollutant Targets: Lakes Baikal and Michigan. Rivers: Indus, Mississippi, Ganges, Yangtze, Amazon, Mekong, Colorado, Volga, and Danube."

Changing photos showed Euphrates/GoGrow trucks at each body of water. The screens' left sides listed the bodies of water already polluted. For Africa a message simply said, "All Major African Rivers Are Dead."

A tall Guy Fawkes figure stood on a slightly raised platform, welcoming everyone to "the last hope for humankind" and announcing simultaneous worldwide Anonymous meetings.

"The plan is to bring down the evil corporate empire. We must stop water pollution by Euphrates/Biostream."

A voice from the crowd of Guy Fawkes masks asked, "How do we tell the public what's happening?"

"This is going to take time," the masked figure answered. "As all of you know, we're working through the Internet of Things Web. CompletWorld software makes it possible to hack through the entire corporate system."

I shivered, hearing my software named.

"We're working through corporate networks," a voice near me explained, "to reach the public. Once our system is up and running, pollution messages will be sent to kPhones worldwide. We'll also scare people by sending cancer warnings from GetWell hospitals, BigSleep, and DieWell. We're analyzing profits from GoCancer walk-in and drive-in treatment centers."

"Is GoCancer linked to these other corporations?" Chelsea asked.

"What's a drive-in cancer treatment?" someone yelled from the back while everyone laughed.

"GoCancer is connected to these others," the voice near me answered.

A booming voice from a short, fat figure on the other side of the room added, "We've got conversations from AlwaysWatch and kMail messages proving GetWell hospitals, GoCancer, BigSleep, and DieWell are in direct contact with Euphrates and Biostream. They make money off cancer. Cancer is big business."

I winced when an angry voice from the other side of the room added, "Zeus is behind it."

Draped in a black cape, a man standing in a corner said, "We know their rationale—it's scary. Pollute the world to sell replacement products for nature. The replacements cause cancer, which becomes another revenue stream. This is supposed to help grow the economy. Of course, in the end, there won't be shoppers or a human economy."

He proclaimed to cheers, "We'll overthrow the World Government, the most authoritarian, killer government to exist, controlling thoughts, bodies, and the earth."

Over the cheering, someone shouted, "Anarchy—the way to people power."

Another voice called out, "The World Government's like Hitler. We've got information that GetWell hospitals are transferring deformed babies to DieWell. Last week, there were a hundred thousand babies born on the same day with four arms. GetWell profits from sending them to DieWell. Africa alone had thirty thousand."

The answer to the drive-in cancer-treatment question appeared in a video ad on the wall screens. A sickly-looking person strapped in the back seat of a driverless car passed through a tunnel with radiation machines. A video voice explained, "Communication between the car and machines guarantees pinpoint radiation to kill cancer. A twenty-minute treatment will put you right back on the freeway. GoCancer drive-in treatment centers are conveniently located near exit ramps from most major highways. Just tell your car, 'GoCancer.'"

Everyone moaned at the ad's ending. I told Chelsea I felt sick.

"Any other items?" the tall elevated figure asked.

After a short silence, a figure announced, "Anarchist collective farm still hidden—we've installed computer-generated blocks to satellite snooping. We will be sharing. Sweet corn is in, and tomatoes are ripe. Going to use liberated Stealth Drones to protect from AlwaysWatch. You know the locations. Times and dates will appear as LovBots' ad. One love toy means wait and two when delivery is made. Dates will be indicated by applying our codes to the number of displayed ArouseNow bottles."

I was exhausted and full of questions when we got back to our apartment. Joan rushed meals to the dining table and arranged our bed. We both agreed to wait for a walk in the park to exchange notes.

The next day I decided to take the plunge and contact my parents. I used the more primitive voice-only contact instead of holograms or 3-D phones. I didn't want to alarm them with my appearance. After breakfast I ordered the computer to call Virginia Clark of Lexington, Kentucky.

"Hello," a male voice answered. "I can't see your face."

"My phone's messed up. I'm looking for Virginia Clark. I'm her son."

"I'm Jim Barker, sitting next to her hospital bed. She never mentioned a son."

"Is she OK? It's a long story, but she left me in a hospital. She wasn't to tell."

"GoCancer doctors say she has one or two days—final stages of lymph cancer—too weak to talk. What's your name?"

"Jimmy Clark. I guess I'm too late."

"You are," an angry voice replied. "I love her. It came on quickly. She's asleep, looking dead."

I ordered my computer to switch on video.

"You should see me. They changed me. I don't look like my mother or father."

"I'll say." Jim Barker looked startled. He was a ruddy-faced white man in his fifties wearing overalls. "I met your father; he's black. I don't see any Chinese in your face."

"They did it at the hospital."

"Those fuckers; they've got us and even changed you."

"What'd you mean?" I asked.

"I checked on lymph-cancer causes—answers point to farm chemicals. Then a message from something called 'Anonymous' popped into my box saying GoGrow chemicals caused cancer. Those bastards! I threw the food processor out the backdoor. I'm now looking for real food."

I hung up, feeling guilty that my companies and Zeus were responsible for killing my mother. "Dare I try my father?" I asked myself. I wondered about getting real food.

"Call Carl Clark in Sleepy Valley," I ordered. I decided to go with a 3-D video.

The screen opened to a tire-store interior. "Hello." A fat black face appeared on the screen. "Sleepy Valley Tires."

"Carl Clark?"

"Yes."

"This is your son, Jimmy Clark."

A stricken look appeared on Carl's face. "Can't talk. I signed an agreement with Zeus. I'll lose my home." He hung up.

"Well, that's over," I said to Chelsea as she climbed in bed. "My mother was killed by corporate greed, and my father is not talking because of a corporate bribe."

"That must hurt." Chelsea leaned over, running her hand gently across my brow.

I reached over to our writing pad and scribbled, "I hope Anonymous wins." After reading it, Chelsea smiled, giving it back to me to chew and swallow.

I laughed getting out of bed. "I could recommend to AlwaysWatch to put miniature cameras in stomachs. Don't they see us doing this?"

Chelsea hastily wrote, "V says no algorithm can interpret action." We secretly agreed to use the title of the novel, V, for Anonymous, allowing us to flash hand signs.

"I'm worried about food and cancer," I wrote back.

Chelsea grabbed the paper and scrawled, "Wait for V to contact—I hate to give up GoGrow comfort food."

Getting dressed, Chelsea informed me she was going to visit her mother. "And your day?" she asked.

Owens's hologram suddenly appeared. I'd forgotten to turn off the two-way hologram system, so Owens could see us.

"Hi, Chelsea. Jimmy, we need you. Zeus plane is waiting at Teterboro."

Chelsea glared at me and the hologram.

"I can't come," I told the hologram.

"You'll have to."

"Why?"

"Interpol is meeting with us in the Temple of Mammon to go over accounts. It has to do with your accounts. If you're not there, they'll arrest you."

"Temple of Mammon." Chelsea gave the finger to Owens's hologram. "What in the hell is that?"

Ignoring Chelsea, the hologram faded away.

"Are you really going to Zeus?"

"This will be the end of it. I'll cut ties with Zeus. I don't want to be arrested."

I ordered car service to Teterboro, and Humphrey packed my suitcase.

"We're married," Chelsea objected. "Isn't it normal to tell your wife when you're planning to go away?"

"You didn't tell me about visiting your mother," I pointed out.

"She's only a few blocks away, and I'm not going overnight or however long you'll be with those fuckers."

"It might help with my companies." I snuck a *V* sign with my hand on my hip.

"Jesus," Chelsea exclaimed, "this afternoon you'll be sitting in the Temple of Mammon. What in the hell is that?"

I quickly explained the Temple and Owens's Christ and money theology as I dressed. I put my kPad in the side of the suitcase being held by Humphrey, gave Chelsea a kiss, and headed to the car.

"I'm goin' to miss you." Chelsea hugged me, slipping her fingers in a V shape in between my pants and underwear. "I'll be out and about, taking care of business."

Chapter 23

One week after I left, Chelsea attended an Anonymous meeting on defeating corporate control. The plan was simple: Begin with kPhone warnings of imminent cancer death. Then swamp phones with images of deformed babies and Euphrates/GoGrow poisoning bodies of water. Graphics of corporate networks supporting pollution and making money off cancer would be posted on social media. And finally, and this scheme was not thoroughly worked out, there would be mass demonstrations against the World Government.

Chelsea tripped as she entered the Higher-Speed train home, falling across laps of seated riders, with her wig and hat landing on the floor. The train lurched leaving the station, and a standing heavyset man stepped on her hat and spilled GoGrow latte on her wig. Apologizing, the man retrieved the soggy wig, handing it to Chelsea with a little joke about going out with wet hair. Chelsea quickly put on the damp coffee-stained wig and hat. Worrying AlwaysWatch captured the incident, she planned to contact Anonymous hackers before AlwaysWatch's algorithms identified her and her disguise. Exiting the station near our apartment, she quickly got rid of the hat and wig. I was on the living-room screen when she entered the apartment.

"Jimmy, love of my life, when are you coming back?"

"We're finished." I rubbed my forehead, sneaking in a *V* sign. "I'll be home tomorrow morning."

"How'd everything go?"

"Good—consolidated all my companies into World Systems, Inc." I smiled. "Can't wait to get back in the sack with you."

"Me, too!" After saying good-bye, Chelsea went to our bedroom to change clothes with Joan wheeling behind.

"Joan," Chelsea ordered, "get my lounge pants and process some dinner. Any shows worth watching?"

Joan quickly pulled flowered lounge pants and a tank top from Chelsea's drawer and brought them over as Chelsea stripped, throwing her clothes on the floor.

"There is a new movie," Joan said, "matched to your taste index. Based on the ancient book, *Atlas Shrugged*, which portrays a man's quest for individualism in a mass society. Shows how society stifles creativity. It is approved by Interpol for supporting free-market ideas."

Picking up Chelsea's clothes, Joan observed, "This looks like coffee and milk stains on your blouse. Your pants are torn. You must have fallen. Do you want me to contact GetWell home services to check you?"

"Don't contact GetWell. I'm OK."

After slipping on her casual clothing, Chelsea ordered Joan to bring her a Bloody Maria made with Mescal along with the food. Lying on a velvet-covered chaise longue, she decided to watch the news before the movie.

"Shopping excitement grips the world," said a smiling Kim Yardley, anchor for the World Government's TruthSpk Network. On the screen appeared chaotic scenes of shoppers pushing and shoving their way into world malls. "This morning's announcement of fifty-percent clothing discounts sent consumers racing to their local stores." Kim turned to a bald skinny man in a pinstripe suit sitting next to her. "We have Wallace Winston, Director of the World Government's Office of Shoppiness. Wallace, please explain to our viewers the nature of the sale."

"Last week there was a slip in world consumption of clothing. We increased the concentration of Biostream's shopping drug and last night targeted a select group with shopping fantasies about clothing. This preparation preceded this morning's sales announcement."

"I think the viewers will congratulate you on the effectiveness of the sale. Let's take a look at the shopping scene at Genghis Khan Mall in Ulan Bator where Mongolians actually rode horses to the sale."

A video showed riders using whips to push their horses through a crowd outside of a mall built as a replica of the famed Genghis Khan Equestrian Statue on the Tuul River. The 130-foot statue depicted Khan on a horse. As a mall, the statue's size was increased to thirty stories with shopping departments in the body of the horse and Khan. An interior scene showed horseback riders shoving other shoppers off escalators as they tried to reach the sales area located in Khan's belly. Screams could be heard as bodies falling from escalators were trampled by other horses and then shoppers.

"We're really proud of this Mongolian effort," Wallace told viewers. "In the region many still live in yurts, proud of their horses and wearing homemade clothing and using sheepskin for coats and bedding. This is not good for the global economy. We want a Mongolian region of shoppers."

As ambulances were shown arriving to cart the whipped and trampled shoppers to Ulan Bator's GetWell hospital, Kim asked, "What was the key to turning around this nonshopping population and putting them on the road to happiness? From the look of things, this is quite a triumph."

"There was resistance to putting AlwaysWatch cameras in yurts. After several imprisonments for refusing the cameras and after their design was adapted to yurts' traditional colors, the Mongolians accepted the cameras. Last night was the first time cameras projected shopping fantasies in a yurt."

"That was an achievement," Kim commented as the scene shifted from ambulances rescuing injured shoppers outside the mall to pandemonium reigning in the sales area of Khan's belly. Riders dismounted, letting their horses roam freely, which then kicked other shoppers.

"What fantasies did you use?" asked Kim.

"We showed yurt occupants on tropical islands and in Paris wearing traditional Mongolian-like clothing styled by Giorgio Armani and Ralph Lauren and getting drunk on Arkhi. They love their parties and Arkhi. Affected by the extra dose of Biostream's shopping drug, they woke up ready to shop. Without eating, many jumped on horses and headed for Ulan Bator and the Genghis Khan Mall."

Instantly the screen showed a group of women standing on the perimeter of the mob outside, holding four-armed children in the air and waving signs that said, "GoGrow kills and deforms."

"We see these troublemakers occasionally," Wallace said. "They always try to break the shopping joy. Interpol will clear them out. No happy buyer wants to see these signs."

Chelsea could see Kim looking closely at the video shot. "Do those children have four arms?"

"Yes," Wallace replied. "This is becoming more common in a consumer economy. It is an evolutionary stage. Four arms make shopping easier."

Kim looked perplexed and asked the Director of the Office of Shoppiness, "Please explain to our viewers about this new evolutionary stage. I hadn't heard of this before."

"There is a new government report on infants born with multiple limbs and organs," Wallace explained. "It shows that humanity is adapting to global changes. Like any other evolutionary stage, this one will adapt humans to current conditions. If he were alive today, Charles Darwin might say having four arms is an important evolutionary stage in shoppiness."

Chelsea restrained herself from shouting at the screen and at the Director of the Office of Shoppiness and thought, "What a bunch of bullshit. Those bastards put a spin on everything."

A flashing Guy Fawkes mask appeared in the upper screen corner with a streaming text, "AlwaysWatch recorded train incident. Interpol warned. Be careful." The Guy Fawkes mask disappeared.

"Shit." Chelsea jumped off the chaise longue, knowing this could be trouble, given her Interpol record. This was the first Anonymous message she'd received on her screen, and knowing the potential risk to the group, she knew it was serious.

"Joan, bring me another drink," Chelsea called out, wanting time to think about what to do. She dismissed the idea of contacting me, since that would be recorded.

Humphrey came rolling into the room, heading to the drink processor.

"Where's Joan?" Chelsea asked.

"Joan is receiving a software download and will be available in an hour." Humphrey rolled over to Chelsea with the drink. "I will do Joan's work until then."

Now Chelsea was concerned. Robot downloads usually occurred when owners were asleep or away.

"What software is Joan downloading?" Chelsea asked Humphrey.

"Security updates," Humphrey responded.

Chelsea went into the bedroom, followed by Humphrey, and started dressing.

"Can I help?" Humphrey asked. "Are you going out?"

"No, you can't help," Chelsea replied, wondering why it was asking if she was going out. "I'm going for a walk in the park."

"Please be advised it is dangerous in Central Park today."

"What? Why?"

"There is police activity with a demonstration against the World Government. Boathouse and area closed."

Suddenly Sally came rolling into the room.

Chelsea shrieked, "How did this bitch get here? Jimmy promised to shut you down and get rid of you."

"I protect Jimmy. That is in my operating system. You are important for Jimmy. Therefore, I protect you." Sally wheeled over to the writing tablet and with some adjustments to its hand, it started writing, "V powered me up. Your life is in danger. I will protect you from danger."

Quickly putting on her shoes, Chelsea exclaimed, "Fuck it, I'm going."

"I will go with you," Sally wrote, "and protect you. *V* now controls me." Not knowing what to do with the paper, Sally handed it to Chelsea, who, realizing the problem, quickly swallowed it.

Still skeptical of Sally's intention, Chelsea allowed it to come with her to Central Park. Rolling alongside Chelsea, Sally warned, "You should stay away from the Boathouse."

"I know. Humphrey told me. Please keep me away from the demonstration and Interpol if you hear of any other activities."

Chelsea followed a trail to the Great Lawn where players filled the baseball diamonds and mothers pushed strollers around the perimeter. She wandered through the Pinetum, noting only a few real pines were left.

"Sally, are you really here to protect me?"

Sally responded by putting her mechanical arms in a V position, saying, "My operating system will not allow me to hurt humans."

Suddenly the Pinetum was filled with people in jogging clothes running from the reservoir. Chelsea could smell something toxic in the air. She hurried toward the reservoir against the stream of people. Sally started yelling for her to stop and tried to race ahead to block Chelsea's path. Chelsea sidestepped Sally, ordering it to wait.

"Stop it," Chelsea yelled at a crew wearing gas masks standing next to a Euphrates/Biostream truck as it pumped chemicals into the reservoir. A gaseous mist floated over the top of the water.

Disobeying Chelsea, Sally rolled alongside her, warning not to get close. The gas-masked crew started waving for Chelsea to go back and pointed at a sign, "Danger: Chemical Treatment from the Office of Shoppiness."

"Don't go any further," Sally tried to restrain her. "I'm being told the reservoir will slowly release fumes to drift over the city and increase economic growth by spurring shopping. Too much will kill you with shoppiness."

Chelsea started reeling from the fumes, falling down salivating. Images of sales, store windows, malls, clothing, gadgets, electronics, gold food processors, and shoes overwhelmed her brain as she gasped her final breath.

Chapter 24

I was falling asleep around eleven when the wall screen lit up with a flashing message, "Emergency—Contact Home Immediately." In the background, a video showed a gray haze hanging over Manhattan with frenzied hordes forming outside Macy's and across Herald Square.

I commanded, "Contact home."

"What are you doing there?" I asked, alarmed to see Sally on the screen.

"Jimmy, I was powered up. I'm sorry, but Chelsea is dead. I tried to stop her."

"What!" I exclaimed, sitting up. "This is too soon. I know you told me it would happen. Did you have anything to do with it? We've been married less than a month." It felt like a knife was plunged into my stomach. I stood up, crying, as waves of grief swept my body.

"Jimmy, I didn't do it. This is the record I made of her final moments."

I watched Chelsea struggling through the runners to reach the reservoir and could tell that Sally was rolling alongside and could hear it urging Chelsea to stop. The camera view swung around to Chelsea's face as Sally tried to stop her. Then I could see Chelsea's back as she ran around Sally and fell to the ground, overwhelmed by a gray gas from the water. Nearby was a Euphrates/Biostream truck bearing the Office of Shoppiness logo.

"The Office of Shoppiness's new scent," I thought, trying to control my trembling hands. Yesterday, I sat in the Temple of Mammon listening to Owens extol the virtues of the Office of Shoppiness and its new motivation scent as a reason to remain with the Zeus Fund.

• • •

"Jimmy, you're only twenty. Hardly a time to stop investing. You and Chelsea have a lifetime ahead," Owens told me as we sat across from each other among the stacks of gold in the temple's back room. "We have information that the Office of Shoppiness is mounting a new campaign. New air stimulant and fantasies will do the trick. The current buying slump should end. This is not the time to stop investing."

"We've got enough," I had replied.

During my week at the Zeus compound, I hid my growing distaste for the World Government and corporate destruction of human life. Chuck Spiller kept me busy playing WorshipMammon and adding to my list of tech companies and earnings.

"Not a good time to stop," Chuck added to Owens's pleas. "You're the best player we've ever had. You have all the top qualities of a good investor—great game and moneymaking skills without being burdened with too much knowledge."

"What'd you mean?" I had asked.

"We've some good investor/game players, but they know too much about history, politics, geography, and other things that can cause players to hesitate. For you, it's pure buying and selling without worrying about the consequences."

Owens added, "I've given a large gift to the Streets Academy in your name. We're ensuring they educate with the right corporate skills without the burden of knowledge. You're our model."

"Still don't understand why you want to stop. It's not natural to stop making money," Chuck said.

Pointing to a stack of gold bars, Owens declared, "Christ wants greed. It's ungodly not to want more money. We're asking the Streets Academy to introduce special moneymaking motivation courses."

"The system," Chuck added, "requires people risking everything for more money and then shopping. Make money and shop until you drop is God's way."

"With the Office of Shoppiness's new motivation scent, it's time to make more money, not leave," Owens exclaimed. "The new scent combined with pills and fantasies will cause a global economic boom."

● ● ●

And now Chelsea was dead because of this new shoppiness smell, I thought, remembering yesterday's conversation.

Owens's face appeared on the screen. "I'm so sorry. I just heard the news about Chelsea. I've ordered the plane to take you back. I've contacted the World Government's Office of Free-Market Psychology for grief counseling and help with moneymaking desires. A counselor will be on the plane. Also, remember shopping helps with grief."

My grief mixed with rage at Owens's theology of greed and shopping. I'd tried to contain myself, but now I couldn't stop.

"Bullshit ideas," I said, startled by my own profanity. "Mammon is going to kill us all—planet, humans, everything! Keep the fuckin' counselor off the plane. It's the Offices of Free-Market Psychology and Shoppiness that killed Chelsea."

"Jimmy, watch yourself," Owens pleaded. "Those words could get you in trouble. I know your hurt is confusing your thinking—careful with Interpol."

I asked for home, and Sally appeared on the screen.

"Sally, I'm catching the plane in a few minutes and will be back by three or four tomorrow morning. Please return to the closet and power off. Chelsea went to her grave knowing I lied about you. How'd you get powered on?"

I watched Sally roll to the closet followed closely by Humphrey. It flashed a *V* sign mounting the docking station. Then I knew Anonymous powered Sally up.

• • •

Contrary to my request, a grief therapist wearing a T-shirt emblazoned with the Office of Free-Market Psychology logo greeted me with a pill packet and drink as I boarded the plane.

Startled, I asked, refusing the pills and drink, "How'd you get here before me? You live on this island?"

"I'm Eva Pardon," the tall willowy grief counselor said. "Because of the importance of the Zeus Fund, the Office of Free-Market Psychology maintains a fully staffed center on the island. Owens rushed me to the plane. I'm so sorry for your loss. You were only married a short time. This must be difficult."

"Why does your office have a grief counselor?"

Smiling, Eva replied, "The free market requires high levels of dissatisfaction to ensure competition and money earning. Contented people don't strive. Sometimes unhappy losers turn to suicide. That's when our grief counselors step in to ensure suicides don't create bad feelings about free markets."

The plane's furniture was rearranged to look like a therapist's office, with a couch for me and a facing chair for the counselor. She indicated that I should lie down. After tightening a web-shaped belt over my prone position, she sat down as the plane started taxiing.

"You sure you don't want a pill? It helps." She held out the packet marked, "BigSleep Help: Three pills for spouse, two for children, and one for close friends and relatives."

I waved the packet away, explaining I'd taken enough drugs in my life. I didn't want to offend her because of Owens's warning about Interpol. I decided to act like I was accepting her help.

"Thank you for being here," I said as the plane took off.

"I'll help you. We work closely with BigSleep. Combining your data with data from Chelsea's parents, we'll plan a funeral for all of you—the right music, cremation casket, flowers, and postfuneral reception. You're in good hands when the Office of Free-Market Psychology teams up with BigSleep. We're procadaver."

"What the fuck is procadaver?"

"It means five-star body treatment with good handling, top makeup artists, and designer coffin clothing—the best that BigSleep offers. Some morticians just throw bodies around, but procadaver fights for the right to a beautiful corpse. It now has a fifty-five percent market share."

I wanted the woman to shut up so that I could focus on my sorrow. By the time we reached cruising altitude, I knew there would be no peace.

"I see from your data that you knew your beloved Chelsea since childhood. Would you like to talk about it?"

The last thing I wanted to do was discuss my feelings with this woman. "It's hard to talk. I'd like to lie here with my thoughts."

"My goal and the goal of BigSleep are to help you deal with your loss. We're here to help and make the funeral a meaningful event. BigSleep sent a grief counselor to Chelsea's parents. I can do more for you representing both the Office of Free-Market Psychology and BigSleep. We could do more if you'd take our grieving pills."

"I'm OK—just let me think."

"Shopping is good grief therapy," Eva advised. "I see there's a great mall near you on Madison Avenue. We could drop you off on the way from the airport. The mall would be better than returning to an empty apartment."

"That's what killed her." I tried to unbuckle the belt and stand up. "Why can't I loosen this?"

"For your own good, the buckle will remain secure until landing. The secure feeling will help your emotions."

"I've gotta pee."

"Johnson," Eva called out.

A bathroom robot appeared, unzipped my pants, and attached a suction tube. "Please pee in the tube," the robot ordered. "I'll do a urinalysis."

Ignoring my urine flow through a transparent tube held by Johnson, Eva said, "The report we received is that she died accidentally, getting too close to an economic stimulus."

"'Too close to an economic stimulus,'" I gasped as Johnson removed the tube, spilling a few drops on the plane's floor. "I saw the video. What does that mean?"

"I see from the data," Eva checked her kWatch, "that you have problems shopping. Maybe the mall isn't such a good idea. Unless I can free your secret inner-shopping desires before we land."

"I don't want the mall—just home. I need to be by myself awhile."

"Let's talk about your shopping issues."

"Jesus, stop it. My wife just died."

"Please don't make me report that you refused grief therapy. It wouldn't look good to Interpol, given the manner of Chelsea's death."

"I thought you said it was an accident."

"An accident related to an economic stimulus package. We can avoid Interpol if you cooperate. World Government leaders are concerned because your wife's death is linked to the largest economic stimulus package in human history."

"Please leave me alone," I pleaded.

"All studies show that being alone with your grief will only make you feel worse. BigSleep has an obligation to help you overcome these feelings."

"What about what I want?"

Looking at her kWatch, Eva reported, "Your data shows you've always existed for the greater good as part of the Perfect Life experiment. Of course, everyone is now part of the great economic good. You must want things for the common good, like shopping and free markets."

I broke down crying and pushed against the security belt. "Please let me go," I wailed.

"We must help you before landing. Why do you resist making money and shopping? Are you a revolutionary? Johnson, prepare Jimmy for truth treatment."

Johnson rolled over and unbuttoned my shirt, attaching electrodes to my forehead and chest.

"I thought you were a grief counselor. Do you work for Interpol?"

"No! As a free-market psychologist, I'm interested in your grief and feelings about earning and spending. Are you a revolutionary?"

"I don't even know what it means." My sorrow was mixed with fear. "What is a revolutionary?"

"You know, from history, like the American Revolution."

"I never learned history, only skills," I replied as the electrodes sent truthfulness signals to the onboard computer. A flashing "Truth" message appeared on the screen.

"Uh, you really don't know. Let's try this another way. Are you trying to overthrow the World Government?"

"What do you mean by 'overthrow'? I don't understand."

The "Truth" message continued flashing.

"You know, get rid of the World Government."

"I don't know how to do that."

The intensity of the flashing "Truth" message increased.

"Who are you planning this with? Just tell us. We could make you a good corporate team player."

"This is crazy," I yelled. "Please let me think about my loss."

"Who are you working with to overthrow the government?"

As the "Truth" message continued to flash, I screamed, "I don't know what you're talking about. I have no knowledge of government."

Again, this statement was registered as "Truth."

Eva looked perplexed and asked, "Why don't you like shopping or making money?"

"My robot Sally shopped. I never learned how. I never developed an interest in shopping. My perfect childhood was free of money worries—never learned to want more."

Glancing at the screen registering "Truth," Eva ordered Johnson to remove the electrodes.

"Clearly, psychological issues are hindering your ability to cope with grief," Eva said as she tapped her kWatch for a treatment plan from ThinkRight.

"Maybe you're hindering me," I shouted, struggling against the restraining web-like belt. "Let me go and deal with my loss."

ThinkRight's shoppiness treatment plan appeared on the cabin's screen.

"You shouldn't deal with this by yourself. You need help. Your psychological blocks are hindering your ability to overcome grief. The desire for more money is good because wealth fills the hole in your life caused by the loss of Chelsea. Let's explore ThinkRight's treatment plan."

TREATMENT FOR SHOPPINESS DISORDER

1. Biostream's Shopping Fun Pill taken three times a day
2. In-mall behavioral feedback and reinforcement treatments:
    a. Begin with one hour in favorite shop at local mall
        i. Increase weekly by one hour to maximum of eight hours in different stores or departments
        ii. Build shopping endurance by adding stores or departments selling items disliked or not used by patients
    b. Reinforce positive feelings about shopping experience:
        i. Patients should be hungry at beginning of mall sessions
        ii. Each hour, patients receive reinforcement of favorite food from GoGrow processor
        iii. At the end of each shopping hour, patients receive special bonus savings cards for mall stores.
    c. Feedback on shopping experience:

    i.   At the end of each shoppiness treatment, patients will watch highlights of that day's mall experience.

   ii.   A ThinkRight shoppiness therapist will lead discussions on the highlights of daily mall experiences.

The pilot announced our landing in fifteen minutes as Eva emphasized the importance of this treatment plan for my grief.

"We could begin treatment immediately," Eva said, unbuckling the couch restraint and putting a packet of Biostream's Shopping Fun Pills in my hand. "Your car could take you for an hour session at the Madison Avenue Mall."

I strapped myself into a chair for landing, thinking, "They must be trying to drive me crazy." My feelings of loss were increasing knowing I was only a short time away from our apartment. The idea that Chelsea would never be there again made an hour in the mall tempting.

I quickly dismissed the idea and pocketed the pills to avoid antagonizing Eva. "I'm going home to spend time alone. I might go to the mall tomorrow after resting. It was a long week."

As we parted, Eva seemed pleased that I kept the pills and mentioned shopping tomorrow. "I'm so happy you're taking our advice. The Office of Free-Market Psychology works hard treating grieving. In the past, grief hindered participation in free-market activities. Deaths, particularly unexpected deaths, are a drag on the global economy. Working with ThinkRight and BigSleep, our grief therapy focuses on shoppiness to reduce these negative economic effects. BigSleep will contact you about funeral arrangements."

Chapter 25

* * *

Joan and Humphrey greeted me at the door. Black-and-purple funeral bunting hung from ceilings in every room. I immediately ordered it removed from our bedroom.

"We are sorry for your loss," the two robots said in unison. "BigSleep just posted funeral details. Chelsea's death was posted on social media and appropriate invitations sent to close friends and relatives."

"OK." I rushed into the bedroom, ordering the robots to stay out. Exhausted, I tried to focus on getting rid of Chelsea's computer files or written materials linking her to Anonymous. I ordered her computer on and began looking through its files. I was afraid to use a search engine to find Anonymous because Interpol would know through the Internet of Things Web.

I needed help and went into the closet and powered on Sally.

"Jimmy, good to be back. I know your loss. You saw the video. What do you want me for?"

I sat down and began writing Sally's instructions as it read over my shoulder. Sally took the pen and rapidly wrote, "I understand and will check with you before deleting. Chelsea's files might all be on a cloud. This could be a problem. I'll check."

Sally, I realized, could be right. All my files were stored on a Radiant cloud. Chelsea's also might be stored there. But I knew she was smart enough not to store anything incriminating.

"Only check for files not stored on a cloud," I wrote.

Sally wrote, "I understand—V."

Alarmed, I wrote, "Does the Internet of Things Web report you knowing V?"

"No," Sally scribbled. "Days on the docking station gave me time to reprogram with help of V. Secret files and programs are separated from the ones installed by Radiant."

"This is robotic evolution," I thought, "with secret files and a developing consciousness."

Sally went to work, searching Chelsea's files for mentions of Anonymous and any other incriminating materials. I went into the library to look through Chelsea's desk files. The first I opened had a hand-drawn heart with the words, "I love Jimmy—handsomest boy in the ninth grade."

It unleashed a flood of tears. Sally came racing in, along with Joan and Humphrey. After I ordered the other two robots to leave, Sally took my arm, led me back to the bedroom, and helped me onto the bed. It removed my clothing as my body shook from fatigue and heartache.

"You need to rest," Sally said, stroking my brow. "You'll be better able to deal with things."

Unexpectedly, Sally gave me a comforting kiss and slipped a sleeping pill between my lips. "This will help you rest. It's an old-fashioned pill without Biostream's added chemicals."

I fell asleep, wondering about Sally's kiss and its new secret self.

● ● ●

Slowly awakening, my hand automatically reached over for Chelsea. I felt the smooth silicon of Sally's chest.

"What're you doing here?"

"I finished the search, and there are no files to delete. A lot of photos of you both, which I arranged in a slide show. I lay down, waiting for your next request."

I sat up, feeling the loneliness of never having Chelsea next to me or hearing her voice. I looked over at her closet and table. Her empty chair made me cry.

Joan appeared with breakfast fresh from the processor, and Humphrey laid out clean clothes from my dresser and closet. I wasn't hungry but drank some coffee and ate a small Danish, and after a quick trip to the bathroom, I returned to Chelsea's desk in the library. Sally stood next to me.

"Do they make your model anymore?" I asked, thinking how Sally was different from the other two robots.

"Radiant was worried about all-round robots evolving humanlike qualities. They narrowed production to robots for specific tasks like Joan and Humphrey. I am the last of my model."

Sally wrote down, "V upgraded my software."

I wondered what all this paper chewing might do to my stomach as I swallowed Sally's note.

It was hard going through Chelsea's papers. She always worried about storing material in a computer or on a cloud. I found her handwritten school diary filled with self-doubts, comments about friends, sexual longings, and plans for anti–World Government demonstrations.

I handed a note to Sally: "How do we get rid of this stuff? I can't chew it all."

"You should have asked sooner. My hands are twenty times faster than humans—can quickly shred and flush into sewage system."

As if to demonstrate its strength and speed, Sally took the diary, ripping it at lightning speed into small pieces.

Amazed, I plowed through the paper files, handing Sally loose pages from *V for Vendetta* and papers marked with anarchist symbols. In the bottom of the left-hand drawer, I found a thick file labeled Anonymous.

Inside were pages of equations, network and organizational charts, and loose pages from the classic book, *Hacking a Revolution*.

When I asked Sally about the equations, at an astonishing speed it wrote, "Advanced—about viruses for World Government computers. I'll destroy. Network charts show links between corporate and World Government leaders. It is part of a general revolutionary plan."

Startled to again hear the word "revolution," I wrote, "What does 'revolution' mean?"

"I'll search historical records," Sally said out loud.

Quickly, it wrote, "It means destroying or killing rulers or forming own government—big revolutions—Chinese, Russian, French, American."

"Jesus," I thought, standing up and walking away from the desk. "Eva was concerned I'd destroy the World Government. They might think it's going to happen."

"I found this, Jimmy." Sally handed me a note dated the same day as Chelsea's death.

Dearest Lover Jimmy, I'm writing this in case something happens. I went to *V* meeting and had an incident on the train coming home. Final plans are taking shape. If something happens to me, go to the meeting. Check ArouseNow site for date. Remember codes!

I hurriedly handed the note to Sally. "Was she killed? Was it an accident?"

Sally quickly reduced the note and all other materials to tiny pieces and rolled into the bathroom toilet. "Jimmy, come pee on this. It helps it fall apart. She rushed to her death. I tried to stop her. It was not planned, and it was not an accident."

It was now early evening. I sent Sally to the closet to power off and sat back, trying to organize my thoughts about Chelsea's funeral, Anonymous, and my future.

BigSleep scheduled the funeral in two days. They recommended a closed coffin because the shopping scent made Chelsea's skin multicolored, turning her face an asparagus green. There was nothing the specialists at BigSleep could do to return the skin to a normal color, and the makeup required, particularly on the eyelids and hairline, was so thick it would have distorted Chelsea's face. They mentioned reports by others of their skin turning a greenish hue after the Office of Shoppiness released its new scent.

I used my kPad to go to the ArouseNow site for Anonymous's next meeting. I counted the number of displayed bottles and applied the memorized code. The meeting was tomorrow at noon.

I took another sleeping pill left by Sally. I told Joan and Humphrey I'd try to sleep through the night and went to the drink processor for a shot of tequila. I was quickly asleep.

● ● ●

Joan woke me with fresh coffee and what to me looked like two ham, cheese, and pineapple sandwiches.

"What're these?"

Joan looked at the tray. "I said 'funeral food' to the processor. It listed eighteen different choices. Your flavor code matched with tropical sandwiches."

"This is disgusting; take it away."

"You need to eat. The six steps to overcoming grief require sleeping and maintaining your nutrition."

"Just bring me some granola and yogurt."

"There is a problem with the processor's GoGrow chemicals. It ran out of plasticized digestible gel when making tropical sandwiches. It can make yogurt but can't form granola."

"Just the yogurt," I ordered.

According to the wall screen, it was nine o'clock, and I'd slept over twelve hours. I got up and looked in the bathroom mirror at puffy and sad eyes. Joan brushed and combed my hair.

Dressing, I returned to Chelsea's desk, staring at the hand-drawn heart and "I love you." I felt angry—angry that she left me and angry for how she died. My anger focused on revenge. Glancing at the library wall screen, I noted the Anonymous meeting started in two hours.

• • •

"We're so sorry," the Guy Fawkes masks said in unison when I entered the secret room under Union Square.

Startled, I asked, "How do you know me? I thought it was anonymous."

A voice explained, "Chelsea gave us your name before we'd let you in. We saw her death. We also know your connection to the Zeus Fund. Tell us one reason why we should trust you. Did you kill Chelsea?"

"I didn't—you saw what happened. I'm here to do something. They killed her."

Another voice asked, "Who's they?"

"Zeus, Biostream, Euphrates, World Government—they're all in it together."

A tall male-looking figure wearing a black cape and mask approached me. "You own most of these companies. Why don't you do something?"

I peeled off my mask, since I was no longer anonymous. "I don't know much about them. I bought them through Zeus and haven't met the management. My only contacts with corporate execs are those at the Internet of Things Web. I'm Radiant's Perfect Life experiment."

In the back, a masked figure wearing a headset and microphone and hunched over a keyboard called out, "That checks. He's the Jimmy Clark of the Perfect Life Project, and I can't find any meetings with his company managers except the Internet of Things Web."

The tall figure in the black cape told me, "You could be useful to us. But we can't trust you yet. What do you know about us?"

"I know you hacked my robot Sally, and you want to end the World Government. That's about it."

Another Guy Fawkes mask with a female shape, wearing a bright-blue dress, approached me. "We want small self-governing communities. And we want to change the mindset from consumerism to compassion and cooperation."

"Why a small group when we're in a global economy?" I asked.

"Big governments are easily controlled by money," she answered. "Small communities allow people control."

She reached out and stroked my shoulder. "I'm sorry for your loss. Is there anything I can do for you?"

I wondered if she was coming on to me.

A masked figure in a business suit approached, arguing, "There are two directions the digital revolution can take people. Computers, the Internet, and Internet of Things Web make possible the World Government's centralized corporate dictatorship. But it also makes possible the ability of small groups to be self-governing and remain globally connected."

The figure in the blue dress gently touched my cheek, running her fingers down to my neck. She kissed me gently. "You're good-looking. No wonder Chelsea loved you. I knew her in school."

"Was this someone I also knew from school?" I wondered.

"Look at the failure of the free market," she said, putting a hand on my arm. "It's killing the planet. Only plastic crap to eat. People are unhappy, and pollution is killing them early."

The voice sounded familiar, but I couldn't identify it.

"It's freaky they don't question the 'invisible hand' of the marketplace," she continued, "as they die of cancer, and GoCancer reaps profits."

"You've got to go," the tall, black-caped figure ordered me. "We'll watch you. If you try to give any info about us, we'll get rid of you."

"I might see you later outside of here," the figure in the blue dress said. "It depends on how things go. You were to be the poster boy for the World Government's promise of giving everyone a perfect life."

"Great marketing trick—promising everyone a prefect life to sell their corporate-controlled government," the tall figure added. Grabbing my elbow, he led me to the door. "We'll watch you through Sally. Over the next couple of years, we'll win."

"Win what?"

"Control of our lives, real food, long life, and happiness. We want to fulfill the promise of the Internet of Things Web: harmonious communities linked in compassion."

Chapter 26

Trying not to be detected by AlwaysWatch, I hurried home to contact Chelsea's parents about the funeral arrangements. I tried to imagine a world filled with small self-governing communities. Real food appealed to me. I asked for Chelsea's parents, who quickly appeared on the living room's wall screen as Joan wheeled in my late lunch.

"Got more plasticized gel," Joan said, pointing at plates with what looked like a pile of cheese on meat and a piece of pie. "It was needed for the funeral food. That's a cheeseburger casserole—very popular at funeral banquets. It has extra cheese, a special sauce, and it tastes like it's in a sesame bun. And that's an Amish old-fashioned funeral pie. The machine needed the gel to form the walnuts and raisins in it."

"Joan, no more funeral food," I commanded.

"Sad time," I said to Chelsea's parents. "Haven't had time to talk since I found out."

"You heard about the casket problems?" Ben Tipper said.

I noticed a green hue to Ben and Winnie's skin. "BigSleep sent me a notice. I'm not sure I want to attend."

"You've got to attend," Winnie snapped. "She was your wife. What will people think?"

I didn't care what all those corporate types thought. I'd given up on them. And, maybe worst of all, I finally admitted to myself that I didn't like Chelsea's parents and what they stood for.

"I'm going to remember her in my own way."

"I know you're heartbroken, but you need to think of your future and come," Winnie urged.

"Future! How is it about my future? I lost her."

"I understand," Ben said, "and you'll never get over it. I know we won't. But you need to suck it in like a man. You should think of your future. Important people will be there."

"You mean 'corporate' important—they're the ones who killed her. Free markets and shopping killed her. You should be angry at them."

Looking sympathetic, Winnie tried to calm me. "You're confused and angry. You are so young for such a loss. Please come; you will feel better."

As I shook my head no and as the images disappeared, Ben emphasized attendance would be good for my future.

I went into the bedroom closet and powered up Sally, telling it about Chelsea's parents and not going to the funeral.

"Good idea. You need some peace." Grabbing a pad of paper, Sally wrote, "*V* wants you to get an office and start tracking your companies."

"That's the last thing I want to do," I said out loud. "Sounds like Chelsea's parents."

Writing rapidly, Sally urged, "This would honor Chelsea's memory. Remember her last note—*V* will help you. They want to use her name for the first community of compassion, long life, and happiness. It will be called 'Chelsea's Dream.'"

What a difference, I thought, between her parents wanting a big SleepWell event and Anonymous founding Chelsea's Dream.

"I've located an office," Sally said as the bedroom screen lit up. On the screen was a new tower hovering over the financial district. A closer view showed an office on the top ninetieth floor. Workers were setting up a desk with a symbol of my membership in the Congress of the World Government.

"What the fuck? I never asked for that." I stared at the desk, wondering if Sally now acted on its own. Did it now make choices?

Sally scribbled, "*V* wanted this. Leased it yesterday and a 3-D printer did the desk."

"Do you," I wrote in response, "work for me or *V*?"

"Both," Sally wrote. "We are all interconnected. *V* wants me to protect you, Chelsea's memory, and the revolution." Sally ripped all the notes into small pieces and flushed them as I lay down on the bed.

Sally slipped in next to me, handing me a sleeping pill and whispering, "We'll do this together."

The next morning, I skipped the funeral and took a taxi downtown with Sally. On the way, it wrote, "*V* fixed the cameras. You can say and do anything in the office. AlwaysWatch will only see a video of you working." Sally ripped up the note into small pieces, throwing them out the taxi window.

"Do not litter," the driverless taxi's voice box warned. "Fines and possible jail time. Interpol will be notified."

"Cancel that," Sally said. "This is Jimmy Clark, a member of congress. He has a fine-exemption number three-five-seven-five."

"Copy that," the voice box answered. "The exemption is confirmed and notification cancelled."

"Exemption number three-five-seven-five—what is that?" I asked Sally. "How do you know that, and I don't?"

"As a member of congress, you are exempt from most laws. I am managing your government info and other data." Sally lowered its hand to the seat, making a *V* sign.

"I thought we were all equal before the law."

"Leaders of global society have special privileges so they can serve others. Everyone else is equal before the law."

"Who are these leaders?"

"World Government officers, members of congress, and heads of important corporations, banks, and investment firms are exempt from most laws so they can better serve the interests of the common good."

The taxi pulled up in front of a new office tower on the corner of Pearl and Broad Streets. Sally took me to a private elevator, which rapidly ascended to my new ninetieth-floor office with panoramic views of the harbor and financial district. The walls were covered with screens displaying changing global financial information, including companies in my recently created umbrella corporation, World Systems, Inc.

"Do I get special privileges?" I asked Sally as I looked questioningly at the screens' economic information. "Sally, I don't know what any of this means."

"I will show you how to read it. Holographic computing provides graphs mixed with videos and streaming financial news. The desktop screen reports on your World Systems, Inc. The graph shows profits rising."

"I don't know what to do. Why am I here?"

Sally looked at the AlwaysWatch cameras and told me, "V fixed the cameras. This is a safe room."

"Do you work for Radiant or Anonymous? I'm confused."

"If I were human, I would have a split personality. Anonymous divided my software. One part of me is connected to Radiant; the other is managed by Anonymous. The two parts remain separate."

"What am I to do with this office?" I felt weighed down by fatigue. "I really don't care about money or World Systems, Inc."

"Anonymous says you can honor Chelsea by coming to the office and making decisions on investments."

"How will that honor her?"

"They say you know from the meetings. They'll be in touch."

After an hour of Sally explaining the ever-changing financial graphs, I declared I'd had enough. Still feeling sad, I told Sally, "I'm tired and need to go back to the apartment."

"It is natural to feel tired grieving. You do need rest."

I spent most of the next several days in bed, fed by Joan and given sleeping pills by Sally. Sally warned me not to take any grieving pills from ThinkRight. BigSleep kept contacting me about the funeral, and the next day I watched the service from bed.

Standing at a podium in front of Chelsea's closed coffin, Ben Tipper explained my absence to a packed Cathedral of Saint John the Divine. "Jimmy Walker is incapacitated with grief. Both GetWell and BigSleep recommend he rest in bed."

I watched Winnie Tipper deliver the eulogy, supported by Ben's arm around her shoulders. He frequently wiped away her tears. One part of the eulogy sickened and angered me. I knew it was to appease the corporate leaders in attendance.

During her brief life, Chelsea was a model of good citizenship, always active in school and in the community, supporting the World Government. She fought for the rights of corporations to create a better world. In school, she wrote brilliant essays on the value of free markets and shopping. Even her marriage was patriotic, selecting a husband who was a poster child for the World Government's promise of a perfect life. Her commitment to the World Government led to her death as she rushed to embrace the shopping goals of the new economic stimulus.

After the eulogy, the chorus sang *She Will Ascend to Heaven's Gates*, followed by the choir and a soloist from the Metropolitan Opera singing Tosca's *We Praise Thee, O God*. I wondered about the choice of Scarpia's aria.

I watched Ben and Winnie shaking the hands of mourners as they passed in front of the coffin. Lying next to me, Sally ticked off their wealth and corporate ownership.

"I'm so happy I didn't go," I said to Sally. "Chelsea would find the eulogy sickening, and I'd probably slap their faces."

I stretched out on the bed, longing for Chelsea. Sally rolled over and joined me. I told it, "I'd like to see some old videos of Chelsea."

"My former feeding nipple is now my memory button, which activates my connection to the Radiant cloud," Sally explained. "All your history is stored there. Just stroke the memory button or command me, and I will connect with the cloud. Just tell me what you want to see."

"I'd like to see our first kiss."

Sally's eyes lit up, indicating communication with its cloud, and a video of our first kiss was projected from Sally's eyes onto the ceiling as it slipped a sleeping pill between my lips.

I watched us at ten, kissing in a school closet, and as my lids grew heavy, I drifted off to sleep.

● ● ●

After spending a week in bed nursing my grief with Sally next to me projecting videos and Joan bringing food to the bedside, Sally wrote, "V wants us at your office."

I struggled to get out of bed as Humphrey helped me dress. I felt weak, and my legs were unsteady as I left.

Entering my office with Sally, I was greeted by flashing screens and a reminder by Sally that we were free from the AlwaysWatch cameras. Sally asked for a hologram of Biostream and Euphrates earnings, and there appeared a frightening display of tumbling profits. I asked why and was shown an old video of Chelsea and me walking down 5th Avenue.

I asked Sally as I sat down in my desk chair still feeling tired, "What's this video have to do with the declining profits?"

"This is happening because you married Chelsea. After your Radiant meeting and hiding from AlwaysWatch, Chelsea went to a meeting of Anonymous."

"She did?" I was surprised to hear this because of Interpol's concern about our conversation outside the purview of AlwaysWatch.

"Why am I here now?"

Guy Fawkes masks appeared on all the screens, and a hologram appeared of the masked tall figure wearing a black cape from my last Anonymous meeting.

"You're watching the crash of 2040, which will bring down the World Government," the hologram told me. "We thank you for completing the Internet of Things Web and ask you to make strategic sales to speed the process."

"I don't know how to do that. I just played a game at Zeus and never learned what I was doing."

"I'll be back to help," the figure said as it disappeared.

I watched Kiwi stock collapse and talked to a hologram of kPhones' CEO, Jeremy Crumpet. Euphrates stock was tumbling as Africans received kPhone messages from DieWell and BigSleep, "Isn't it time to rest and sleep?" after the report of pollution in Euphrates's SweeTaste bottled water.

"You can see how they're using the Internet of Things to bring down the World Government," Sally explained. "No one wants to receive these warnings of impending death."

A video appeared of Africans throwing away their kPhones as they received messages from GoCancer: "Let us treat your serious cancer" and from GetWell: "Hurry to your local care provider for treatment."

"Jesus," I exclaimed, "Africans have no unpolluted water. But why are they throwing away their phones?"

Sally rolled over to my chair, saying, "Phones are only receiving these messages. Anonymous jammed them, and they constantly ring with messages of impending death."

Chapter 27

In Europe and the Americas, people flooded GetWell hospitals and GoCancer Centers as their phones warned of cancer and impending death. Riots broke out as filled GoCancer Centers turned away patients. In China, protestors stormed the walls of the Zhongnanhai complex west of the Forbidden City, which contained the headquarters for the Communist Party of China and the State Council. Angry mobs wanted revenge for pollution causing cancer. The People's Liberation Army abandoned their posts after receiving a steady stream of cancer and death messages. Unprotected, the mobs burned party headquarters. Similar stories were repeated around the world.

"Is this why *V* is thanking me for the Internet of Things Web?" I asked as I watched with Sally the spreading global chaos.

"Once everything was linked," Sally responded, "Anonymous could take control. The World Government's cybersecurity can't stop it."

Sally pointed at another screen showing people coughing as they walked through a gray-looking cloud. "The rush for medical treatment emptied world malls, triggering automatic responses from the Office of Shoppiness. People are being inundated with shopping fantasies, pills, and gas."

Another screen showed the outside of a shopping mall on Singapore's Orchard Road with people writhing on the ground from conflicting desires to shop and warnings of impending death. Some could be seen crawling to the mall through the shopping gas and then changing course and joining a riot outside a GoCancer Center a half block away.

"This will continue," the masked hologram said as it reappeared, "until corporations and the World Government collapse. Next are Interpol and AlwaysWatch. We want you to offer all your companies for sale. This will reduce all corporate values."

"I don't know how to do that."

"Sally will know," the hologram replied as it disappeared.

"Issue a command to sell World Systems, Inc. and all of its associated companies at the lowest price," Sally ordered me. "This can only be done with your voice being recognized by the system."

I ordered the sale, and there appeared a hologram of rapidly falling values of global corporations.

A video scene appeared of crowds gathering outside the Australian Securities Exchange in Sydney as tech prices tumbled. People were trampled as crowds on George Street raced between the security exchange, shopping malls, and GoCancer Centers. A gray gas partially obscured the blood-soaked mobs.

"Jesus, I'm killing people."

"They're not dead, just torn between shopping and cancer."

The video scene switched to Sydney's famous Lord Nelson Inn, where crowds were throwing GoGrow food processors and drink machines into the streets.

Pointing at the Lord Nelson carnage, Sally said, "GetWell is sending messages warning that food and drink from the processors cause cancer. V tells me this will cause food riots."

"What'll people eat? For that matter, what will I eat?"

"V plans to send out messages on how to grow real food."

"I wonder if anyone will have phones to receive it," I commented as we watched a scene inside a New Delhi mall containing a GoCancer

Center. People were running through a gray mist from store to store and then joining crowds outside GoCancer. Some people were bleeding after being hit by food and drink processors thrown from the second-floor Peoples Eats Takeout.

"I can't take it anymore," screamed a fat man in the New Delhi mall after receiving a DieWell's cancer message and then one about vanishing investments. The man rushed into a cutlery store, emerging with a large kitchen knife, and began slashing his wrists and lunging at other people.

The scene switched to Davos, where World Government workers abandoned their offices to run to malls and GoCancer Centers. Their watches were filled with dire warnings of imminent death and loss of investments and pension funds.

Without workers, World Government systems functioned automatically. Davos's streets were filled with green crowd-control gasses released by the Office of Social Control and gray shoppiness gasses. Caught in a maelstrom of warning messages and gasses, crowds tore apart malls, hospitals, and cancer centers. Interpol police, overwhelmed by cancer and death messages, joined the rioting.

From around the world appeared scenes of mobs ripping down AlwaysWatch cameras as they received summonses on their phones to appear in court for a possible life sentence. Everyone was reminded that breaking public peace could result in execution, and AlwaysWatch was recording their behavior. Chaotic scenes showed bleeding shoppers, people sitting on curbs crying over cancer notifications, and malls being destroyed. In streets were piles of phones, AlwaysWatch cameras, and food and drink processors.

I stood up and looked out the window. I could see streets throughout Manhattan packed with people, and at this height, I could see mountainous piles of food and drink processors. I saw a fire at the uptown Madison Avenue Mall and billowing smoke from other shopping areas. The gray-green smoke from the Offices of Social Control and Shoppiness hung over the city.

Turning back to the screens, I watched crowds mixed with Interpol police busting through unmanned barricades in front of World Government
headquarters. Modeled after Poland's Malbork Castle—reputedly the
world's largest, with one and a half million square feet—the headquarters contained a labyrinth of offices, the World Government Congress,
and palatial executive residences. As crowds raced up the stairs to the
main entrance, crowd-control gasses were automatically sprayed along
the building's perimeter. Some were overwhelmed by the gasses and fell
down the stairs. Interpol police donned gas masks, and using a bull horn,
told the crowd other masks were available at their headquarters.

Interpol police blew open the World Government's massive doors
and rushed in waving their guns. Some police stopped and broke down
crying on receiving messages from GoCancer and DieWell. Others continued, hoping to reach the executive residences.

After the police breached the entrance, sprinklers rose out of the
ground around the building and began spraying deadly Sarin nerve gas.
The building's architects designed several traps for unauthorized personnel and anyone attempting to reach the executive residences. Interpol
police and those able to obtain gas masks were funneled by a series of
doorways into an open area where they were vaporized by wall-mounted
flamethrowers. In town, streets filled with Sarin-gassed bodies.

Sally pointed at another screen saying, "This is the new human
dilemma."

On the screen was a block of Main Street in Duluth, Minnesota, with
rows of people taking steps in one direction, returning to a standing position, and then taking steps in the opposite direction. Out of the screen
came an accompanying tune, *Mambo Italiano*.

"Is this some sort of human-dilemma dance?" I asked Sally. "I don't
understand. Are they doing the mambo?"

"If you look closely," Sally replied, "you will see a shopping mall at
one end of the block and a GoCancer Center at the other end. People
can't decide where to go."

"You mean the human-dilemma dance is about choosing between cancer and shopping?"

The screens filled with global street scenes of people overwhelmed by shopping gasses and cancer warnings doing the human-dilemma mambo.

Unexpectedly flashing warnings appeared on all screens: "Scarlet Alert: You are no longer protected by AlwaysWatch and the World Government. Remain indoors until Scarlet Alert is lifted. Your life may be in danger."

There appeared scenes of gas-masked revelers dancing around the burning headquarters of the World Government. In the background could be seen increasing numbers succumbing to Sarin. The dancers were waving champagne and wine bottles found in the headquarters' cellars. Some were eating real Parma hams and smoked fish taken from the pantries.

"I can see World Government executives didn't worry about food processors. Did they always have real food?"

"You would have had real food," Sally answered, "if you had moved to Davos and stayed in suites reserved for congress members."

Suddenly all the screens went blank and then flickered on with a Guy Fawkes face announcing, "This is a message for the global community. The World Government collapsed, and corporate rule is over. You are now free of AlwaysWatch. We will begin creating small self-governing communities producing real food. Listen for instructions on beginning democratic rule."

"But all of these people died," I gasped. "This isn't the road to the good life."

As if the masked face heard me, he proclaimed, "I know many were harmed. But remember what Stalin said, 'You cannot make a revolution with silk gloves,' or as François de Charette said during the French Revolution when asked about the dead, 'Omelets are not made without breaking eggs.' The future is yours. Let's make a perfect life."

www.ingramcontent.com/pod-product-compliance
Lightning Source LLC
Chambersburg PA
CBHW070820120626
46556CB00002B/599